the HUNTER the BEAR and the SEVENTH SISTER

World of Arcas

By B.I. Woolet

ARCAS ARTS

THE HUNTER, THE BEAR, AND THE SEVENTH SISTER
Copyright © 2014 by B. I. Woolet
Published by ArcasArts.

ᴀRCASᴀRTS

For permission requests, bulk discounts, or other information, contact ArcasArts at the following address:
ArcasArts
P.O. Box 731
Notre Dame, IN 46556

www.arcasarts.com

Appendix star charts and pronunciations were adapted with the courtesy and written permission of IAU and *Sky and Telescope Magazine*.
Image Credit: Star Decoration Clip Art from Vector.me (by johnny_automatic)
See more at:
http://vector.me/browse/160463/star_decoration_clip_art#sthash.9aGxxHb4.dpuf

Cover designed by Regina Wamba of www.maeidesign.com
Copyediting and Interior Design by Amy Eye of www.theeyesforediting.com
Printed in the United States of America

ISBN: 978-0-9898735-0-5 (paperback)
978-0-9898735-1-2 (eBook)

Visit us on the web: www.worldofarcas.com

First Edition

For our children who will inherit the ancient tales and create their own adventures inspired by the glorious heavens. May you always see shimmers of light piercing through the darkest night.

TABLE OF CONTENTS

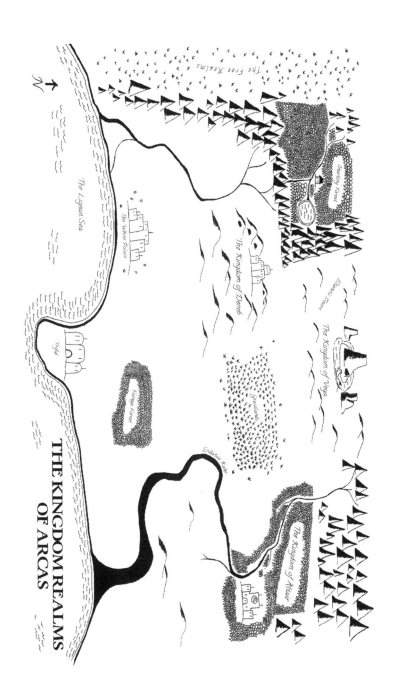

THE KINGDOM REALMS OF ARCAS

Canst thou bind the sweet influences of Pleiades, or loose the bands of Orion? Canst thou bring forth Mazzaroth in his season? Or canst thou guide Arcturus with his sons? Knowest thou the ordinances of heaven? Canst thou set the dominion thereof in the earth?

—Book of Job 38:31-33

CHAPTER 1

A STRANGER IN THE NIGHT

Jackson held his sword firmly with both hands, for one would be foolish to challenge the powerful Draco with mere one-handed swordplay. Circling around him, the beast roared from his gut, flinging embers of fiery saliva through the air. Each hazardous droplet sizzled against the doubled-edged steel blade. Jackson dove to the ground on his knees, slicing the dragon's leg. His sword did no more damage than a mere twig, bouncing off each armored scale, merely scraping off the top layer of cool, thick oil, which protected the dragon from both water and flame.

Jackson sprung to his feet, sparing not even a moment for Draco to take advantage of the failed attack. Rolling behind the creature, jumping to his feet, then running from the hurling flames, Jackson determined he must aim behind the ears where the tough scales smoothed into thick flesh. Dust and wind whirled around him as Draco rose in the air. The dragon arched his hovering body and flared his heated nostrils for the final attack. No decent strategy would save Jackson now that the beast was suspended above him.

Jackson knelt on the ground in surrender, digging his hands into the earth as if the ground would help him cling to his endangered life. As the powerful reptilian wings swooped one last time and the head leaped downward to finish him off, Jackson cast two fistfuls of dirt at the dragon's eyes. Stunned, confused, and temporarily blinded, the creature fell to the ground and shook its head rapidly from side to side, clawing at his own face to remove the grainy intruders.

Jackson ran up close—unnoticed by the preoccupied beast—jumped on its back, and sliced across the nape of the neck just behind the ears. Blood squirted and spit from the wound. Flaring with anger and pain, Draco blindly turned to spit fire toward the direction of the blow. But Jackson had calculated the beast's reaction. Swooping underneath the dragon's neck as it twisted, Jackson slashed a last blow across the trachea, cutting the very breath from Draco before the mammoth creature collapsed heavily to the ground. The intense battle left Jackson with pink, warm cheeks and his slightly heightened breath formed tiny clouds in the crisp autumn air.

At Jackson's childhood home in the city, a teen would

never have this freedom to fight imaginary beasts without ridicule. There were too many eyes watching, judging every movement outside the closed blinds and closed doors. The only acceptable form of fantasy came from a screen and a gamepad. But in the forty acres of woods bordering his backyard, and the hundreds of acres of farmland surrounding them now, he could grab a stick and thrash at the air, trees, and bushes as much as he desired. Holding the large sword-length, bark-covered, rough stick like a javelin, he torpedoed it through the woods since its use against dragons and otherworldly beasts had ended in triumph, and he had no other use for it now.

The stick may have traveled far in an open field, but the thick Indiana woods altered its path after several feet as it knocked against bark, tangled and spun in branches, then finally dove on top of the leaf-covered undergrowth. Jackson paused to pull a small flashlight from his pocket. He knew the trail by heart, and he wasn't usually scared of the dark, but logic told him wandering in the woods blindly in the night lacked judgment. Plus, a little light on the path would usually frighten off the occasional rabid raccoon or crazed coyote.

Ahh, there's the spot!

His favorite place to stargaze was a large, circular clearing in the middle of the woods. Several log benches surrounded an enclosed, gigantic campfire created by small boulders taken from Farmer John's fields through the years.

3

On a warm summer's day, Jackson would lie on the soft grass and gaze at the sky. But with fall dew saturating the ground's surface from the cooling night air, he chose to lie on one of the benches instead. The bench was sturdy and heavy and long enough to stretch out his legs. It was homemade outdoor furniture assembled back when Farmer John's son was still a kid living on the farm and working with his dad. Grandpa and the farmer were good old-fashioned friends and good old-fashioned neighbors.

Though Jackson grew up in the nearest medium-sized city forty-five minutes away, he always loved visiting his grandpa in the country. Grandpa would often take him out to the clearing. They would lie on the ground and look at the constellations in the clear night sky. Almost three years had passed now since Gramps died. Jackson's family moved out to the country soon after, inheriting the old farmhouse. Though he had no one to share the night sky with anymore, Jackson still enjoyed gazing solo and reading through the constellation books Grandpa had given him years ago.

No one else shared Jackson's love of the stars like Grandpa. No one else seemed to have much knowledge or interest in constellations or gazing at the starry night sky. That was okay though. Lying out in the clearing, he often pretended Grandpa was still right there next to him. Time had passed, but the scenery was the same, and he still felt his aged mentor's calming presence.

Sometimes, Jackson would bring the constellations to

4

life, making up stories about Leo and Orion fighting battles together against Ursa, the giant wild bear. Jackson missed his bright-belted friend, Orion. He wouldn't roam this fall sky until around midnight, but once full winter hit in late December, he could find him before 10 p.m., which was usually the latest he was allowed to stay out.

Wait! There are the Pleiades! The seven tightly clustered, individual sparkles were barely visible over the eastern horizon and shining through the bare branches of a tree. Orion wouldn't be far behind. Jackson chuckled as he remembered the Greek tales of scandal surrounding these beautiful, bright stars. *Ha! Even when beautiful women are frozen in time and space, they still manage to create drama and spontaneous lunacy in the men around them.* Continuing to scan the night sky for dippers, heroes and other mythical creatures, Jackson's eyes grew heavy.

It was a perfect night to be outside—no mosquitoes, no gnats, no flies, and a gentle wind rustling the browning leaves. Some leaves still held on to branches and some floated to the ground with each trickle of wind that whispered past. A brief rest before returning home wouldn't hurt, and his parents always knew where to find him, so he relaxed further, pulled his hoodie over his chilled ears, set his phone on the bench just above his head, and gave in to the peaceful surroundings.

"Jackson! Jackson, wake up!" a voice beckoned him from his dreams.

It must be his dad, who often would come out to fetch him when it got too late. The air felt slightly warmer, the wind blew rapidly across his hands and face, and he heard distant thunder echoing through the sky. Jackson turned his head toward the light, slowly opened his eyes, and squinted at the face above him. But this time, the light was not from his father's flashlight. This time, it was neither his father's face looking down at him nor his father's voice speaking to him. Jackson's stomach instantly tightened, and his eyes shot open as every nerve exploded with adrenaline.

"AHHH!" Jackson yelled, jumped from his seat, and sprinted toward home. Heart pounding and head spinning, he tried to reason what he saw. The most logical conclusion would be a ghost. What other creature would be glowing white against the darkness? But, ghosts were translucent, right? Well, not that anyone he knew had ever met a ghost, but that's how it was in the movies. This creature was definitely solid, alive.

Jackson's knowledge of the trails paid off. He didn't see anything behind him and just around the corner should be a clear, straight path back to the farmyard. Maybe he over-reacted; maybe he was just dreaming. But just as Jackson rounded the wooded bend, something was wrong. He was back at the campfire, back at the clearing, and back within sight of the glowing creature.

Something was definitely wrong! No one knew these trails better than Jackson. Perhaps he turned himself the

6

wrong way in panic. Backtracking, he raced away from the clearing again and turned the corner anew. Terror consumed his eyes and numbness tingled through his extremities as the next turn revealed, once again, a path back to the clearing.

"You can't run from me, Jackson." The calm, clear voice pierced through the darkness immediately behind him.

"UHH!" Jackson bellowed as he turned and ran from the being who appeared without warning.

Jackson could hear the creature rapidly pursuing him. Yet, he did not hear the sound of feet thumping behind him; it was more the sound of wind. This wind moved differently than the constant rush of air the coming storm pushed through. This wind rushed against his neck with rhythmical reverberation. *Phooom, phoom, phoom, phoom.* The leaves rustled and clattered in response and even the branches appeared to sway in rhythm. Running past the cold fire pit again, Jackson headed toward another familiar path, but the trail was entirely gone.

All paths, which he knew should be there, seemed to be covered with a waving kaleidoscope of impenetrable trees and brush. Jackson did a one-eighty, scanning the tree line for any final route of escape. But as he turned, the blazing, lighted creature hovered right in front of him. Jackson fell to his knees and covered his head as if protecting himself from a blow. Surely, if the being didn't vaporize him, he was fated to die this very moment of a heart attack. He cowered on the ground, awaiting certain death. Jackson's arms involuntarily fell from his head to the earth beneath him as he vomited repeatedly from both exhaustion and fear.

CHAPTER 2

THE WHITE SWAN

"I'm sorry, Jackson," the voice apologized. "I hadn't expected my arrival to cause you such stress." The celestial being relayed both strength and compassion in his voice. "I'm not here to hurt you. I need your help."

Jackson wiped his mouth on his sleeve and breathed deeply, staring into the moist grass and leaves beneath him. Though he was positive an aneurism would strike him dead any moment, curiosity overcame his dizziness, exhaustion, and fear. Jackson slowly lifted his eyes toward the brightly glowing being in front of him.

The first sight to behold was the creature's shoes: smooth, silky, and bright white. They resembled boot-high moccasins in size and shape, yet they were so white and unscuffed they appeared to have never touched the ground. Golden topaz gems fastened the middle of each shoe.

Jackson's gaze ventured farther up to a diamond-contoured cloak made of the same silky white material as the shoes. The body appeared to be that of a man's: feet, legs, hands, arms, and shoulders. His muscles were developed and powerful, but not overwhelming like a Hercules or a professional body-builder. The garment reached his neck with a split, rounded collar that stood up. In perfect coordination with the shoes, the middle was buttoned down from the lower neck to the waist with golden topaz gems. Diamond designs flowed intricately throughout the chest and arms. Behind this incredible suit of clothing, there appeared to be a beautiful display of feathers. At first, Jackson assumed this was part of the garment, as its color perfectly blended with the fair white. Refocusing his eyes, Jackson realized that these feathers were not an adornment. The man standing in front of him had wings: large, powerful, feathery, real-live, working wings.

An angel! thought Jackson. Excited, though still terrified, he straightened his torso upright, still sitting on his calves and gawked at the face. Bleached blond hair shone off his head like fiery sunshine waving wildly in the violent wind, while emerald green eyes pierced into Jackson's soul with a concerned urgency. His skin was smooth but well defined by his clear, strong chin and cheekbones. With a new calm and awe, Jackson thought that this must be the most beautiful creature he had ever seen.

"Are you an angel?" Jackson managed to release the words spinning around his brain.

"My name is Cygnus," he revealed with his voice fighting through the wind and a crack of thunder. "There's no time to explain now. We must leave. Don't be afraid, Son of Earth. You can trust me."

Cygnus immediately began drawing a door in the air. Like a flaming laser, light shot through his fingers. Once the arched drawing was complete, reality collapsed to the ground like falling water. The trees and the darkness vanished behind shades of blue and orange dancing about in the dazzling portal.

"It's time. Let's go," ordered Cygnus.

Still on his knees, absorbing the sight of the shimmering doorway and the celestial being with both awe and confusion, Jackson remained frozen, motionless.

"Go where?"

"There's no time to explain. We need to go now!" Cygnus urged just as a bolt of light shot down through the sky, piercing a thick sycamore. Jackson startled as his eyes leapt toward the sounds of creaking and snapping nearby.

"HEEELLLLPPP!" Jackson yelled as half the tree collapsed downward, headed right for his body. With one hand, Cygnus grabbed Jackson off the ground as effortlessly as if he were a mere toddler, and threw him into the portal away from the crashing tree and away from the world he knew.

Falling.

Falling.

Falling.

He flailed his arms and legs as if swimming through the air would slow his descent. Jackson attempted once to open his eyes, but the intense wind quivering past his face and the unfeigned fear of immediate death kept his vision sealed shut.

If Jackson could have relaxed and ceased his continuous, panicked screaming, he may have enjoyed the serenity of the nearing world below him. Bright air and a smooth breeze emitted perfect warmth around his terrified, free-falling body. The calm, encompassing heat of coral, crimson, and gold radiated through the soft blue sky while the land below teemed with green.

Lush grass blanketed a valley, which was outlined by a forest climbing upon rolling hills and mountains of thick trees and brush. Behind the soft, rounded tops filled with trees and shrubbery loomed taller peaks edged with steep, sharp rock and topped with light speckles of fresh snow. The valley revealed deer-like creatures feasting on grass, gray rabbits chasing one another, and black squirrels skipping amongst the trees. An abundance of animal life filled the surrounding forests. Songs of birds, bellows of goats, and gobbles of turkeys accompanied the vibrant yet secluded woodland hills.

Just as Jackson was losing consciousness in preparation for a deadly collision with the ground, he felt large spurts of wind behind him increasing in speed and proximity. Instantaneously, his yelling ceased as his breath was nearly taken from him by an arm swooping around his chest. The rapid descent relaxed from a free-fall to a glide.

"Don't worry. You're safe."

Cygnus had grabbed him. Catching his breath and calming a bit, Jackson slowly lifted his eyelids. In the distance, he saw flying animals silhouetted through the clear sky while bright light and warmth radiated on all sides of his face. Jackson looked both to the right and overhead several times, perplexed that the light and heat he observed was being emitted from two separate suns.

"Do I see two suns?" Jackson asked baffled by the sight.

"There are actually three suns here. Much of the time, we see all three in the sky, though part of the day, only one or two remain visible." Cygnus turned his position of flight. "See? You were just looking at the golden sun and the setting crimson sun. On this side, you can see the rising coral sun."

Each of the three suns appeared unique and distinguishable. The golden sun looked to be the smallest and shone bright yellow like Earth's sun. The crimson and coral suns were larger and both similar in size but one rose and set with an orange hue and the other a warm red. Thus, the inhabitants of this world could easily tell the passage of time by the differing colors and location of these three suns.

"Where are we?" Jackson asked with both awe and confusion.

"My home. Welcome to Arcas."

Nearing the ground, Cygnus and Jackson's horizontal flight position moved to vertical as they glided to the ground. Before them rested a small cabin in the valley. It wasn't elegant or large, but it felt inviting, just like a cabin should feel in a green valley surrounded by wooded hills and mountains. After all the heart-racing terror Jackson had just encountered, it felt like a place of rest, a place of peace.

But a dark cloud was rising out of this paradise.

"Is that a fire?" Jackson pointed at a tower of billowing dark gray smoke in the distance.

"I'll check it out. Get in the cabin. I have a turkey sandwich waiting for you there." Cygnus's brisk walk turned to a run as he spread his wings and ascended over the cabin toward the distant smoke.

Jackson stood baffled, stunned, and alone. He looked to the west until the winged man disappeared over the hills. Abandoned in a strange world by a strange being, he studied the lively solitude around him. If he had grown up in the lush Smokey Mountains, perhaps the thick surrounding forest climbing upon mountains, weaving around streams, and echoing with wildlife would feel less massive and terrifying. But this wasn't a flat Indiana woods. And if Arcas was home to a powerful, winged man, what other fearsome creatures roamed this world?

Jackson knew what he could possibly encounter in his backyard, and the scariest thing there was a white-faced opossum. Not because it is the most deadly creature in the Midwest, but because when one hissed at him from atop a tree branch with its freaky fangs and beady eyes, Jackson was certain he'd seen the devil incarnate.

Maybe it would be safest to just hide in the nice, little cabin, Jackson reasoned as he felt an eerie sense of being watched out in the open, exposed valley. The cabin was a better option than being trampled or eaten by any wild, alien animals running away from the distant fire. Jackson decided it was best to obey the man-angel and briskly walked to the cabin while his heart continued racing. As he crossed the threshold of the small home, he noticed a round, rock doormat lying before the front door decorated simply with three large circles and one diamond shape.

The quaint cabin looked as if it belonged to several different time periods. He twisted a glass doorknob screwed into an old, painted, manufactured door surrounded by rustic log walls, which appeared to come straight out of the American frontier. Inside, a homemade wood table stood in the center surrounded by two rusty folding chairs. Out of habit, Jackson's hand slid down the side of the inner wall for a light switch. But in a world with several suns, apparently there was no use for an amenity like electricity. He walked over to window, hoping to glimpse Cygnus again or the fire, but the window's direction only displayed more green hills and trees.

Jackson's stomach growled. Perhaps his mind and nerves were going to remain over stimulated and uncomfortable, but the aching in his stomach could be remedied. So, he sat at the rustic table in front of a blue plastic plate topped with a sandwich and a blue plastic cup already filled with dark red juice. It was apparent that he was an expected guest though plasticware "made in China" is not exactly what he would have predicted being served from in another world.

As he finished chewing his first bite of turkey sandwich and took a drink of the sour-sweet liquid nectar before him, Jackson contemplated his strange situation in a fantastical world revealed by a fantastical being. Though the alleged turkey was cut into large, uneven pieces lacking the moisture and frailty of typical deli meat, it still tasted relatively normal. Like real food, it calmed his uneasy stomach. Although Jackson had a hard time accepting what had happened so far, he knew what he'd felt was real: the intense fear, the increasing questions, the warmth on his skin from the three suns. Sure, he'd experienced dreams before that looked real, felt real, and sounded real, but they'd never tasted real.

Jackson had barely met his rescuer and couldn't even remember his name from the brief, traumatic encounter. But whatever type of creature he was, he constantly emitted a sense of power, beauty, and authority. Jackson felt drawn to him like someone who was so amazing in every way that upon shaking his hand, one immediately claims him. Perhaps, he was just grateful that this magnificent man saved him from the falling tree or from colliding with the ground. Perhaps, this angel creature was merely the only hope of safety and answers in this strange world. Whatever the reason, Jackson knew full well that the winged man had not only chosen him but chosen him by name.

A flying shadow interrupted the bright and warm light of the suns flowing through the windows. *Phoom. Phoom. Phoom.* The sound of slowing wings rattled against the outside door followed by a *knock, knock* against the solid wood. Jackson left his meal to reach for the handle as he searched for some logical reasons to excuse his embarrassing behavior in the forest earlier. His panicked run followed by barfing episode was not exactly the first impression he liked to give.

Jackson smiled awkwardly as he prepared for a fresh introduction and pulled the door open. The terrifying creature standing in front of him and glaring at him with dark eyes was not Cygnus.

CHAPTER 3

OTAVA AND THE BEAR-EATER

Jackson slammed the door and jumped back, but the giant bird's claw grabbed the doorknob and pushed it open again. *Caw! Caw!* The solitary avian shrieked a message toward the sky as Jackson scurried under the table. It was the only hiding spot in this simple, one-room cabin. Four claws clinking against the wood floor with each step, the raven ducked his head and walked inside.

The urge to run overwhelmed Jackson's tingling extremities. Even if he could get past this ebony goliath alive, these constant, reoccurring panic attacks might kill him before he got the chance to flee. The bird twisted his head down, peering at Jackson sideways underneath the table. For a moment both froze. Then another *Caw!* aimed directly at Jackson's face vibrated every last nerve in his body.

As a black talon reached under the table after him, Jackson bolted back near the wood-burning stove and grabbed a fire poker. The raven hopped on top of the table and turned his head from side to side as if he were examining the best angle of attack. The bird methodically flexed one foot of talons open like he was cocking a gun in slow motion to prepare for the dramatic shot. Jackson edged around the walls, keeping the poker steady with both hands and aimed at the beast.

With eerie flexibility, the bird slowly notched his head around, following Jackson, though the rest of his body remained motionless. As Jackson grabbed the handle of the open door with one hand, the raven's wings sprung open, filling the room with black. It jumped up, and shot both legs out at Jackson. Jackson flung the poker, causing the bird to squeal and leap back. He slammed the door shut and ran for the forest, but Jackson could still hear the creature scratching, banging, and pulling at the door.

As Jackson reached the river flowing down through the woods, he heard another *Caw! Caw!* echoing through the valley. He turned back and saw the bird outside the cabin, raising its wings in flight. In moments, it was hovering just behind Jackson, lowering its tail, and extending its monstrous talons. While Jackson dashed from the open air near the riverside into the cover of the forest, the claws jolted out in attack, grabbing each leg around the ankle.

"Uhh!" Jackson bellowed as his face and arms slammed

to the ground. He flailed his arms, grasping at sticks, rocks, and tree branches. While his body jerked up from the land, he reached out and grabbed a branch.

"Help! Help! Somebody help me!" Jackson cried. He held tightly while the limb rustled and bowed. The twigs behind his hand bent and broke one by one from the force of the bird pulling him away. Just before the last stick of branch slid out of his grasp, something whizzed through the air, hitting the bird in its face. The raven shrieked, dropped Jackson, and jerked backward in the air.

Jackson scrambled up and bolted into the thick of the forest. The black shadow raised itself above the tree line and circled around. Then he saw it. A small, flat clearing on the side of the hill in front of a cave entrance. Jackson scurried past a campfire blazing underneath a large pot and into the shelter of the cave.

Hours seemed to pass as he crouched on the floor behind a rough wooden bench, wondering what made the bird shriek and drop him. Jackson hid just past the glimmer of the crimson and coral sunlight but not far enough into the darkness to be swallowed by it. The once-inviting, soft valley and homey cabin had abandoned him to the unknown wilderness. When the flying shadow of the raven finally left over the hills to the south, Jackson came out from behind the bench. A soft aroma of leeks and vegetables simmered through the air as he stood on the clearing near the safety of the cave to examine his new surroundings. Someone lived here and would be back soon. The fire was going too strong, and the soup was full of fresh vegetables appearing to be crunchy as if they were just added to the broth.

Jackson scanned the length of the river below and caught something red hovering over the surface of the water with the corner of his eye. *Splash! Splash!* A school of unique and colorful fish was swimming and jumping through the water. Reds, oranges, purples, blues, and greens soared through the air then dove back down. They reminded Jackson of the Beta fish he'd often seen in the local supermarket. These fish were five times larger than Beta but with the same flowing fins and vibrant hues.

Jackson felt the outside of his pants pocket to grab his camera phone, but it was missing. It either fell when Cygnus chased him through the woods or was still sitting on the bench where he laid it. Jackson desperately wished he had a camera to capture this place. Who would believe him? Giant birds, vibrantly colorful fish, a winged man… Would he even believe his own memories if he ever made it home again? One thing was determined. He would now take walks in the woods with his phone plus his small sketchpad for emergencies.

Snap! Snap! Snap! Jackson ran back inside the cave and rapidly scanned the woods. A rustling of leaves continued.

"Hello?" he asked, hoping for a friendly response to the obvious proof of life nearby. "I'm sorry to intrude, but a giant bird was attacking me."

"Just sit back down and relax. I'll be right there to help you," a deep, gruff voice called out.

Thankful for some civilized life in this strange world, Jackson accepted the invitation. Hopefully this person would know how to get back to the winged man without being eaten by ravenous birds in the process.

Just as Jackson sat again on the bench, a loud crash thumped the ground beside him. His body jumped in alarm at the noise. A portcullis made of large, rugged sticks crashed down from above and now blocked the large mouth. The cave instantly became a cage.

"What's going on? Why did you lock me in?" Jackson yelled, bewildered and scared.

"I'll ask the questions here. What type of creature are you? How did you find me? Why did you bring that black southern corvus to my northern home?" the same voice growled from the brush.

"Please, sir. I didn't find you. I don't even know where I am. My name is Jackson. I was brought here by a tall guy with white wings."

"White Wings, huh? Cygnus?"

"Yes! Yes! Cygnus was his name. He was going to meet me back at the cabin, but I ran here because that monster bird attacked me." Jackson's explanation was a plea for his freedom, a plea for help, and a plea for his life, a life he no longer seemed to control.

"*If* that's true, then where is Cygnus?"

"I don't know. He brought me here and then… he flew away."

"Reeeaaally? I want the truth, Son of Earth… Did you eat him?"

"What? No! No, that's gross! Like I said, he flew away. There was some smoke coming out of the woods, and he left to check it out."

"If you didn't eat him, then what do you eat?" the voice questioned.

"Uhhh, I don't know. Food. Fruits, vegetables, beef, chicken…" Jackson was confused, not knowing which answers would gain his release and which would gain torture or death.

"What about bears? Do you eat bears?"

"Bears? Um, no. I've never eaten bear before."

"I don't believe you, Bear-Eater! I've heard stories." The stranger growled. "Horrible stories. Dead bears standing stuffed next to human fireplaces, bear skins lying on the floor like a rug." He changed his voice to sinister, mocking tone. "'Look at that creature! It's big and thick and will feed a whole town of Earthians!'" Returning to his low growl, he continued. "It's barbaric!"

"Look, I'm really sorry… about the treatment of bears on Earth. If you let me out, I promise to be a best friend to every bear I meet." The voice went silent in thought for a moment.

"So, if I let you out, you will promise to never eat a bear and never to use a bear as decoration?"

It felt as if all that was left was for Jackson to sign the dotted verbal line of official agreement. He replied swiftly, eager to be released from the cage.

"Yes, yes, of course! I won't hurt them. I won't stuff them. I am not a Bear-Eater."

A large bush about thirty feet away started to rustle and shake… and walk. As it grew in length, Jackson realized that underneath the leaves was a brown, furry body. Black eyes, a brown muzzle, and fuzzy round ears peered through the greenery. Jackson stepped back from the portcullis in shock.

It can't be!

A large, brown bear walked out of the brush toward the cave wearing full-body, real-leaf camouflage. In a different scenario, the cautious bear would have looked quite comical. Being trapped, however, with a large, talking, camouflaged bear coming toward him was a bit bewildering, frightening, and surprising, especially since this large, talking camo-bear was apparently afraid of being eaten by humans!

"My name is Otava. Because I trust Cygnus, I'm going to let you out. Remember, Son of Earth, you promised to keep your scheming, ravenous, naked hands off my fur." Otava slowly walked toward the cave, holding out a spear aimed at Jackson in warning.

"Mr. Bear… I mean Otava, I have absolutely no desire to touch you or harm you or eat you… I've already promised multiple times." Jackson was no longer sure he wanted to be released from the cage, which now felt like a safe barrier between him and the large-toothed, paranoid bear, ever threatening and questioning him. "To be honest with you," he continued, "this cave is looking quite comfortable and safe right now, so I'm perfectly fine waiting in here until Cygnus finds me."

Otava stared at Jackson a little longer, sizing up whether he seemed harmful or truthful. At last, he went to the side of the cave and started pulling on a large grapevine. The wooden portcullis slowly lifted to its original position hidden behind the tree branches hanging over and around the top of the cave. Afraid the gate would come crashing back down on him or that the creature would reveal his vicious teeth and claws in attack, Jackson waited to exit.

Otava dropped on all fours, then headed toward the pot full of bubbling soup. He sniffed, stood, and grabbed a large ladle from the tool belt around his waist. The belt was thick leather with pouches like one might expect on a carpenter's belt. Only this belt's pouches were hanging with cooking utensils. Otava dunked the ladle in, pulled the steamy mixture up to his mouth, and slurped his sacred concoction.

"Ahhh, perfection!" Otava exclaimed.

"It smells and looks very good." Jackson commented, edging slowly out of the cave. "Do you cook often?" Maybe a little polite small talk would smooth the rough edges of raw hostility from the talking grizzly.

"Do I cook often? Ha! Let me tell you, Bear-Eater, I have been basting since the beginning and simmering since the three suns shined upon Arcas! And I'm proud to say that I haven't missed a meal yet," Otava boasted.

"Wow. That's impressive. I miss meals sometimes on accident, and I don't really know how to cook. But please, let me clarify again. I am not a Bear-Eater." Jackson was still slightly worried that this crazy bear would lock him up or— worse—let him fall into a prepared tiger pit.

"Well, if you don't eat bears, then come try some of my stew. No guest of mine is going to miss a meal while sitting right in front of me!"

Otava handed him a wooden bowl full of a brownish mixture packed with a variety of vegetables and meat that appeared to be some type of fish. It smelled decent enough. He never got to finish his meal in the cabin, and Jackson wasn't about to give the bear another reason to be upset with him. He was determined to at least try it out of respect for his host. Only, he wasn't quite sure how to properly eat it.

"Well, what are you waiting for? I can see your scrawny bones. You must be starving! Eat the soup!"

"I'm sorry. I was just wondering how I should eat it. Where I come from, we usually eat soup with a spoon."

"What's a spoon?" Otava glanced across his tool belt as Jackson explained.

"Well, it's curved and you dip it down in the soup to

bring the soup up to your mouth." Jackson motioned with his hand like he was scooping a spoon into the bowl.

"Ahh, yes, I have one of those."

Otava seemed pleased that he figured out exactly what a spoon was. He reached down to his belt, pulled out the large ladle, and handed it to Jackson.

"A spoon for you. Now eat, eat! I'm anxious to know if you like the depth of flavors!"

Jackson examined the ladle. The bear didn't quite understand. The ladle handed to him was just as big as the bowl. He decided the best option would be to dump the contents of the bowl into the ladle and carefully sip it from his new and improved long-handled bowl. He didn't want to be rude, so he used what was handed to him. Jackson brought the ladle to his lips and sipped. Otava eagerly watched every move, waiting for a response. The warm liquid filled his mouth with flavors of tomato, chives, and fish. Tart but slightly sweet, mild but slightly spicy, hearty but simple, it was surprisingly delicious. Jackson made sure to reassure the chef.

"It tastes great."

"Of course it does!" Otava agreed proudly, overly satisfied with the simple compliment.

Otava had been holding his bowl in his paws while waiting for Jackson to eat. Now that the first taste was affirmed, he brought his own bowl to his mouth between his thick pads and protruding claws and swallowed it all in one gulp. He looked over at Jackson, who was still trying to hold firmly to his table manners by gently slurping from the ladle. Otava shook his furry head with a slight mixture of confusion and comedy in his expression.

"Ya know, for a Bear-Eater, you sure eat dainty like an Ilmatar!" he teased.

Jackson smiled awkwardly. He didn't quite get the joke, but he got the point. He returned the soup back to the bowl, set the ladle down, and brought the bowl to his mouth, mirroring his companion's eating style. Otava nodded, then returned to the pot to refill his bowl.

"You scared that bird away, didn't you?"

"This is my home." Otava glanced up from the soup with a slight nonverbal hint that he would boot Jackson out as well if he made a wrong move. "I scare every unsavory creature away."

"Thank you." Jackson smiled earnestly.

Otava replied with a brief grunt and shrug as if it was no big deal.

"This stew feels a little tingly on my tongue. What spice does that?"

"That's just your buds responding to ultimate culinary euphoria," Otava explained with passionate satisfaction.

"I don't know… My fingers are tingling too." He set his bowl down and wiggled his fingers around, inspecting them. Black splotches slowly appeared everywhere, crowding his vision just before his limp body collapsed, sending the ladle and bowl sitting next to him flying off the log into the dirt and grass.

Otava jerked his head around to see what all the fuss and noise was about.

"Hey, Bear-Eater! You could have asked for a bed before hibernating." He went over to Jackson and jostled his body with his soft paw to wake him. No response. He lifted Jackson's arm, and it flopped back to the ground. "What a waste," he mumbled, looking at Jackson's spilled soup soaking into the dirt.

Otava walked back to his seat and finished his fresh bowl once again with just a gulp. He looked at the pot of soup and then back at Jackson.

"Ursa Major!" he cursed. "Now I have to take two trips. The soup or the boy, the soup or the boy?" He scratched over his ear with blunt claws.

Otava made up his mind. He went over to Jackson, lifted him with one paw up on his thick back, and walked over to the cave. The bear laid him down and then proceeded to collect some nearby branches to cover Jackson. Satisfied with his work, he exited the cave and collapsed the portcullis again. He returned to the pot of soup, grabbed it, and bumbled off.

"Otava, what are you doing?" a bewildered voice demanded.

"I'm just taking my stew home."

"Why is that boy trapped in your cave?"

"I just put him there for a bit, so I could take my pot home."

"It is crucially important that no one finds the Son of Earth. You really decided to haul off the soup instead of the boy?"

"Of course." He was positively confident with his decision. "After all, it's a Bear-Eater, and I've only just met him. This stew and I have been in a relationship since the crimson sun met the horizon. The boy can't escape. He can't even move, and he still feels warm. My pot, on the contrary, is getting cold. Anyway, he's your problem now. Do what you want with him."

CHAPTER 4

SON OF EARTH DISCOVERED

Jackson's fingers twinged as he slowly regained consciousness. He was not yet mobile from the food-induced coma, but in the darkness of his mind, he could hear people talking. His eyes fluttered and his muscles flexed. Peeling his eyelids open, he lay still, trying to collect his thoughts and figure out what was going on. Wet. Wiping his hand down his shirt and then swiftly moving to his forehead, he realized his body was covered in sweat.

Why does my mouth taste weird?

He moved his tongue and felt something on it. Out of reflex and repulsion, he yanked it out. A moist leaf smashed between his fingers. Slowly sitting up, Jackson realized he didn't recognize this place. He was lying on a bedding of leaves covering a raised wooden platform inside a log cabin.

The voices continued in the next room. He stood up and walked toward the cracked door to hear what they were saying.

"But you could do it. With your skills and weapons, it would be easy for you."

"No. No. No. I won't kill him. I won't look at him or touch him. I want absolutely nothing to do with him. You want him dead, you kill him!"

"You know I have more urgent matters to deal with. What about The Hunter? Would he do it?"

"Maybe. I'll tell you what. I'll help you find The Hunter. But then I'm done! You two can figure out how to kill him."

Jackson's heart was racing, a terrifying yet familiar feeling of late. He recognized the voices. There was no forgetting that gruff, growly tone of the psycho, talking bear. *I bet he planned this from the start! He must have drugged me so he could hand me over to... Cygnus?* That was the other voice! The bear acted like he was a friend of the winged man. *Great. They brought me to their planet to kill me! I'm probably their next science experiment!*

Jackson had to escape. He had to get far away before the bear and his accomplice found him awake and decided to complete their deadly task, which surely would involve a form of torture. Cygnus brought him to Arcas, so there must be a way to get back home. Escaping was a better option than hanging around for Otava and Cygnus to introduce him to the hired killer. Jackson crept to the front door and quietly opened it.

Creeeaaak. The small, high-pitched squeal blasted through Jackson's nerves like an avalanche. He stopped moving on the threshold of the open door, hoping that no one heard.

"Hey, Bear-Eater? You done hibernating yet?" Otava called out.

Jackson wasn't waiting around to chat. He flung the door shut behind him and bolted into the forest. Jackson dodged mammoth trees and flew under giant branches. He ran with great speed and agility like a cat escaping the clutches of a pursuing toddler. Jackson could plan his return to Earth later. The important thing now was to get away. Far away.

No sounds of chase rustled from behind him. But wait… Something else was running through the forest, not behind him but coming toward him from the side. He knew the sound well, horse hooves. With hooves and clanking armor, it couldn't be the bear, but maybe The Hunter they mentioned was riding after him to claim his alien prize. Jackson turned away from the pursuer and darted behind a thick, tall tree.

Clomp-clomp, clomp-clomp, clomp-clomp. The hooves stopped along with Jackson's breathing.

"I know you are close, Son of Earth… Tell me. What you are doing here in Arcas?" the deep, guttural voice asked. "What profit have you been offered to sell out both our worlds?"

Before Jackson knew what was happening, a sword flew from the side of the tree at his throat. Cold, unwavering steel edged his trachea, giving new urgency to each breath.

"Answer me or die. What are you doing here?"

The creature who moved around the shadow of the tree to join his sword was not what Jackson expected. His life was being threatened by both the horse and the rider, a centaur.

"Please, don't kill me. I don't know why I'm here!" Jackson pleaded. *Any place on Earth has to be safer than this crazy world!* Jackson screamed inside. *God, whatever sins I've committed to deserve having my neck sliced by a mutant creature on this alien planet...* But before he could finish his final prayers, the sword jolted away from his throat with the clash of a rival sword. Jackson dropped to the ground as the centaur backed away quickly, regaining control over his weapon.

"Get out of here! You centaurs don't belong in these woods," commanded his rescuer.

Jackson swiftly crawled behind a bush to distance himself from the impending fight. Peering through the leaves, he recognized a familiar, tall figure clothed in white. Cygnus! Cygnus and the centaur cautiously circled each other from a distance beyond the touch of their swords.

"I know who you are, White Wings, but I didn't know you were a traitor. This boy doesn't belong here!" the Centaur accused.

"If you know who I am, young foal, then you must

know that I have been around since The Bridge still stood between Earth and Arcas. From the ancient days till now, never once has there been a law written that forbids Earthians from entering our world," Cygnus retorted as they continued to circle each other, engaging their swords to fight.

"You know this isn't about laws. It's about allegiance, and it's obvious now where your allegiance lies."

"My crossbow has its allegiance pointed right at your heart, clunky feet, so I suggest you put your sword down!" yelled Otava heartily as his camouflaged head rose up out of the distant brush.

"Alright! No need to shoot, soldier. I'll put the sword down." The centaur slowly lowered the long blade as he turned his body to the side. He found Jackson's face through the bush and gazed right through him. "You may be safe at the moment, Son of Earth, but we will find you soon enough. You will not defile our land with Earth's darkness. Go back while you still can!"

Just as the centaur's sword stroked the ground, he twisted and kicked his hooves backward against the dirt, flinging dust, leaves, and small rocks into the air. While Cygnus and Jackson reflexively shielded their eyes, Otava shot his crossbow into the dust. But the distraction was a success, and all that was left of the centaur was thumping hooves echoing through the forest. Cygnus looked back at Otava.

"On second thought, Otava, maybe I won't send you

to kill Eltanin!" Cygnus yelled out, partially jesting and partially irritated because Otava missed the centaur.

"Don't start with me, Cygnus! You know I let the centaur go on purpose. I can't have all of his friends trampling through my quiet forest looking for his body. This crazy boy here is the one you shouldn't be sending to Eltanin! Everything was cozy and safe in my perfectly armed fortress, but he decided to trample through the forest like a wild bull right into the enemy's grasp!" Otava retorted, directing the conversation away from his missed shot.

"Safe? I heard you in the cabin! Didn't you bring me here to kill me?"

"Why would I want to kill you?" asked Cygnus. "I told you I need your help. While you were waking up, we were discussing your journey and how to find The Hunter."

"But still, you were talking about *killing* someone. Are you going to kill this hunter?" Jackson was a mess of confusion and still trying to grasp a piece of the whole picture. He picked up a stick, fiddling with it against the undergrowth to calm his nerves from the last twenty minutes of adrenaline.

"Hahaha! Kill The Hunter? You see, Cygnus? The boy is missing something here," Otava bellowed, pointing a claw toward his head.

"Don't be so hard on him. You're the one who fed him the volantis and made him ill." Cygnus turned his attentions back to Jackson. "We're going to ask The Hunter to get rid of Eltanin so you can safely enter the Pillar of Vega and take the gem from Earth."

"I'm sorry, but I have no idea what you're talking about." Every explanation spoken from Otava and Cygnus was filled with foreign names and foreign places. Jackson felt like each shard of new information was spinning around his head in a whirling storm of nothingness.

"That's right. I never explained why you're here. A thousand apologies, Jackson. Let's return to the safety of Otava's cottage, and I'll tell you everything.

Once they covered their tracks and Otava set all the intruder traps outside his home, they settled at the table to explain everything to Jackson.

"Long ago, three kings of Earth and three kings of Arcas held sacred gems," Cygnus began. These gems had the power to create passageways between your world and ours. The kings created pillars for the gems to provide safe and guarded locations of trade between our two worlds. All of the kingdoms grew in wealth and power until a great, dangerous water filled the Earth. The kings of Arcas had no choice but to remove the gems from our world's pillars in order to end all transportation for the safety of our people and our world. After thousands of peaceful years, our enemy, Gurges Ater, is trying to open these pillars once again. If he succeeds, he will steal weapons and humans from Earth to turn into his slaves. He would rule all of Arcas and control all trade with Earth. You're here to make sure these portals between our worlds stay closed."

"Okay… But why me?" Jackson felt small and awkward and weak sitting with these two strong, large, otherworldly beings. He chuckled slightly, trying to lightly dismiss their choice in a hero. "I'm sure there are more qualified people to help you stop an evil dictator."

"We have learned that Gurges Ater now holds all three gems of Arcas," Cygnus continued. "He is amassing his armies to move toward the ancient pillars of Vega, Altair, and Deneb. But the portals cannot open for him unless one gem on Arcas is connected to one gem on Earth. We need you to remove the gems still on Earth, so the passageways will close beyond his reach."

"That's right!" Otava piped in. "The little cubs used to chant 'Arcas to Arcas. Earth to Earth. Steal a gem from life to dearth!' Those yellow gems are deadly for us."

"You see, only a Son of Earth can remove a gem of Earth. That's why we need you. That centaur was most definitely a scout from Gurges Ater. His army has reached the Starling Forest. They are terrorizing beings everywhere they go and capturing people with the black corvus who dwell in the ruins of Trifid."

"So, the bird that attacked me was also from this Gurges Ater person?"

Cygnus nodded and continued. "Between the centaur and the corvus, it won't be long before Gurges Ater knows an Earthian is here. Gurges Ater will send his armies straight to Vega to secure his first pillar. We must leave soon to find

The Hunter and get you to Vega first. Here, I brought a few turkey sandwiches to rebuild your strength for the journey."

Jackson shoved one in each hoodie pocket, and then bit into the third to be polite. His stomach turned but not in reaction to the sandwich. It was the unpleasant yet familiar feeling of fear stampeding through his mind. He couldn't do this. He wasn't a hero. He couldn't fight some alien dictator. It was all too much. He didn't know what day it was or what time it was or how many police were at his house right now looking for him. His poor parents wouldn't have a clue what happened. For crying out loud, he still didn't have a clue what was happening! Otava already verified in the woods what a scared, incompetent boy he was for such a huge task. Surely, Cygnus knew it as well. Perhaps Jackson just needed to confirm their suspicions.

"I'm sorry, but I really think you should just take me home and find someone else to fight your evil dictator. Our world has powerful governments and armies and secret agents and weapons. Get them to help."

"Do you really think your leaders and kings and armies would just come and help us with no strings attached?" Cygnus leaned forward and stared into Jackson's eyes with somber severity. "We have resources and creatures and valuables your people have never seen. Would they simply rid us of Gurges Ater and then leave us in peace?" He sat back to finish his case. "You know the answer. No. They would become hungry for our land, our treasures, and our endless youth. We've seen it happen before, and many people died in both our worlds because of it."

"But I'm not a hero. I'm just a kid."

"I don't need you to fight. I don't need you to be a hero. I just need you grab a few stones. Then I will return you safely to your family with a generous reward for your service, and our worlds can continue to live peacefully and separately." Cygnus leaned forward and locked eyes with Jackson as his voice fell quiet to a compassionate but firm tone. "Listen, Jackson. I've saved your life in both your world and ours. You have nothing to fear. I will protect you."

Jackson didn't know how to get out of this mess. He wouldn't go on a risky journey in another world for mere riches, but it would be nice to bring home some alien treasure to show his parents. It might help explain his random disappearance. Cygnus *had* saved his life twice now: once from the tree, and once from the centaur's sword. Maybe he owed it to Cygnus. The white-winged man had obviously gone through much trouble to bring him to Arcas and had saved him from death already. Jackson couldn't fight an evil dictator, but with Cygnus protecting him, he could easily grab a few ancient stones. One thing was certain, there was no way he could face Cygnus and declare, "I won't help you."

Bellowing barks and lingering howls bounced off the thick trees in the forest and entered their way into the cabin.

"Do you guys hear that?" Jackson snapped out of his thoughts by the distant noise that reminded him of Farmer John's old hunting dogs.

"Hear what?" Otava asked, peering out the window with his crossbow to threaten any foe who may be near.

"Dogs," Jackson replied.

Everyone listened.

"You're right. That does sound like dogs. Otava, do you think it could be *him*?" Cygnus asked with a sudden urgency.

"He usually isn't this far north yet, but we don't typically hear any other dogs in the Starling Forest."

"Well, if it might be *him,* we'd better not miss our chance. These thick trees won't allow me to fly or see well from above, so, my friends, it's a race on foot! Let's chase down some dogs!"

Cygnus motioned them forward as they followed him out of Otava's cabin. The three dodged trees, ducked under limbs, and jumped fallen branches, using their auditory senses to track the distant, continuous canine calls.

CHAPTER 5

THE HUNTER

Little chance remained to catch up with the swift, mission-bound canines until the duo of dogs suddenly stopped underneath a tree. Bouncing upward on their back legs and pounding their front paws against the thick tree bark with their voices and heads raised, the dogs guarded their prize. When the excited creatures were within eyesight, Cygnus motioned for Otava and Jackson to stop at a safe distance. A man silently appeared from the leafy shadows, pulling out an arrow, aiming it, and firing in one smooth motion. As a black squirrel leapt to reach the unguarded branches of the next tree, a *thoomp!* stopped him mid-air. *Plop!* The furry-tailed rodent fell to the ground with an arrow stuck straight through its skull. This was not just an ordinary huntsman.

This man was The Hunter. Slowly and cautiously approaching from behind, Cygnus called out to him.

"Rigel! Many suns have crossed since I last had the pleasure to speak with you."

Acting neither startled nor surprised, The Hunter hung his bow over his shoulder and leisurely turned his head to look at the audience.

"Cygnus, old friend, thousands of suns have crossed since I have heard that name uttered by a kingdom politician." Shifting his attention back to the latest kill, The Hunter bent down, picked up the arrow, and balanced it between two tree branches with the squirrel limply hanging off the center of it. "I'm sure you remember Rigel disappeared long ago when the great waters consumed the Earth, and the Kings of Arcas drowned their sacred oaths of friendship vowed at the great pillars. The Hunter is all that's left now."

If any name is renown in Arcas yet veiled with mystery, it is The Hunter. Many in present-day have never met him, but upon sight, no one would question his identity. Though a prominent warrior in the ancient days, he removed himself from the laws and loyalties of the three kingdoms before the last great battle waged at the Pillar of Vega. Since then, his path has remained consistent: the northern mountains surrounding the Starling Forest during winter and the southwestern Free Realms during the summer.

The Hunter lives off the land and travels only with the

companionship of his two dogs: Procyon and Sirius. The legends proclaim he bears the height of a centaur, the strength of a minotaur, the stealth of a leopard, and the cunning of a wolf. Looking upon this mammoth of a man with brown hair, a ruggedly shaved face, tan leather clothing, and a thick belt with three identical silver pendants, Jackson would have easily believed every story.

"Well, Hunter, it is because of those very pillars I am standing beside you once again. I'm sure through your vast travels you have heard rumors of Gurges Ater?" Cygnus paused until The Hunter gave a slight nod of recognition. "Then, you must also know he has gained power over the years and an extensive army. He is no longer a creature hiding in the darkness of the ancient ruins of Trifid, and Earth is no longer a desolate world buried under water. Gurges Ater has somehow acquired all three gems of Arcas and plans to use them."

"So, the pillars will be blazing with trade and friendship once again, eh?" The Hunter spoke with a hint of sarcasm that turned to a hint of regret. "Don't let me waste your time then. As fond as I was of the Sons of Earth, the bitter taste of the past remains. I will not be wedged between the men of Earth and the men of Arcas. Not for the rising power of Gurges Ater. Not for the kingdoms. Not for anyone."

"Gurges Ater means not to re-establish treaties and trades with Earth. He means to create his empire on the backs of stolen slaves. He will plunder and kill to control the pillars, so he alone can gain access to Earth's weapons, wealth, and people. If he reopens the portals, he will use his new powers to take all of Arcas by force." Cygnus allowed the severity of the situation to settle in The Hunter's mind for a moment. He lowered his voice. "You know the weaknesses of men like no other. Bound by fear, they will drift into long Arcasian lives, an eternity in chains."

The Hunter knelt down, petting his two dogs that waited, patiently alert, at his sides. Suddenly, he seemed to notice Jackson's presence and turned his attention toward the boy.

"Son of Earth, where do you fit in this tale of war and woe?"

Jackson turned his eyes from the strong, fine-looking dogs to the imposing presence of The Hunter. It was time to breathe deeply, think clearly, and give the right answer. It was time to prove his commitment and worth to Cygnus.

"Cygnus asked me to go to the pillars and remove the gems of Earth so Gurges Ater can't access my world," Jackson answered, hoping he sounded more confident and courageous than he felt.

"Very good, White Wings. You have chosen a young but brave Earthian." The Hunter smiled, remembering his fondness. "Well then, that leaves only one reason for you to seek me out..." Cygnus nodded once in agreement as The

Hunter stood, looked him directly in the eyes, and announced with a stone face. "Eltanin."

"I would go myself, but I can't fly the boy that distance, and I need to gather the resistance to distract Gurges Ater from reaching Vega first."

"What about your furry friend over there? The rare sighting of a disguised Ursa could provide a good distraction." The Hunter seemed to chuckle at Otava's elaborately camouflaged attire.

"I could kill Eltanin if I wanted to! I just prefer to feel fire burning in my stomach and not on my fur!" Otava retorted, attempting to cover his fears and save his pride.

"Otava the Ursa has already shown great courage in the face of danger. He rescued the Son of Earth from a black corvus, and just moments ago, he scared off a centaur who attacked the boy. He has already given much to this cause for Arcas. I can ask no more from him."

All eyes and ears studied The Hunter, awaiting his reply. It was clear he could not be coerced or ordered or bribed. He would answer as he chose. He would go where he chose. He would live as he chose. As if his dealings with Cygnus were over, The Hunter looked directly into Jackson's eyes and with a slow cadence announced his reply.

"A hunter requires two things when he rises with the suns: a path and a purpose. Well, boy, you have placed both before me. I suppose I should know your name if we are to embark on this epic quest together." The Hunter radiated a relentless yet light-hearted courage.

"Well, sir, our large, furry friend over there calls me a Bear-Eater. Others here call me a Son of Earth, but at home, I go by Jackson."

"Furry friend, indeed! Cygnus, do you see why I don't trust these Earthians? They openly speak with jealousy over our dark rich coats of fur while they secretly scheme to wiggle their dainty, naked toes in it!" Otava wiggled his clawed foot in the air.

Everyone chuckled. Difficult times were coming, but the laughter helped lighten the heavy road the boy and The Hunter would soon travel.

"Otava, if you wait for me while I give a few instructions to my friends here, I will gladly journey back with you."

"I guess I can wait a little longer. The boy didn't eat much, so I still have plenty in my pot for dinner!"

Cygnus pulled Jackson and The Hunter aside. Within their tight huddle, he held out his hand, revealing a polished stone. It was about the size of a strawberry and displayed a mixture of intertwining red and yellow hues.

"Many years ago, I found this special transport gem," he whispered. "It possesses the self-contained power to create a small, temporary passage anywhere between our two worlds. With the gems of Arcas in the hands of the enemy, this is the only way you can transport between our worlds. It will allow you to walk from the pillars of Arcas to the pillars of Earth, so you can remove the gems."

"So, this is how you brought the boy to Arcas?"

"Yes," Cygnus answered The Hunter, then carefully instructed Jackson. "When you're inside the Pillar of Vega, press a finger on each of the four corners of the gem. Then, draw a door with the light, and walk through. But be sure to keep hold of the gem. The door only remains open as long as all corners are pressed."

"Can I use this gem to return home anytime?" Jackson asked excited by the prospect of quick access back home.

"Not quite. With this gem, you can return to *somewhere* on Earth. If you use it apart from the pillars, however, it is very dangerous. The pillars were created as safe places of transport between our worlds, but one must be careful when transporting through unmapped locations. You may end up in the middle of the ocean, in a lion's den, among savages, or falling from the sky as you personally witnessed earlier. I would not risk it, Jackson. Do not use it outside of the pillars."

"What happens after we get the gem from Vega?" The Hunter asked.

"I will send my eagle, Aquila, to collect the gem. Then, you will receive thanks and reward from the kingdoms for your services, and Jackson will journey to Altair for the next gem." Cygnus gave Jackson a pat on the back, signifying his task was far from over. He then motioned for the bear to join him. Looking back at The Hunter and Jackson a last time, Cygnus added, "Be swift, my friends. If you do not succeed quickly, Gurges Ater surely will. Not even the three suns will be able to fight the darkness he will bring to both our worlds."

Jackson waved good-bye to his two new friends, wondering if he would ever see them again. He wasn't quite sure whether to smile with a false courage or release a cry of despair. Cygnus brought him here and promised to protect him but was abandoning him again. Jackson agreed to help, but he never imagined Cygnus would leave him so quickly to journey alone with a stranger. Thankfully, The Hunter was good at displacing sentimental emotions with raw, immediate action. He grabbed the squirrel still hanging from the tree, pulled the arrow out of its skull, cut it in half with a knife from his belt, and threw a piece to each dog.

"Well, Jackson, Son of Earth who eats bears, there's no reason for delay when adventure awaits! Eltanin's desert lies ahead to the northeast. Sirius! Procyon! Let's go, boys." The Hunter commenced the journey as they steadily conquered the forest tree-by-tree, hill-by-hill.

As Jackson followed behind, he noticed the terrain was gradually changing. The soft, rolling hills he first laid eyes on in Arcas were now growing more jagged and rocky. The gigantic leafy trees, which appeared to be similar to oaks and aspens near the valley, were slowly intermingling with the mountain-thriving pines and firs. He marveled at every mountaintop and every shoot of vegetation; they looked new and old, vibrant and weathered.

Following the swift pace of a skilled outdoorsman, Jackson's legs soon reverberated with burning sensations. Regardless of his past physical excursions of swimming in the winter and baseball in the spring, mountain hiking evidently required muscles he didn't know existed. Every sensation in his brain and body screamed, *You can't do this! You don't even know what you're doing! You are on a different planet!* And all of it was true. For a quiet teen who never traveled much farther than Grandpa's house, even mountain ranges on Earth would have felt a world away from the flat, corn-filled plains he was used to.

After several hours, however, the strong, confident presence of The Hunter gradually covered Jackson with a sense of safety. But this temporary peace would quickly shatter to panic once Jackson realized they weren't traveling alone. Something was following his foreign footprints, steadily gaining ground behind the weary Son of Earth.

CHAPTER 6

SHELTERS AND TURKEY SANDWICHES

Climbing, ducking, slipping, sliding, and gripping, the inclining forest trailed on endlessly and the passage of time blurred with the continuous sunlight. Not wanting to appear whiny or weak to The Hunter, Jackson silently wrestled with his endless, exhausted thoughts.

How long have we been traveling? Every ounce of my body is throbbing! Surely we are going to stop and rest soon. I'm so hungry. Don't these people ever sleep? Have I been in Arcas for hours or days? I am so not the person for this job! I wonder if my family is searching for me. I wish I could tell them that I'm okay... Well, I'm kind of okay... at the moment at least. What will happen to my body if I die here?

Nearly ready to pass out from exhaustion, Jackson

suddenly stopped, obeying The Hunter's silent hand gesture. Sirius and Procyon froze, pointing in the same direction. Jackson's eyes slowly followed the gaze of the dogs, scanning the bushes and trees for whatever ceased their travels. Two tan-and-white pointy ears interrupted the green foliage of a nearby bush. Just as Jackson realized they were all staring at a deer—alert and sniffing the air for danger—a faint *thump!* pierced the air and into the doe's chest. The doe stumbled off wildly, but a short thirty yards away, she fell to the ground. With a flick of The Hunter's wrist, Procyon and Sirius ran ahead to guard the lifeless body.

"Do you know how to make a shelter?" The Hunter asked as they followed the trail to the doe.

"Kind of. I've made a fort out of sticks, and I sometimes watch a TV show that teaches you how to survive in the wild."

"What type of creature is a *teeveeshow*?"

Knowing how difficult it would be to explain what a television show is to The Hunter, Jackson cunningly replied, "Well, a TV is a creature that lives in a box and talks to you whenever you have nothing better to do."

The description seemed to satisfy The Hunter's half-interested question. His mind was focused on much greater things, like surviving the hazardous journey ahead and facing the dangerously deadly Eltanin.

"We need a shelter that blocks out the light, so we can

get some sleep. Did the *teeveeshow* teach you to make a shelter like that?"

"I think I can figure out how to make it dark inside."

"Then, start gathering sticks for the fire and shelter. I'll skin this deer and find a few greens to go with it."

"Are you sure I can eat a deer from Arcas? The last thing I ate almost killed me, and Cygnus just keeps giving me dry turkey sandwiches," Jackson asked, slightly worried that he would either be starving or poisoned the whole journey.

"Dry turkey sandwiches? Hahaha! Cygnus thinks he knows so much about your people. Worry not, my boy. There's plenty for you to eat here. The turkeys along with many other animals and plants were brought over from Earth during the early days, but not everything native to Arcas will kill you or make you sick. A deer surely won't." The Hunter's confident knowledge satisfied Jackson's fears.

Following instructions, Jackson began to wander through the forest. Slowly breathing in the surroundings after the swift-moving journey thus far, he began to fully appreciate the beauty all around him. The lush, untamed forest felt remarkably serene and safe. As he scanned the area for good firewood and shelter-building materials, he recognized a creature he could only dream about on Earth. His eyes grew wide. His heart pounded excitedly, but his breath ceased. *Am I dreaming?* Jackson asked himself. *I can't believe it!*

The animal's tan nostrils hovered above the ground as it sniffed and grazed at the grass near a stream flowing through the distant valley. It moved slowly around as it yanked up roots and grass with a long, ivory horn pointing out from its head. Jackson watched with awe and unbelief as it jolted up and galloped off to join a whole herd of the mythical horses trampling from the valley over another hill, sending vibrations through the forest floor. All Jackson could think about was running immediately and telling The Hunter all about the amazing sight.

"What took you so long, kid? I could've gathered the sticks, setup camp, grilled, and ate this entire doe by the time you got back with those twigs," The Hunter shouted playfully to Jackson as he returned to the flat campsite. He hadn't cooked or eaten yet, but The Hunter had indeed gathered his own sticks and leaves for the shelter, setup the campsite, skinned a deer, and staged the fire pit all while waiting for Jackson to return.

"I'm sorry it took me a while, but I found a whole herd of unicorns! There must have been a couple hundred of them! They were white and black and brown and spotted, but every single one had a horn coming straight out of its head!"

"Oh, you mean the monoceros?"

"Uh, maybe. We call them unicorns. I have seen sketches of them from mythology, but they don't exist on Earth! People don't know whether or not they've ever existed or are just stories."

"Really? How sad that you no longer see the mighty monoceros. They actually came here from Earth in the early days with other imported animals."

"No way!" Jackson felt as if he were living in the past and future simultaneously with new knowledge to bring back to mankind. "Why did they bring them to Arcas? Aren't they more dangerous than horses, stampeding around with long horns in front?"

"The monoceros are mostly peaceful creatures—stronger than an ox for hauling wood and faster than a horse if you dare mount one. Respect them and you should not have to fear them. Why don't you work on the shelter? I'll start cooking." The Hunter's driven focus remained unimpacted by Jackson's enormous discovery. He quickly returned attention to the immediate tasks of food and rest.

The pile of materials The Hunter found was a bit different from Jackson's meager collection. These leaves were as tall and wide as a man, some as thick as a plastic shower curtain. Jackson rubbed his fingers over top one thick, rubbery green leaf before turning his attention to the pile of sticks for the frame of the shelter. In his father's garage, he would have plenty of necessary tools to create such a construction. He wished for conveniences he often took for granted—tape measurer, hammer, nails, and a saw. All he had now were thin vines to use as rope. While he began tying the vine around large sticks, he could hear The Hunter hitting stones together. Soon, the rustic smell of smoke permeated the air and fire rose from scraps of vine and bark.

"The TV survival shelter is now complete!" Jackson exclaimed in earnest excitement.

The Hunter turned around from the makeshift kitchen and stared. "Is *that* what your talking box creature calls a shelter?" asked The Hunter sarcastically.

"What's wrong with it?" Jackson thought the little stick fort looked great.

"It doesn't look very sturdy."

"We'll, I don't want to make a home out of it, but I think it will work for sleeping a few hours." Jackson patted at the stick structure covered with the large leaves.

"Okay, little man. Climb in there and tell me if you can still see the suns through your roof," The Hunter challenged.

Jackson got on all fours and squeezed into his newly crafted shelter for two. Just when he got situated and looked up—*CRACK*—the poorly supported masterpiece fell crashing down on top of him.

"Ha! Ha! Ha!" bellowed The Hunter as Jackson crawled out from the rubble, flinging small twigs and debris from his clothes and hair. "Well, it was at least good for a laugh. Let me show you how it's done by a real woodsman."

With the skill of thousands of years of practice, The Hunter quickly constructed a sturdy, nocturnal-worthy dwelling place. Jackson intently studied every placement of wood and vine on the structure. Then he helped The Hunter weave the large leaves over and under the top layer of sticks like a tapestry. Except the small amount of light that entered in through the short, open door, it was very dark inside. The Hunter then instructed Jackson on how to use the extra leaves to make bedding and pillows. When the final touches were completed, The Hunter returned to the campfire.

"Now *that* is a cool shelter!" exclaimed Jackson as he entered the dwelling.

He laid his head on the leaf pillow and stared into the darkness above him. Oh, how he missed the darkness. Jackson closed his eyes and imagined the stars shining around him. He recreated their shapes slowly dancing across the night sky. As much as he missed the beauty and quiet of nighttime, what he missed most of all was sleep.

"Now, next time, I expect you will be able to build a dark, sturdy shelter yourself. Then, when you return to your teeveeshow friend, you can teach him a thing or two about survival!" The Hunter enjoyed sharing his skills once again with an Earthian. It reminded him of a time long lost, and of a fondness that time never altered. "Come, Jackson, this wild venison will soothe your stomach and boost your energy for the road ahead."

The Hunter began eating, but soon noticed that Jackson did not join him at the fire. He walked over to the shelter and gently kicked at Jackson's shoes. Smiling at his exhausted, immobile companion, he returned to the campfire, finished his meal and threw some scraps to Procyon and Sirius. The Hunter carefully separated some of the meat, wrapped it in smaller leaf sections, and then wrapped all of it in two large leaves tied together to form a traveling bag for the journey. He wrapped up the last large steak, but carefully surrounded it with warm embers on the outside of the fire. He positioned his dogs to guard the entrance of the shelter and joined Jackson for a time of rest.

After hours of slumber, Jackson groggily turned, yawned and stretched, lifting his heavy eyes. Every muscle, bone, and joint ached with stiff pain from long hours of travel, tight sleeping quarters, and the lack of a mattress. The most pressing ache, however, echoed from his grumbling stomach. He stared at the dark stick roof above him, wondering if it was morning yet.

"Oh, right. This is the land of perpetual day," Jackson remembered out loud.

He heard a small scraping sound outside the shelter. The Hunter was not inside, so the noise must be him working again on cooking or skinning something or perhaps building a horseless carriage out of sticks. Jackson smiled. He was just about to wiggle his way out of the shelter when his feet hit something soft. A head popped up and began growling.

"Sorry, boy. It's ok, boy," Jackson whispered while jerking his feet away from the creature, hoping the dog wouldn't bite them off. The growling grew louder. Jackson covered his head, moved to the fetal position, and froze.

Please don't eat me! Please don't eat me!

But the growling turned into barking, and soon the large dog was on his feet. *Clank! Crash! Thump! Bang!* It sounded as if the whole campsite fell apart. When Jackson realized he had not been eaten yet, he opened his eyes to see that Procyon was not barking at him but at something outside the tent, something in the campsite. Fear of a bite turned into fear of the unknown. Something was out there.

Though his heart pounded, ready to explode, Jackson felt slight comfort because the large barking dog had not moved from his post at the edge of the shelter. Jackson slowly crawled around in the tight space, trying to peer out the opening beyond Procyon. Heavy footsteps were running in from the forest followed by additional barking. Just as Jackson managed to peer around the dog, The Hunter and Sirius showed up.

"What happened? Are you harmed?" The Hunter asked, sword drawn and breathing hard.

"I'm fine. I don't know what happened. I just woke up and Procyon started barking at something in the camp," Jackson answered, crawling out of the shelter.

"Did you hear anything? Footsteps? Talking?" The Hunter expertly scanned the area for clues while he questioned.

"Nothing. I just woke up, the dog was barking, and then something crashed."

"Good boy, Procyon!" The Hunter petted and scratched the fearless guard's head. "Well, I don't see anything missing, but your food was knocked into the fire either when the intruder ran away or while the intruder was trying to steal it." He poked it with his sword and pulled out the black, crispy meat. "I can get more from the traveling pouch."

"Don't bother. I'll just eat Cygnus's last turkey sandwich." Jackson's worries turned the conversation quickly from food back to foe. "Who would've done this? The centaur said he was going to come after me! Could it have been him?" Jackson feared that Gurges Ater and his army had already found him.

"If there were tracks, I'd have a good idea about who or what the intruder was, but there are none."

"Cygnus said those freaky black birds were flying around the forest. Are there any signs of a giant bird?"

"Not a print, not scratch from a corvus claw, not even a broken twig. This creature did not want to be discovered... Whatever it was, we'd better leave before more come."

In just a moment, The Hunter tore down the shelter till it looked like a random pile of forest remains. He expertly covered their tracks and the fire, and they headed northeast toward Eltanin's Desert. While Jackson feared that danger was stalking them from behind, The Hunter knew the most threatening danger lurked ahead, guarding the Pillar of Vega.

CHAPTER 7

ELTANIN'S DESERT

One sun, two suns, three suns. Three suns, two suns, one sun. As far as he could tell, Jackson must have been walking through the desert for about two Arcasian days now, though it seemed more like two weeks. This world transitioned through time, but it felt like a blurry transition: light followed light followed light from the colorful, revolving trinity of fireballs in the sky. If he had his phone, Jackson would futilely attempt to text his brother to find out the day and time in Indiana right this very moment. He couldn't keep track of how long he'd been gone, and Jackson worried about his family often. He continued to remind himself that the best thing he could do to get home soon was just to focus on the mission. Since leaving the forest-filled mountains, the suns were really the only varying things to look at now besides sand, rocks in the sand, and wind ripples in the sand.

No clouds today and no shade today—it was a hot, hot, hot wasteland of nothingness. Jackson ached with desire to pour his remaining water rations over his gritty hands, his sweaty feet sticking to browned socks, and his dusty head. His legs had recovered from the mountain climbing days prior, but his current unspoken complaints were his cracked lips, arid eyes, and sweltering skin, which couldn't cool off while the suns of Arcas constantly beamed down upon him. He also couldn't shake the creepy feeling they were being followed. Every time The Hunter turned to glimpse behind them, Jackson also turned, expecting to find an army on horseback or giant birds in full pursuit, but their eyes always met the same view of unending sun and sand.

Jackson imagined riding Farmer John's horse, Thunder, through the desert instead of suffering through each never-ending step on foot. The powerful brown thoroughbred raced over the sand as the wind cooled Jackson's face and instantaneously dried his sweat, creating a natural air-conditioning. Of course, Jackson was also drinking an ice-cold pop in this dream sequence and was chasing a more intriguing adventure than collecting ancient, polished stones.

He galloped onward in the blazing sun to save a beautiful princess from the clutches of a dragon... Well maybe a princess was a little too high maintenance. He galloped onward in the blazing sun to save a beautiful maiden who was stolen from her quiet village by savages and chained next to the dragon's lair as a pagan sacrifice.

"I recognize this area. We have less than two days till we reach the mount," The Hunter explained to Jackson, interrupting his fantasy.

"Do we have enough water to make it?" Jackson partially complained and partially really wanted to know if he would survive.

"As long as you don't keep giving it to the dogs to drink, we will be fine. These hearty Arcasian dogs are full of vigor. They can go days without water."

"Okay. I'll try not to. They just looked really thirsty. Do you guys ride any regular horses in Arcas?"

"Getting tired, Son of Earth?" The Hunter seemed to chuckle at his feeble companion while the mammoth of a man displayed few signs of fatigue.

"Well, I was just thinking about a horse back home that would come in pretty handy about now."

"Yes, we have horses on Arcas, but most of the tame ones are found in the kingdoms. Occasionally, you may find a wild horse, but good luck catching one of those beasts. You'd have better luck riding a wild monoceros than a wild horse."

Up ahead, the barren terrain was starting to change. The sand was becoming slightly lighter and nearly transparent, almost like golden glass. It still moved like sand underneath them though it felt a little stiffer and occasionally a little crunchy beneath their shoes. Every couple hundred paces, they would spot a cactus that rose for what seemed like miles in the sky. Since the crimson sun vanished under the horizon again, the high golden sun and lower coral sun now angled upon each cactus from one side, creating a slight shade for them to rest under. The travelers took advantage of the new shade often.

The thick, unique cacti bore neither fruit nor needles. The vertically rippled desert growths were large, green, spongy, leafless trees—a stock of life surrounded by nothingness. Jackson tried to scratch a hole in one to see if water would leak out as he rested against the giant green pillow. A thin layer of mucus seeped under his fingernail. He thought about licking it off, but during the minute he studied the substance, its moisture evaporated, leaving only tiny, white, powdery flakes. He squished the flakes between his fingers and let them float off in the growing breeze.

Jackson and the Hunter stood and stretched from a quick rest in the shade. Ahead, the once-level yet lightly rippled terrain became bumpy and jagged. The same golden-glass sand carpeted the ground, though with less uniformity than before. One solitary rock pile silhouetted the horizon. Jackson was about to comment on the odd change in scenery when he felt a faint vibration move from his feet to his hands to his head. He grabbed for his water and leaned his hand against the smooth cactus, assuming his body was reacting to weariness or heat exhaustion. The wind blew stronger, cooling their bodies while distributing particles of sand through the air.

Jackson rehydrated and steadied himself against the plant, but the vibrations did not cease. As his senses awakened, he didn't just feel a rumbling anymore—he heard it. Jackson and The Hunter simultaneously twisted around to see where the sounds were coming from. The sight produced momentary paralysis, which quickly changed into a terrified sprint to escape. An enormous, golden-brown wall galloped toward them in the distance with columns of earth-toned wind leading the charge.

"Haboob! Run to those rocks!" The Hunter directed, pointing to the only source of possible protection.

"What is that!" Jackson yelled through the deep, intense moaning of the currents.

"A sandstorm!" The Hunter hollered back as they continued darting away from the impending danger.

Jackson nodded, then focused more on the ground in front of him than the destination ahead. The heavy sand sunk beneath him as each foot plunged into it. Walking on sand was definitely easier than running. Jackson noticed he was nearing the small, bumpy hills of sand. He determined they must be caused by wind, and so he decided to run right through them rather than waste energy dodging them. Jackson threw his foot and his weight on the first one he came across, expecting to sink a little and continue on. The soft landing he'd foreseen was met with startling solid rigidity that jolted his knees, hands, and face to the ground. Spitting the sand from his mouth, then bouncing back up, Jackson continued the race with a new strategy of either hurdling the bumps or evading them, as he could no longer trust what lie underneath.

The Hunter and his dogs rounded the pile of large rocks and disappeared. Jackson could feel pricks of sand beating against his exposed extremities. The rumbles grew louder and the lights of Arcas darker as the soaring shadow blocked their rays. Jackson curved around the boulders and met The Hunter, who was seated with his back against them, working meticulously to ready the area for the stormy blast. The Hunter handed Jackson a wet cloth.

"Lightly tie this behind your head to cover your nose and mouth. Close your eyes, pull your shirt over your head, and rest on your knees," The Hunter instructed.

The Hunter peered over the rocks, gauging the distance. He jolted back down as the coming darkness roared just seconds away. Pulling the cloak from behind him, he encompassed both his body and that of Sirius and Procyon. Jackson closed his eyes and hid his head. The intense wind cooled his body and the rumbling darkness could have even lulled him to sleep if it weren't for the flinging armies of sand attacking his bare, exposed legs. He blindly reached down to release his rolled-up pants. Success!

His hands were now stinging from the tiny attackers, but his legs were covered and the flying grains and boisterous winds against his back were bearable. The darkness continued, the vibrations continued, and the roaring winds continued.

"Jackson, wake-up, boy, the storm is over." The Hunter's large hand firmly shook his left shoulder. Words faintly flew through the expanse of Jackson's mind as he regained consciousness.

But it's still dark. It's still bedtime.

He obediently reached up and pulled first the hoodie then his shirt off his head, squinting through his weighty eyes. The perceived darkness was just The Hunter's large shadow over him, blocking out the suns. Jackson removed the cloth from his face. It was mostly dry now, but contained a layer of thin mud on the outside. Though he felt disgustingly dirty and thirsty, he was thankful the high winds dried his sweat or he, too, would have a layer of mud blanketing his skin. He stood up and shook the thick dust from his shirt and pants. Many miles away now, the faint, brown wall of grainy, flying particles continued rolling through the desert.

"Take a look behind us. The storm uncovered a little bitter history between our worlds."

Jackson stood on the small rock he had used as a seat during the storm, gripping the larger one overhead. The ground previously carpeted with bumpy sand—the same sand he tripped on while running from the storm—was no longer just bumps in the desert. Hundreds of black metal fragments and wood shards now broke through their sandy covering. As their eyes rolled over the open field, the sun sparkled specks of light off tiny spots still bearing the original metallic shimmer. Most of the helmets, spearheads, and broken pieces of shield appeared warped with dull brownish-green hues encompassing them.

"After the great water consumed Earth, there was a mighty, final battle that took place on these very grounds between the Sons of Earth and the Sons of Arcas. The Sons of Earth did not want the pillars closed. They still had hope that there was life on the other side, and so they overtook the northern kingdom and made their final stand at the Pillar of Vega where the last door to Earth remained open." The Hunter grew more animated, pointing into the desolate land as if it were alive in front of them.

"At that time, Eltanin was a powerful dragon that had the strength of a thousand men. It has been said that the three kings sent Eltanin to destroy Earth's army with the mighty fire from his mouth. With similar cunning, the Sons of Earth brought their guiding light Thuban, who was also Eltanin's brother, to fight and destroy the Arcasian army. As the battle began, the dragon brothers circled over the armies with strength and ferocity, but when the two beasts saw the pupils of each other's eyes, they each turned against their own soldiers and nearly wiped out all flesh at the scene. The few Sons of Earth who survived were banished from Arcas.

They chose to enter the portal one last time and face the wrath of the waters rather than face the wrath of the sword. The surviving kingdom soldiers finally killed Thuban, but the wounded Eltanin was punished for his betrayal. They removed his greatest power, leaving him bound to the waters at the Pillar of Vega. He would forever protect the pillar he betrayed in battle." The Hunter finished his colossal tale while Jackson rebuilt the grandeur and horror of the scene before him.

"Wait a minute... Eltanin is a dragon?" Jackson was suddenly hit with the reality lying before them.

"Of course," The Hunter answered confidently though slightly puzzled that Jackson had agreed to a task when he didn't fully understand the dangers of the mission. Jackson's stomach began to turn into a hundred tiny knots. Though the dry sandstorm seemed to vanquish every drop of liquid from his body, sweat moistened his forehead once again.

"You said his greatest power was removed, so he can't breathe fire, right?" Jackson asked, trying to find some logic and hope amidst the growing presence of monsters and danger.

"A dragon's greatest power is not fire, Jackson." The Hunter explained, "Fire contained in a pit of rock or a pool of water will not singe a home. But fire that rides on the evening wind will consume a village."

Jackson thought over the riddle for a moment.

"So, Eltanin can't fly?" The Hunter gave a nod of

affirmation. "But, flight or not, you're still telling me that we have to waltz past a fire-breathing dragon to enter the Pillar of Vega?"

"No, Son of Earth, *we* are not going to pass Eltanin. You are."

CHAPTER 8

THE PILLAR OF VEGA

In the distance, the weary travelers spotted three great mountaintops. Now, these weren't like the Colorado Rocky Mountains—a range of continuous, pointed, dark rocky tops dusted with snow that Jackson studied for a geology project last year. These mountaintops were vertically striped with reds and tans, flattened on top, and pillaring straight upward like a New York skyscraper. Though the triune mountains were grouped tightly together in comparison to the vast wasteland that surrounded them, each mountain stood alone, separated by a football field's length of flat, sandy land in between. Towering palm trees and short bushes spotted around the two side mountains. But dense green vegetation surrounded the mountain in the middle.

"There she is—the tallest mountain in the fallen

kingdom of Vega, home to the last open portal between our worlds."

"This doesn't look much like a kingdom."

"It was a small kingdom, but a strong and wealthy people. They dwelt in tents as far as your eyes can see, and King Adhafera's palace rested high on top of Vega's mountain. All traces of their homes were consumed in the dragons' flames."

"How can there be palm trees and grasses growing around it in the middle of the desert?"

"Just hidden past those trees and grasses rests the kingdom's water supply, a large, natural oasis of fresh ground water. Now, it only quenches Eltanin's thirst." Reaching a stone's throw away from the lush vegetation, The Hunter sent the dogs ahead. "Go check it out, boys. Go!"

Alert and eager for action, Procyon and Sirius raced forward to circle the mountain. Jackson and The Hunter slowly and quietly crept through the surrounding brush, hoping to drink some water and freshen their faces and hands. A slight breeze rustled through the green life springing up from the water's edge. Their voices now turned to whispers as Jackson and the Hunter crouched behind a bush and through some grass to fill their goatskins with water. The swift dogs returned minutes later, joining Jackson and The Hunter to lap up the cool, fresh spring. Once Procyon and Sirius were refreshed, The Hunter sent them around the entire mountain again, but this time, they jogged cautiously through the grasses and bushes, sniffing and listening for the slightest sign of the beast.

Silence. Though calm in sight above, they could feel the energy below: hunger, anger, and revenge rolling underneath the blue, waiting to taste the rarity of flesh once again. There were more strange vibes emanating from the tranquil water than Jackson would have liked. Both life and death swam in this oasis. And every breath of wind, every rustle of brush, every interruption of the water's stillness screamed to Eltanin, *Someone is here!*

"The water is calm. It should be an easy swim," Jackson remarked hopefully.

"It may be calm, but it is not still."

"Maybe no one's here…" Jackson whispered, hoping the deafening silence was proof the dangerous dragon no longer resided at the mountain's moat.

"Maybe, but the longer we stay, the more likely something *will* be here. If you quietly wade across, perhaps we will go unnoticed." The Hunter grasped Jackson's arm and stared into his eyes as if he were forcing courage into the boy's very soul. He then nodded to signify the moment was now and released him.

The time to think was over. The long desert days were for pondering different scenarios, different dangers, and different deaths, but today, today was the day for Jackson to act, and now was the time. With clammy hands sticking uncomfortably to grains of sand and fibers of grass, he crawled to water's edge again. Jackson pulled off his shoes slowly, methodically placing each sandy sock inside and arranging them next to each other in the grass. Each motion felt like a step closer to death. Jackson breathed out, silently slid his legs around front, and turned to grab the earth behind him while sinking into the wet blue.

The water felt surprisingly cool and refreshing against Jackson's parched, dusty body. His fully saturated jeans, which they cut off into shorts after the sandstorm, felt weighty but manageable. The sensation of a smooth, cool bath relaxed his tense nerves, but Jackson stopped himself from the strong temptation to close his eyes and dunk his head in. Ever so slowly, he stroked his hands under the water, moving from his chest outward. He paused slightly between rapid deep kicks, hoping to stir few ripples and remain as quiet as possible by keeping his feet well beneath the surface.

Jackson's mind traveled back to the first time he swam through Farmer John's pond. The water was clean as far as pond water goes, but it was still dark and murky; one couldn't see more than six inches past the surface. At ten years old, even with his grandpa swimming just a few strokes away, he kept feeling like some hungry fish or underwater terror would snap off his toes or drag him underneath. His juvenile terror was really the fear of the unknown, the fear that darkness always conceals the most unspeakable danger.

74

Yet in this moment when danger was most likely to come upon him, the water was clear. He could see colorful underwater flowers swaying gently twenty feet or so below his feet before the clear blue turned into a soft navy. Though vegetation flourished next to the sweet water, Jackson didn't see any animal life within. Fifty yards to go and half way there, he turned his head to make eye contact with The Hunter, who nodded him on. Jackson increased his speed, locking his eyes on the steep rock stairs carved up the side, which led to a large entrance inside the mountain.

Suddenly, Procyon began barking loudly from the bank. Jackson noticed the silhouette of Sirius running from behind the mountain toward The Hunter and Procyon. The barking continued. Jackson knew something was happening, so he abandoned the calm, quiet swim and flew into the fastest freestyle of his life. The Hunter took cover behind a bush amidst the tall bank grasses, pulled back his arrow, and searched the water for the creature.

Jackson could hear the *splash-splash, splash-splash* of his arms alternating through the thick wetness. His legs and arms began tightening into a slow, familiar burning sensation. Through the rush of water against his head, he could still hear the continuous, maddening barks that heightened his pace, his nerves, and his heart. As Sirius reached his companion guarding The Hunter, Procyon dove into the water and swam after Jackson.

Where is it! He was waiting for it, but he could not feel

it. Every nerve in his body expected to feel a clamp on his leg, a tail whip under his belly, or a claw drag down his back. Instead, he only felt the smooth, yet grainy rocks as he grabbed the stairs and pulled himself out of the water. Jackson ran and ran and ran, up and up and up, focusing on each step to get as far from the water as he could.

"Jackson, STOP!" The Hunter yelled out.

Jackson froze and whipped around, facing The Hunter. Sirius continued barking not at the water, but directly at Jackson, while The Hunter's arrow was pointing not at the water, but directly at Jackson.

"What are you doing?" Jackson yelled in confused horror. "Where's the dragon?"

"Duck!"

"What?"

"DUCK NOW!" The Hunter shouted as he shot the arrow straight toward Jackson. As Jackson fell upon the rocks underneath him, a shrieking roar flew over his body and skidded partially down the mountain. The beast twisted his long neck around to yank out the arrow, which pierced his leathery, scaled shoulder like a mere thorn. Eltanin's bright green, cat-like eyes whipped back toward the boy who was crumpled on the ground, peering through his arm at the enormous creature.

Thwoosh. Thwoosh. Two more arrows bolted through the air, one into the front leg and one into chest of the beast. The dragon became increasingly irritated and increasingly wild as he ripped the puny arrows out and turned his fury on The Hunter. Eltanin hurled spit and fire as he bellowed across the moat, singeing grasses and shrubs but missing The Hunter, who rolled out of the path. Procyon bolted out of the water and ran with bared teeth toward the dragon. Another arrow flew at his face, but missed as the giant reptile dove into the deep blue water.

"Hurry, Jackson, run! Go with him, Procyon!" The Hunter yelled as he sprinted with Sirius to a new location, preparing to face the next move from the wingless dragon.

Jackson raced up a couple dozen more stairs, finally reaching the entrance as the faithful dog joined him. The large, hollow room inside the mountain was decorated only with a bed of grasses and a pile of dry bones. In the back, a single light shined down upon a sparkling white spiral staircase. Jackson hurried up the milky quartz spirals with lungs and legs still burning until he finally made it to a room just below the top of the mountain.

When the staircase ended, Jackson's eyes were overwhelmed with walls full of gems, precious stones, and glorious texture. The ceiling contained two large skylights in the rock above; one lit the stairs and the other lit the pillar. Across from the pillar, words written in an unknown character language sat etched into the wall. The Pillar of Vega consisted of three circular columns that rose to Jackson's waist. On top of three columns, a large flat sheet of rock rested. It was precisely carved, containing three large circles, one on the left, right, and top. Underneath the circles, a large diamond shape was carved with a smaller, vacant gem-shaped hole in the middle of it. The stone looked surprisingly familiar, but there was no time to scroll through his mind to access the memory.

Outside, The Hunter and Eltanin played a deadly game of cat and mouse. Eltanin would jump out of the water to spit fire at The Hunter, who used his mighty sword to repel the fire back toward the dragon, already diving beneath the surface in time for the flames to flow over empty water. Sirius paced back and forth along the edge of the water, trying both to contain the beast and to alert The Hunter of his whereabouts.

"Come on and fight, Eltanin!" The Hunter taunted. "You used to fly over the heads of men, commanding the skies and respect. Now you swim under men's feet and hide behind a fading flame. Do you really want to die like a coward? Come out and face me, you wingless, slithering serpent!"

Jackson heard deep pounding against the mountain as if a semi-truck were ramming into the side of it. Procyon perked up his ears, analyzing each noise outside. It was clear the battle continued. He pulled out the red-and-yellow transport gem. One, two, three, four, Jackson squeezed each point of the gem with a finger. Vibrations, energy, and light flew out of the gem and into the room. Just as Cygnus had instructed him, he drew an arched door, held his breath, and stepped through the dancing portal.

Jackson hadn't really thought about what he would do or how he would feel once he stepped onto Earth again. One would think he would be full of emotional explosions of relief and comfort after so many days in another world. His immediate physical discomfort, however, took over any other feelings. First, he fell a few feet to a cold, slick floor. After picking himself up, Jackson saw a white hall covered with snow and ice. A few dark walkways sprouted out from the main room. Shivering, he remembered his hoodie lay by the oasis outside, and his body remained damp from the recent swim.

Jackson scanned the room; it felt similar to the pillar on Arcas. Rather than a collage of decorative gems, the iced walls displayed elaborate carvings and engraved designs underneath. The frozen room glistened off the portal lights like a thousand diamonds. In the far wall sat the same type of circular rock that rested on the Vega's pillar; it was the only part of the room that wasn't coated with ice.

Different from Vega, however, this round, flat slab was designed with a circle on top, a crescent moon on the left side, and a cluster of stars on the right. The bottom section again displayed one large diamond shape, but this time, the diamond-shaped slot had a stone within it. There was an inscription over the rock, but it again displayed characters he did not recognize and a language he could not read. The bright-yellow stone slowly turned within the deep groove. Jackson held his breath, reached in, and removed it. It felt as if the gem fought its departure with a slight magnetic tension before the release.

Then DARKNESS. Cold darkness surrounded him everywhere. Jackson panicked. *What did I do? Where did the light go?* Finally, through his shivering worries of a frosty death, he remembered Cygnus's instructions. The portal only stays open while all four fingers continue to grasp the corners of the transport gem. Upon holding the gem of Earth, he had released his precision points on the transport stone and shut the portal. Jackson blindly explored the jewel in his hand, pressing each finger on a point until light shot through the room again. He drew another door and ran back into the warm desert cave. Procyon was gone and Jackson's fears grew wild again. After one last glimpse of the remarkable grotto-like pillar room, he ran back down the stairs to the cave entrance.

The Hunter and Eltanin now fought face-to-face on the dry ground between Vega and the left mountain: flame meeting sword, snap chasing swipe. Procyon was already panting and paddling through the water to join his battling companions just as Sirius was violently thrown near the left mountain by the blunt swing and force of the dragon's head against his body.

Jackson dove back into the oasis to meet The Hunter for their final escape. But as Jackson swam, the dragon lunged at The Hunter, spewed a quick flame, and then whipped his tail around, knocking The Hunter flat on his back. Before The Hunter could regain his footing, the dragon was on top of him. One large, clawed foot held down The Hunter's legs while only the sword's blade separated the dragon's teeth from The Hunter's face. Hot drops of spit flew down, sizzling the clothes on his chest as Eltanin snarled, roared, and snapped.

"AHHH!" The Hunter bellowed in pain as the dragon put all his weight on The Hunter's legs and reared up, flinging the sword into the water by swiping forcefully with one front claw. Eltanin then shot thick flames at Procyon who was nearing the battle. Awaking from his stupor, Sirius darted to join the fight while Procyon ran from the raging, fiery breath.

"NOOOO!" Jackson screamed in anguish as he crawled onto the bank and watched the mighty Eltanin arch his neck for the final attack.

A growling roar rose up, echoing between the three mountains, but the sound did not come from the dragon. A large, flying, desert-camouflaged creature bound on top of the dragon's lower back, sinking its teeth and claws into the beast. Scales ripped off like shingles on a tornado-ravaged roof. Warm blood gushed out from the fresh, exposed meat. As the dragon swung his head and body around to strike, the creature jumped off and rolled behind a large group of boulders. Eltanin roared and sprayed fire out over the rocks.

"Otava?" The Hunter called out, jumping to his feet. His clothes were a little singed, and he was dripping in dragon spit and his own sweat but still strong and ready to fight.

"Don't worry! I'm not on fire. Hey, Jackson! Can you distract this reptile for a minute? I need to get a weapon to The Hunter!"

With no weapon of his own, Jackson picked up stones and threw them at Eltanin, distracting the beast's attention away from the others. The Hunter joined Otava behind the mountain boulders to find a pile of artillery laid out: a battle-axe, javelin, bolas, flail, military fork, and a crossbow were a few of the many, which were unraveled from an arsenal-filled bag and displayed for the choosing.

"Ha! Which one am I supposed to use? All of them at once?" The Hunter chuckled.

"Use what you want. You volunteered for this. I just know better than to bring a mere knife to a dragon fight!" Otava answered back.

With one hand, The Hunter grabbed the bolas and whipped the tight rope connected to three balls over and around his head several times to gain speed. Jackson, Procyon, and Sirius were all providing a hearty distraction now as the three sprinted around, dodging the rapidly hurling dragon's breath. Still swinging the bolas, The Hunter picked up the javelin with his other arm and torpedoed it at the beast. Feeling the danger whizzing through the air toward him, Eltanin flung his body around, facing The Hunter once again and avoiding the javelin.

Once their eyes met, the bolas spun through the air and flung around the mouth and nose of the dragon, dampening his flame and muzzling his bite. As Eltanin clawed at the ropes on his face, Otava popped out from the rocks with his crossbow, shooting a large net over the dragon's body. The Hunter and Otava promptly secured the netting down by stabbing several sharp, long weapons through the net into the ground and by pushing a few boulders on top of the corners. Then, The Hunter and his dogs guarded the trapped Eltanin as Otava returned his arsenal into his traveling bag, and Jackson recovered The Hunter's sword sticking in a few rocks not far below the water's surface.

Jumping back in the oasis to retrieve the sword soothed him, like aloe on his hot skin. Jackson's arms and face still glowed red from the dragon's heat that had blazed past him. He yanked the sword out and climbed back on the bank. With the sandy grime washed off his toes, he realized his feet were covered in scrapes, cuts, and skid marks. He shook the dust off his dry socks, replaced them on his weathered feet along with his shoes for protection, and tied his hoodie around his waist. As he met the others guarding Eltanin, he now noticed thick, dark-red scars where wings once sprung from the creature's back.

"Are you going to kill him now?" Jackson asked, giving the heavy sword back to The Hunter.

"No. We'll leave him in peace. In a few days the cords

will loosen, and he'll find a way to free himself. You have the gem, and we all have our lives, so there is no reason for further bloodshed," The Hunter replied.

"Heed. Heed. We won the battle with little injury, and we will let him lose the battle with little injury," Otava agreed.

The unique team of three gathered some water and their weapons, then veered east into the desert. Jackson smiled as he thought about all of his previous "battles" with "Draco the Dragon." Like this one, he had always finished in victory. But today, he had completed a real task and won a real prize, and it wasn't the little yellow gem in his pocket. It was the combat-earned friendship of a man, a boy, a bear, and two dogs.

Jackson battled with friends today, and none fought for pride or prestige; they fought for the greater substances of life, peace, and unfettered freedom. On the path toward the next pillar and the next gem, Jackson would reflect upon every scrape, bruise, and sore muscle with keen fondness. He had conquered his worst fears. Jackson looked death in the face, survived it, and he had never felt more alive.

The round crimson sun set at their backs, the golden sun warmed their heads, and the coral sun rose up on the Eastern horizon, lighting their path to the Eridanus River and the Altair Kingdom.

CHAPTER 9

THE SEVENTH SISTER

Merope floated atop the sand as tiny grains of dust bounced and swirled underneath, flicking the hem of her long, brown cloak. For a few hours now in her journey through the desert, she listened to muffled roars, grunts, and thumps as Eltanin tried to loosen the woven binds. Finally, her silver eyes met his. With his mouth wound shut, Eltanin's blazing breath remained stifled to a mere steam exiting his nostrils. His flailing claws, legs, and tail had managed to twist and tangle their way into further bondage.

Merope glided over to the beast, examining his binds. She moved near Eltanin's glossy, scaled face as he continued to writhe and twist. Sitting down next to him, she gazed in his eyes, touched the top of his muzzle, and hummed a deep, enchanting song through her body. Her lips never moved. Eltanin relaxed. His heavy, large eyes softened their glare and closed. Merope's song continued as she waltzed around the dragon, carefully cutting and unwinding his binds. Lastly, she stroked his head and tenderly removed the bolas from his muzzled mouth.

Merope moved backward, keeping her eyes steadily focused on the dragon. When she was just past the three mountains, she stopped humming and dropped her bare feet to the ground in a light thump. Eltanin's eyes shot open, and he jumped to his feet. After quickly surveying his surroundings for a threat, their eyes met once again, and he calmly returned to the water. Merope then examined the five sets of footprints and followed their trail. The rugged, chuckling, and adventure-dirtied comrades she was tracking were quite the contrast to her mysterious grace and beauty.

Merope was the youngest and darkest of her sisters. Her thick, black hair, highlighted with deep purples, slowly danced around her silver eyes, illuminating her olive skin, and flowed down to her waist in a gentle wave. Though her looks were unique among the seven Ilmatar sisters, all shared the same shimmering silver eyes and the same swaying power of song.

It had been six days since she last saw her sisters. The ambush and confusion were still fresh in her mind. Merope had been returning triumphantly from picking mushrooms. She had finally reached the last elegantly chiseled step up the wooden staircase to their treetop home and threw open the door.

"See, Asterope? I told you I would find a bag full of mushrooms!"

As soon as Merope spoke, the bag dropped from her hands, bounced off the side of the tree and scattered on the ground below. Her six sisters were all surrounded by weapons and masked raiders who were tying their hands and gagging their mouths. One man reached for her, but she jumped from the top platform, slowed her fall midair and rolled to the ground. The raider, who attempted to grab her, wasn't expecting her to leap off and reached too far. Hitting a few tree limbs first, he came crashing down with a loud thud. While he groaned on the Starling Forest floor, two others rushed down the stairs to pursue Merope. She took off running as her eldest sister Maia cried out to her.

"Merope, find White Wings! Find White Wings!"

Hiding beneath a concealing thicket of bushes for what seemed like hours, Merope watched her sisters being carried off through the sky in burlap sacks by large, black ravens. The masked raiders cut down the sisters' tree, sending their beautiful home crashing to the forest floor. As a few of the villains built a fire and congratulated themselves over a feast of stolen food, Merope snuck behind the rubble of her broken home. The ravens were long out of sight. With no available tracks to follow her sisters, Merope gathered a few items from the wreckage and left in search of White Wings.

Along the journey, she came across the mumbling of voices bouncing off, around, and through the thick forest trees.

Is this the rest of the ambush party? she wondered. Merope crept closer and carefully found a hiding spot to listen. Perhaps the raiders would reveal information about her sisters' whereabouts.

"My brothers, many of you have heard legends and stories of the one known as White Wings. The three suns have only passed Arcas one time since last I saw him with my own eyes. But that is not all I saw. While traveling through the Starling Forest, I found a Son of Earth."

The shocked crowd gasped with hushed variations of "No!" and "What?" and "It can't be!"

"We all know that the presence of even one Earthian in our free Arcas threatens us all." Weapons pounded the ground in agreement. "White Wings and some disguised beast protected this human from my sword, and then attempted to kill me."

Since the owner of the voice speaking stood tall on the side of a hill above the others, Merope could easily see the centaur. He described his encounter with urgency to a group of fellow horsemen and Arcasian men who, similar to the raiders, did not wear the tunics or emblems of the kingdom realms. One man then stepped forward and took over the oration.

"We believe White Wings is taking the Son of Earth to the ancient pillars. This boy could destroy everything our people have worked for. Our orders from Regulus are to wait here for additional legions arriving tomorrow. Then, part of us will head to Vega with Regulus, and the others will go to the Eridanus with Arcturus to intercept them before they reach the Pillar of Altair."

For as long as Merope could remember, these woods—her woods—had been a place of quiet and peace. Now, something big was brewing, something that smelled of war. Merope would not wait around for more soldiers to arrive. She took off through the forest heading toward the desert and the Pillar of Vega. She didn't understand how a Son of Earth could have entered Arcas again or why White Wings was with him, but that was the least of her worries. Her home lay in shambles, and her sisters were captured. The only option was to find White Wings before the army did, warn him of their plans, and figure out how to rescue her sisters.

Yet, after all these days of tracking a Son of Earth, an Arcasian man, and a burly bear, Merope still hadn't seen White Wings and still wasn't certain whether these travelers were friend or foe. Though Merope saw no faces when she clumsily crashed their campsite after their watchdog's nose and ears caught her, it was evident by the shadowy silhouettes that none bore wings. She held back a bit in fear of being caught, only to witness the camouflaged, furry brown bear also following their path to Vega. Thus, Merope waited even longer, insuring a safe distance between her and the bear before she continued tracking.

One thing felt certain: somehow these travelers were connected with White Wings, and somehow their story was connected with the disappearance of her sisters. So, for many days the Ilmatar continued to follow the bear, who followed the boy, who followed the dogs, who followed The Hunter.

Merope was pleased to free Eltanin from his binds. She fervently hoped someone noble would find her bound sisters and free them as well. It was obvious a battle had been waged against this beast, and she was intrigued as to why the dragon was left alive. Determined to find answers to the multitude of questions brewing inside her, Merope persisted after the fading footprints while the rippling grains of sand underneath gradually transformed into a savanna of fluttering grasses, shrubs, trees, and bushes.

CHAPTER 10

RIDE THE RIVER ERIDANUS

More than one creature was tracking the path of an Arcasian man, a Son of Earth, a bear, and two dogs. A large golden eagle, its body the size of a man's, was gaining ground overhead and began circling the travelers. Its sharp beak was colored black at the tip and pale yellow toward his eyes. The eagle's feathers mainly displayed shades of dark brown though variations from black to white echoed through his wingspan and tail. His head and back, however, were highlighted with golden tans. Bright blue talons shot out of the bird's yellow feet.

The Hunter's sword and Otava's crossbow flew out in reflexive defense as a preying bird this size could easily carry off a boy or a dog. But the bird did not swoop down to grab or attack. Instead, it dropped a small leather bag from its sharp, blue talons right in the middle of the group. The Hunter grabbed the bag, opened it, and pulled out a message that he read to Otava and Jackson.

To The Hunter and Jackson,

If you are reading this message, then you have surely conquered and killed the great Eltanin and sealed the first pillar. Well done, my friends!

The knowledge and resistance against Gurges Ater is mounting successfully, but there is still much to be done before leading an army against the Trifid Fortress on the Ligeian Sea. Be on guard and trust no one, as there are spies busy in search of the Son of Earth. If The Most Skillful Hunter will be generous and guide him just a little farther, I have a boat waiting for Jackson at the Eridanus River.

Please put the yellow gem from Earth in the satchel, and Aquila will bring it safely back to me. It is unwise for Jackson to carry it farther in case of capture or loss on the journey.

Arcas and Earth owe you both a debt of gratitude for your bravery and service at this critical hour.

– Cygnus

All were silent for a moment as they considered Cygnus's letter. Aquila stood at attention, fixing his yellow eyes in turn on each person and dog, waiting to fulfill his current mission.

"Will Cygnus be upset when he learns we didn't kill the dragon?" Jackson asked.

"No," The Hunter replied. "He does not have the right to be upset over Eltanin's spared life. The same grace was extended to him once before. If there's a problem, I will deal with Cygnus."

"So, I guess when we reach the river, then you guys are done, and I continue alone, right?" Jackson mustered up enough courage to announce this more as a fact than a question. After all, Otava and The Hunter might find it perfectly acceptable to leave soon, though Jackson dreaded continuing on into the unknown world without his new companions.

"No," The Hunter stated clearly and firmly.

"What do you mean? You fulfilled your word to Cygnus. You can return to the mountains hunting, and Otava can return to cooking and… trapping humans." Jackson smiled fondly though his stomach ached at the proposition of them leaving.

"No, Jackson. We go together. There are two more pillars to visit and two more gems to collect from Earth. I wish to see them. Otava, thank you for coming a long way to fight by our side. We will neither forget your courage nor your satchel full of many, many interesting weapons."

"As sure as the three suns shine upon Arcas, I'm not leaving! This Son of Earth turned out not to be a Bear-Eater, and he certainly showed the courage of a dragon-slayer. My weapons and I are going to stick around to see what else this little man can do!"

It was settled. The three would continue the journey to the pillars of Altair and Deneb together. Jackson placed the yellow gem in the small bag and held it out toward the large bird. Aquila raised himself above the ground then swooped past Jackson, extending his blue talons and grabbing the bag with one motion. In moments, he disappeared into the sky.

Jackson felt relieved to have completed the first task, but he also felt a strange warmth. Now, he'd felt physically warm many times since the three suns fell upon his head in this new land, but it was the first time that he felt inner warmth here. It was like he was home again. It was like he was with family. The kind of family who tease you and harass you and confront you and push you to your limits, but never ever leave you and would fight with you against any foe on any day to the very ends of the universe.

Merope was gaining ground on the travelers as she reached an area of tall, thin trees, which gradually blossomed into the jungle surrounding the Eridanus. The wide, deep flowing waters of the Eridanus River were a powerful force, changing the hot, barren land into a lush green for miles around it. The army she spied on in the Starling Forest fulfilled their promised strategy. Merope stumbled upon them again in the east. Hundreds of well-armed, unbranded soldiers hid behind a naturally hilled ditch awaiting the party she tracked to appear. Apparently, the scouts had arrived at the lookout minutes too late to intercept the companions as they entered the forest unnoticed.

Merope's eyes darted upward as Cygnus's eagle, Aquila, flew over the depths of the woods toward the river. It would only take one noise or one scout for the entire army to leave their ambush site in a full pursuit. She silently drifted away from the gathering, and then proceeded to sprint off, following the eagle from below. Her feet lightly touched the ground and bound up off the earth with the swiftness, grace, and spring of a deer running through the forest in springtime.

Ahead, Jackson and the others arrived at the wooden canoe. Inside rested two oars and a cloth sack with a note on top.

Jackson,

Here is a turkey sandwich for you. Ride the Eridanus River downstream until you reach the royal pier of the Altair Kingdom. Someone there will escort you to Queen Cassiopeia. Her people guard the Pillar of Altair and will assist you. May the three suns continually light your path.

– Cygnus

"Well, Jackson, would you like to suffer with Cygnus's special turkey sandwich again, or shall Otava catch some pisces in the river for you as well?" The Hunter motioned toward Otava, who was effortlessly scooping fish out of the river and tossing them on the bank. Occasionally, he would catch one in his teeth, flip it in the air, then swallow it whole. Each gulp required a comment noting possible spicing and flavor enhancements that should be added to the fresh aquatic dish.

"No, thanks. I've barely recovered from the last meal that Otava fed me. I think I'll stick with the sandwich."

"I resent that!" Otava rumbled back with a fish still between his teeth. After swallowing, he added, "My cooking was supreme. You even said it tasted 'great!' It's not my fault you Earthians can't handle quality Arcasian cuisine."

"Don't feel bad about it. I know you're a great cook. Hey, Cygnus keeps feeding me turkey, which is mostly known in my country for knocking people into a random deep sleep. We have an entire holiday where we stuff ourselves with turkey, thank God for our full bellies, and then take turns passing out."

Jackson drifted off for a moment remembering Thanksgivings as a child. Before Grandpa passed, Jackson's family used to come out from the city and spend several days at the farm house. His aunts and cousins would come in from out of town as well to help cook up a splendid meal. His two aunts and mom took on the matriarchal role of preparing all the holiday meals in their 20s as Grandma died at the early age of forty-six.

Grandpa often invited Farmer John and his wife, Nancy, over for Thanksgiving. Their son rarely made it home anymore for holidays as he had made a career in the Navy and was usually on some coastal base or out to sea on a ship. Jackson and his cousins would saddle the farmer's horses and toss around footballs on the warmer years, while the dads watched football and passed out on the recliners and couches.

Thanksgivings had been small since Grandpa died. Now that he thought about it, Jackson hadn't seen his cousins or aunts and uncles since the funeral. His family still ate turkey, but no more crowds of people pushing around the kitchen to smell and taste, no more backyard games. Jackson's mom would finish the dishes and then bury her face in a book. His dad would pass out watching football by himself, and Jackson would take his brother and sister to visit Farmer John and go horseback riding.

"Jackson, is The Hunter out collecting firewood?" Otava asked, bringing Jackson out of his other world. Jackson looked around, confirming to himself that The Hunter, Procyon, and Sirius were all gone.

"I don't know. I thought he was still here." Just as Jackson finished talking, the dogs came bounding out of the forest followed by The Hunter—walking swiftly but carefully—with a serious expression under his brows.

"We have to leave now." The Hunters voice was quiet but firm.

"Surely we have time for a properly cooked meal first?" Otava asked as if they hadn't eaten in days though he was the only one who had been eating nonstop since they reached the river.

"My dogs caught scent of something. I followed them and came across a military scout. He asked me about the boy and White Wings and a large, furry, highly armed bush creature. Apparently, an army is waiting for us to appear from the desert, and he is investigating the surrounding areas. I managed to direct him upstream, but we'd better leave now before we're discovered." As The Hunter was explaining the need for an urgent departure, he gathered their bags and covered their tracks.

Otava, as the heaviest, sat in the middle of the canoe to keep it from tipping. In order to still feel useful without an oar to row, he grabbed a leaf-filled branch and propped it expertly against the inside of the boat to shade them with a little camouflage. Jackson sat on the front bench with Sirius and one oar while The Hunter steered the boat from the back with Procyon sitting alert at his knees.

The Eridanus River was much deeper and darker than the cool, fresh mountain river in the Starling Forest or the crystal-clear oasis surrounding Vega. It didn't feel dirty like some of the murky Midwestern rivers, always transporting particles of thick, rich black soil to a new field. This dark blue surface appeared more like a thick veil tossed over top of the river to conceal the secretive world teeming with life underneath.

Jackson crouched low, hiding behind Otava's branches. The river flowed quickly enough that little effort was required to move the wooden canoe forward. The Hunter softly guided them to the middle and occasionally steered away from rocks, branches, or logs obstructing the smooth path forward.

The jungle around them remained still with only the sounds of birds and small, scampering creatures echoing within. It was peaceful and calm, but the companions felt watched, like at any moment some danger would bound out at them from behind the green, leafy shadows. But it was not from within the woods where the dangers truly lay. Danger lurked within the waters where little torrents of ripples slowly penetrated the surface, increasing in size, speed, and number. The canoe gradually began to sway lightly until the front and back end rocked up and down, not in a rhythmic, parallel motion but in a jagged, chaotic tumult as if an ominous war was waging underneath the water, and the heat of the battle was moving up from the deep toward the canoe. The Hunter turned his gaze from the woods and the curvy bend ahead to the waters underneath and then glanced behind him.

"Hold on!" The Hunter commanded.

"What's happening?" Jackson gripped the sides of the canoe.

"Ursa Major! I knew I should've brought my harpoon!" Otava grabbed a spear instead and searched the water for a target.

Merope was close now. She sprinted out of the tree line onto the shore just behind the increasingly warring waves thrashing onward toward the powerless travelers. By the time she recognized exactly who she was following, it was too late to warn him. As The Hunter stood, facing a beast, Merope cried out—first softly in recognition and then loudly in warning:

"Rigel? RIGEL!"

CHAPTER 11

MIRA THE WONDERFUL

The Hunter neither saw Merope nor heard her cries of warning because the sounds and sights before him demanded the presence of all his senses. Less than twenty feet away, a giant whale-like creature leapt out of the river, thrashing and twisting through the air. Though visually solid in figure and form, it appeared to consist of pure water. Its large mouth and head was bound in a bridle, its back ridden by two swirling, translucent water creatures, pulling and gnashing and screaming in languages unknown. As it whipped around in the air, a thousand specks of water sprayed over the travelers, who were now paddling rapidly toward the bank in escape.

The whale-like beast was too ardent, too swift, and too riotous to miss them in spite of their attempts to flee. Flying over top of them, its body and whipping tail came crashing back into the water immediately in front of Jackson. The weight and impact of the beast sank the front end of the canoe deep into the water and flipped the back end over top, sending The Hunter flying into the bank, the bear into the waves, and Jackson straight down into the depths of the river.

Merope raced to The Hunter's body, which was lying facedown in the tall, unkempt grasses. The right side of his face and arms seeped tiny blood drops from skidding and scraping across the ground on impact. She pushed and rolled The Hunter onto his back. With one hand on his cheek and one stroking from his forehead through his hair, she beckoned him tenderly as her eyes reddened, welling up with the pain and the passion inside of her.

"Rigel, oh, Rigel, wake up." A tear fell freely down her cheek.

He gave a shallow gasp as he inhaled to regain the breath the impact stole from him, yet his eyes remained closed.

"Merope?" He softly breathed out the question with closed eyes.

"Yes! Yes, it's me." She wiped the tears away, smiled and laughed softly.

"I don't want to wake up, for then you will be gone again."

"Rigel! Wake up! I'm really here, right in front of you!" She shook his shoulders until his eyes shot open. "What about the boy, the Son of Earth?"

"The boy?" The Hunter jumped up. "Jackson! Jackson!" The Hunter scanned the water. About ten yards upstream, Otava was shaking the water off his thick, brown coat and regaining his land legs. The capsized canoe followed the path of the river whale around the bend and out of sight.

"There! Your dogs!" Merope pointed to where Procyon and Sirius were swimming close together. Both of their necks were sticking out to the side as they paddled rapidly, their teeth clamped around Jackson's shirt pulling him through the water beside them.

The Hunter rushed into the river, praising his dogs as he pulled Jackson from the weight of the water's grasp. He laid Jackson on his back and then moved to the side as Merope knelt next to him. Jackson had a swollen red-and-purple lump on his forehead and was motionless though still holding color in his cheeks.

As if an expert, Merope plugged his nose and opened his mouth. Clasping her lips to his, she breathed into him not just breath but a three-note melody: up for air, down singing "Oo, Oo, Oo." The notes began low but each moved up higher as if she were breathing life into him from the bottom of his toes to the top his head. After three lyrical-breathing repetitions, Jackson sputtered out water from his mouth and nose, coughing vigorously until he regained his air and enough strength to sit up.

Only, Jackson did not sit up. He remained lying down, staring in awe at the vision in front of him. It was the second time in his life he was certain he was looking at the face of an angel. Though the first was an angel he might fear, obey, and admire, this was an angel he might follow forever at her heels like a lost puppy, anxiously awaiting just one look, one smile, or one pat on the head.

"Am I in Heaven?" Jackson asked with genuine curiosity and solemnity.

"No, Jackson." The Hunter laughed. "Do they not tell you these things on Earth?" The Hunter smiled at the boy and then fixed his eyes on Merope. "Angels may travel freely to Heaven, but their most important work resides below with us mortals." Merope kept a cool, stoic composure in response to the compliment, though a slight blush whispered across her face. She held out her hand to help Jackson up and then introduced herself.

"My name is Merope. I have been following you for many days in search of White Wings. Do any of you know where he is?"

"He apparently knows where we are, but we really don't know where he is." Jackson felt sorry he didn't have a better answer. He coughed, then started shivering from the swift breeze stirring through the woods, rippling the river, and waving the grasses.

"Come, Merope. The boy needs to dry off. We'll exchange stories over a fire and food," The Hunter suggested.

Jackson sat on a rock, scratching the ears of the damp dogs thankfully as The Hunter gathered wood. Otava, who was apparently too tired and hungry to fish the old-fashioned way, rigged some cloth on two spears and pulled out a dozen pisces in one swoop. Merope cleared out an area for the fire.

While Otava cooked the fish, occasionally running off in the woods and returning with an array of wild herbs, the other three kindled the fire and exchanged stories. Merope began with the raiders attacking her home and abducting her six sisters. When she described the corvus ravens, Jackson joined in with his own encounter of the black monster birds. Each took turns sharing their unique perspectives in the adventures that brought them together now.

At one point, Jackson wished they could be reveling in their stories under the glimmer of starlight and campfire. Instead, they were under the coral sunset, still faintly fighting against the breezes to warm the grassy bank swaying next to the river. The rising crimson sun in the east gave a nice, warm ambiance of velvet against the surrounding jungle. When a necessary pause of thought occurred during the stories, Jackson suddenly remembered a question that perhaps Merope could answer.

"Since you were trailing us all the way from the forest, do you have any idea who or what raided our campsite there? We knew it wasn't Otava because he would've left paw prints." Merope blushed, squinted her eyes, and held her hand over her mouth.

"Yes, Jackson, I do have an idea, but I'd rather not say," she replied, covering her eyes. At this, The Hunter started to chuckle, first a small rumble like deep, rapidly rolling outbursts from the gut and then an all-out manly laugh.

"Why, Merope, you light-footed little thief! After all these years, you still surprise me."

"I didn't mean to be a thief! My house was destroyed. I didn't have any weapons except a small dagger. I was famished. Besides, I was hoping to find White Wings or get a glimpse of a real live Earthian or at least get a small morsel to hold me over. If I knew *you* were there this whole time, my journey would've been a lot simpler. Plus, I only saw one dog in the camp, and he was partly hidden. I had no idea whether you were friend or foe." Merope threw out a firm defense for her abnormal behavior.

"So, all I really needed this whole time was a pet Earthian and a morsel of food to get you to follow me around…." The Hunter teased with both an air of fondness and sarcasm.

With that comment, Merope threw a three-cord, braided vine at his shoulder that she had been twisting together for quite a while now.

"And maybe a little more tact," Merope added, giving him the all-too-familiar feminine look of I-might-actually-kiss-you-if-I-didn't-want-to-kick-you-so-badly.

"Well, if you wanted a good meal, you should have raided my camp. These guys don't know the first thing about the culinary arts." Otava chimed in after sniffing and testing a ladle full of pisces soup.

Biting her lip, Merope responded, "I actually did raid your camp a time or two. I kept my distance from the others after crashing their campsite, and then you came through mumbling about a Son of Earth and a dragon, so I followed you instead. You left your pot to forage in the woods so often that I couldn't help myself. But once we hit the desert, I had to keep at least half a day behind because there were few places to hide."

"Haha! So, you *are* a light-footed little thief! But you have excellent taste, my lady! You may swipe from my pot any day. In fact, come be the first to taste." Otava pulled a few bowls out of his belt, which were stacked snugly and resting in a leather pouch. He filled one and then handed it to Merope. Otava then proceeded to pour three more, handing one to The Hunter and one to Jackson, but also gave Jackson the large ladle as a "spoon." Merope and The Hunter looked curiously at Jackson and Otava.

"Otava, is the boy going to eat from the bowl and the pot?" The Hunter asked.

"No, that's how these Earth creatures eat. He requested my big dipper the last time," Otava replied matter-of-factly.

"Thank you for remembering, Otava." Jackson smiled and chuckled as he offered it back. "But I think I'm becoming accustomed to the Arcasian ways. I'll eat without a spoon as long as you promise me again that this fish won't send me into a coma."

"You'll be fine," The Hunter reassured.

"Speaking of unusual fish—I'm just a lone Ursa from the Starling Forest. What in the light of the three suns was that watery beast?"

"I haven't journeyed far from the forest either, but there is a song I remember about a creature of the Eridanus called Mira the Wonderful," Merope replied. She began humming, looking up to the sky searching for the tune and the words as if her memories were floating amongst the clouds. Jumping right along with the hummed melody, The Hunter sang in a deep smooth voice:

Mira, Mira
one name for two
the river Eridanus
a playground for you
riding mighty Cetus
the creature of the deep
oh, lovers beware
two quarrel, one leap

"Lovers?" Merope asked with raised eyebrows. "That's not how I remember the song."

"Yes. Lovers." He affirmed the last word directly at Merope and then looked away toward Jackson and Otava to explain. "You see, two royal river nymphs were in love, but the princess refused to give up her family name. In order to marry her, the prince had to take her name as his own, throwing away his very birthright. He eventually relented for he could not bear to be apart from her any longer, and so the two both carry the name Mira. But after marriage, neither could decide who was the leader of the family. So, when riding their river whale, Cetus, they often fight over who should drive the beast. When the quarreling gets out of control, Cetus is pulled in too many conflicting directions, causing the beast to leap from the river into the dangerous, suffocating air until one of them gives up the reins, and they all return to the safety of the water."

"That is *not* how the story goes." She sang the last phrase of the song, "Oh, *sisters* beware; two quarrel, one leap." Merope returned the mannerism by throwing a glance at The Hunter with the word "sisters" and then explained to the others her version of the story. "Mira is actually the name for conjoined twins. Their queen mother died during childbirth. Her last words were to name the child 'Mira.' So, the two share the same name, the same body, the same blood, but two distinct minds. When the sisters quarrel over the reins, one commanding each arm, it leads the confused

Cetus to leap from the water causing the near-death of them and any travelers on the river."

As playful and interesting as these varying versions sounded, there was something brewing underneath the stories that felt deeper than legend. The Hunter's and Merope's versions felt more personal, filled with love, pain, regret, and a fleck of self-righteousness.

"Well, whatever Mira may be, that creature would be quite wonderful to behold if we weren't the unfortunate souls in its path of destruction," Otava remarked.

"I agree! I'd like to see it next time from the bank of the river!" Jackson piped in enthusiastically.

They all chuckled, but Otava and Jackson could feel the underlying tension in the air between Merope and The Hunter, so they moved the discussion back to the soup and the weather and the travels ahead. Before they all relaxed under spots of shade to sleep, it was agreed that Merope would continue journeying with the group in hopes of their path crossing with Cygnus again soon. At the latest, they were certain to meet Cygnus once all three gems were collected, for the winged man was Jackson's guide back home. With Cygnus's knowledge and resources, they could then each decide how to proceed with finding and rescuing the other six Ilmatar sisters.

CHAPTER 12

THE RING AND THE LYRE

The Hunter sat on a felled tree, watching the golden sun peek over the horizon while his companions slept. His sword lay in its sheath next to his leg. A spear stabbed into the rich ground below stood up to his shoulders. Because of Otava's insistence, the bear's arsenal bag lay unrolled on the branches near his side like a surgeon's sterilized utensil pack, ready for operation if he had need of it.

For a while, The Hunter performed the persistent job of a watchman and scanned the tropical forest towering beside them, the river rolling gently below, and the parallel forest decorating the other side of the Eridanus. Otava and Merope fell asleep quickly, but Jackson tossed and turned, occasionally coughing violently in effort to expel the lingering fluid from his lungs. Finally, he threw his hoodie over his head and relaxed in the artificial darkness. When all movement ceased in the camp and it was apparent that the others were now lost to the world of dreams, The Hunter stroked his dogs' heads and watched Merope.

His eyes displayed a mixture of old sadness and new hope as he studied her soft, rhythmic breathing. The wind danced lightly among the leaves, sending tiny rays of sun shimmering upon her body. He smiled at his thoughts of jealousy. If only he could take the sun's place bringing light to her countenance and warmth to her body. No, not yet. He couldn't caress her cheek or surround her in his arms with warmth, but he could watch over her and journey with her, slowly illuminating the darkness that had enshrouded her heart and destroyed her home.

The wind picked up, creating a light whistling, and The Hunter surveyed their surroundings for intruders once again. A foggy mist was gathering over the river, which was strange considering the air was neither humid nor recovering from rainfall. The fog appeared to crawl across the water toward their camp. Upon reaching the bank, the cloud formed a ring swarming round and round, displaying blues and greens in the center along with golds and reds on the outside. The colors were vibrant yet muted by the white haze. A beautifully haunting tune quietly radiated through the ringed cloud.

As The Hunter watched the swirling cloud, he couldn't help but walk over to examine it. The melody of a lyre rang sweeter the closer he got. Afraid of nothing and intrigued by the sights and sounds, he reached out to touch it, and the fog wove around his fingers as if it were clasping his hands and leading him inside. Almost obediently, he entered the vortex.

Music saturated the inner ring with depth and beauty like he was surrounded by an orchestra in a great ballroom with the entire room a spinning ballet for his entertainment and delight. As the world spun around him, The Hunter's breathing became slow and deep until he fell asleep, collapsing into the arms of the cloud. It held him above the ground and carried his entranced body across the river.

Just inside the edge of the forest, the lyre's tune changed and the ringed cloud slowly released his body onto the ground. Dressed in the clothes of a royal knight and skillfully strumming the powerful lyre made from a white turtle's shell, Sulafat commanded his four soldiers with a hushed voice.

"Now! Quickly, tie him up and throw him on Sheliak."

Procyon and Sirius were not unaware, however, of the danger that surrounded and captured their master. Wet and panting from swimming across the river, they leapt through the grass at the kidnappers. Procyon's teeth grazed Sulafat's arm, ripping his shirt, throwing the lyre from his hand, and nearly knocking him off his horse. The immediate cessation of the lyre's tune freed The Hunter from his trance. He awoke, surrounded, with a knee in his back and a man wrapping rope around his wrists while Sirius and Procyon growled and snapped, circling the other four men.

The Hunter twisted and jumped up, hurdling the man off his back. But another soldier was already behind The Hunter and knocked him out cold with the blunt of his sword. In the soldiers' confusion between the canine attack and the near escape of their hostage, Procyon and Sirius were able to leap inside the group and put themselves between the men and The Hunter. All four soldiers on the ground had swords drawn. The dogs with unsheathed teeth continued to snap, lunge, and growl, defending their motionless man.

"Do you want the whole Eridanus to be alerted? Kill them!" Sulafat commanded.

Dog and man, both with their own weapons ready for attack, stared each other down, contemplating who would make the first move. Sirius's gaze shot toward Sulafat. Teeth bared, he jumped over the heads of the other men, aiming for Sulafat's neck. Spit flew through the air from his ivory fangs. Sirius's propelling flexed body fell limp in an instant as Sulafat's spear drove into his heart. The impaled dog fell to the ground, twitching right beneath the horse's girth.

Procyon barked fearlessly and lunged into the crowd of villains. He was struck in the gut, sliced through his back, and one of his paws rolled to the ground, severed from his body. As the life bled out of him, Procyon slowly rotated his head and eyes to look at The Hunter once more, whimpering a high-pitched note of pain and loss from the back of his throat. There the three lay: The Hunter, Procyon, and Sirius. All bleeding, all wounded, all loyal companions, but only one was still breathing.

CHAPTER 13

WITHOUT A TRACE

When Jackson had settled down in a soft patch of grass under a tree, the golden sun was joining in the chorus of light and warmth with the setting crimson sun. The coral sun, which glowed with the depth and richness of a harvest moon, had passed beyond sight. As he untied the increasingly ragged hoodie from around his waist and threw it over his eyes, he thought again about how very strange sleep was in Arcas.

Jackson tossed and turned while his mind journeyed to memories of his Uncle Leonard on his mom's side that everyone called Larry. Uncle Larry didn't sleep much. He owned his own shoe shop, and small business was his life. Sometimes, Uncle Larry would wake up at 3:00 a.m. and not be able to get back to sleep, so he'd just head to the shop. Even when he got a decent night of sleep, he was always up early to make phone calls and prepare for the day's customers, then always up late to balance receipts and check the inventory.

Jackson went to stay with their family one summer to hang out with his cousin Jared who was roughly the same age. They lived in a suburb of Chicago, which was fun to visit, but Jackson didn't find it very appealing to live in. He much preferred the fresh country air, wide-open fields, and fewer neighbors. Jackson thought it was the funniest thing that his uncle would constantly fall asleep in the strangest places: at the dinner table, while reading the paper, on the church pew, and even in the chair by the store dressing room while waiting for Aunt Tami to try something on. Uncle Larry didn't sleep at the standard intervals and times; he slept whenever his body exclaimed, "I'm tired!" That's how it was on Arcas. There were no set sleeping times for the ordinary folk. They just went to sleep whenever they were tired, whenever it became convenient, or whenever they needed to store up rest before a long journey.

"Son of Earth, Son of Earth, wake up," the lovely melodic voice beckoned him from his sleep.

"Try his name, miss. It's Jackson, remember?" Otava tried to help delicately but his voice reflected somber overtones.

"Jackson, Jackson," the angel visited him again in his dreams. As her hand gently shook his shoulder, the warmth of her touch released him from the visions in his mind to the vision kneeling next to him. As his eyes pried themselves open, he couldn't help but smile in happy pleasure at the sight before him. Though he quickly contained his glee because the angel inviting him to join her for another day in this world was not his angel. It was clear at least to Otava and Jackson that she was, indeed, The Hunter's angel.

"Is it time to go?" he asked, sitting up.

"Soon," Merope replied, doing her best to control the fear in her voice. "Have you seen Rigel? I mean, The Hunter. Have you seen The Hunter recently? Did he talk to you? Did he say he was going somewhere?"

"No." Jackson shook his head. "The last time I saw him, he was sitting on the tree over there. I've been sleeping ever since."

"I can't believe him!" Merope yelled quietly under her breath and began pacing. "We had a plan. He was supposed to wake me for the second watch—not disappear and leave me... I mean, leave *us* without a word and without a guide. How are we supposed to find Queen Cassiopeia or White Wings now?"

Merope felt betrayed and abandoned. She fell asleep dreaming of Rigel's strong arms and piercing eyes waking her for the next watch. Perhaps, he would offer his hand to pull her up to stand next to him. Perhaps, he would stay awake and watch with her for a while, sitting hip-to-hip on the felled tree. Perhaps, they would finally be able to talk alone, the other travelers still sleeping and no sisters to interrupt or interfere. Perhaps, it could have happened, but Rigel never woke her from her dreams, and The Hunter with his dogs was nowhere to be seen.

"I'm sure he's just out… hunting," Jackson offered the most logical explanation.

"That's what I thought at first too. But his tracks end close to the edge of the river, and his dogs' tracks go right through it. It's mighty strange to go hunting across the river when there are plenty of creatures in the forest around us," Otava explained.

"I'm sorry to say it, but he went through the river because he didn't want to be followed," Merope added matter-of-factly.

"Maybe he heard something? What if Gurges Ater's army was getting closer, and he wanted to throw them off? Last we knew, they were on the other side of the river." Jackson refused to believe The Hunter abandoned them. It was all too strange and seemed out of character for a man he'd journeyed so far with and grown to admire.

"Miss Merope, we are all confused and upset by *Rigel's* disappearance. But he is our friend, and we must believe it was for a good cause." Otava rolled up his armory bag and grabbed the spear from the ground where The Hunter left it. "Let's say we pretend for a moment that we are soldiers. We're fighting in the colossal battle of our time, and the enemy lies in wait just over that river. If The Hunter left to throw the enemy off, what would he want us to do next?" Captain Otava took on the persona that his precisely camouflaged clothing and extensive knowledge of weaponry always intended for him. Mustering a little courage and resolve, he attempted to take charge of the ragtag, lost-in-the-forest sojourners in search of the second pillar.

"*The Hunter* wouldn't care what we did. He would handle things all by himself just the way he likes it." Merope paused. "But *Rigel* would want us to continue to the Altair Kingdom and meet with Cassiopeia. He would have a plan, and he would join us when he could."

"Good thinking, soldier Merope, very good. Then, we will continue to follow the river by foot till we reach the pier. Cygnus wrote to us that there should be guards at the royal pier who will direct us to the castle."

They quickly but solemnly ate the remaining fish soup. The thickened broth still hinted a slight warmth from the fire's fading embers. As they followed the river downstream, just inside the cover of the forest, it was easy to tell that none of them were accustomed to the dense, plush, tropical life within. Otava led the group with a machete. Between grunts and growls, he chopped down thick leaves, vines, and twigs that grabbed at his fur and blocked their path.

Being from the Midwest, Jackson walked in anxious awe of the wilderness around him. When he thought of the tropics, his vision was usually consumed with poisonous spiders, snakes, tigers, and alligators. Even coyotes and the unspeakably horrid opossums were generally more afraid of humans than tarantulas or snakes or tigers or alligators.

Merope, on the other hand, seemed to be gaining energy from the fresh environment, like a child in a new playground for the first time. Her grieved countenance over The Hunter's disappearance subsided slightly as she hummed different little tunes, bringing out an array of wild creatures fluttering through the trees or scurrying on the ground near her feet.

"I enjoy your songs, Miss Merope, I really do. But if you're going to call the whole forest here, I do hope you can also call them away again before they get hungry for a thick bite of bear leg," Otava fretted.

"Now, now, Otava. We are both from the rich mountainous forests of the north teeming with life of its own. Surely, you can handle a few little colorful creatures in the Eridanus." She playfully held her hand up by her face, which carried a blue and pink swallow.

"Not so at all. If I trusted the creatures in the north, then I would live in a cave like a common bear. But I prefer my cabin where I can shut the door and lock the creatures out!"

"Are you really from the north?" A girlish voice flew out of the trees.

"Who's there? Show yourself!" Otava waved his machete around in circles looking for any possible threat.

"Someone who can help you... if you put your silly

sword away, of course," she bartered. Jackson caught a glimpse of a dress hanging down alongside some vines in a tree.

"Otava, it's just a girl." Jackson looked Otava in the eyes to release him from the flight-or-fight instinct momentarily overpowering him. "I think you can put the weapon down." Then, Jackson firmly but gently assisted in pushing the machete down from its attack pose.

"*Just* a girl?" She flipped out of the tree and landed on her feet right next to Jackson. "And what are you?" Standing as tall as he, she looked right into his eyes, challenging him. "*Just* a boy of Arcas?" Jackson cast his eyes down, slightly surprised and overwhelmed by the sight and a little embarrassed that he offended her.

The girl may have been a little wild looking with dirt streaks on her face, small rips in her dress, and green leaf particles stuck in her hair, but her purple eyes surrounded by tan skin and wavy, amber hair thrown back in a swift ponytail were strikingly intriguing and beautiful. Merope gently touched her shoulder to free Jackson from the girl's pressurized playful gaze still challenging him.

"You said you could help us?" Merope inquired.

"Of course, I can. I know who you are, and I know why you are here." She enjoyed their perplexed and worried looks, so she continued cheerily. "Let's see… You lost your boat. You're traveling with *just* a boy. And you would like an audience with the most magnificent Queen Cassiopeia of the Altair Kingdom."

The three were speechless not knowing whether she was a spy or a friend. The girl, on the other hand, was loving every minute of this conversation where she held both the power and the information.

"My name is Andi," the spunky girl continued. "I was waiting for you at Her Majesty's pier to escort you to the castle. But the guards informed me that Mira the *Terrible* ravaged the river's surface again followed by a stray boat, so I figured it would be more exciting to come find you than to wait."

"We appreciate your help, Andi. Have you seen anyone else in the forest? A man with two dogs?" Merope questioned, longing for some clues as to The Hunter's whereabouts.

"No, I haven't seen a soul or heard a dog since I've been out here looking for *him*." She fixed her eyes back on Jackson and circled around him. "I'm quite surprised by you. I thought a Son of Earth would be much taller and much older looking…Well, little Earthling, what do they call you in your world?" Andi questioned and teased with a superior smirk, which appeared slightly silly considering her untamed appearance. Jackson wasn't sure if he should be offended or excited by the mannerisms and words of this wildly beautiful, yet sullied jungle creature.

"My name is Jackson, and I'm tall enough where I come from," he replied with a temporarily deepened voice, while also subconsciously attempting to both heighten and buff-up his shoulders in the introduction.

"Welcome to the Altair Kingdom, Jackson, who is *just* a boy from Earth." Andi gave a shallow but dramatic bow, as she was not the type to curtsy if she didn't have to. "Shall I take you to my leader?"

CHAPTER 14

QUEEN CASSIOPEIA

The castle looked as if it were under siege by the jungle around it. Moss crawled up the stone walls; vines twirled around the towering conical spirals. Untrimmed multi-colored roses sprang wildly from the outer garden. It was obvious the bridge over the moat had not been raised in many years. There was a passable path in the middle, but weeds and overgrowth wove around the gate, blending it in with the grasses around it.

"See, I told you I knew a short cut!" Andi pointed to the entrance. "Be prepared. When you meet the queen, you will neither speak much nor learn much. But when she's through with you, the Old Miser will tend to your requests. I can't enter this way, but go ahead past the bridge and knock on the inner door. See you later!" Andi frolicked off around the side of the castle.

Past the bridge was an outer courtyard, which was empty save for a few servants sitting around a fire, eating and laughing. When they saw Jackson, Otava, and Merope enter, they grew silent and stared. The trio moved steadily forward, ignoring the gaping eyes. Merope grabbed the large cast iron doorknocker shaped and decorated as a hand mirror. *Klunk. Klunk. Klunk.* A butler of sorts opened the heavy castle door. With grayish-white hair, slender bones, a stiff walk, and a slightly bent back, he looked to be about a hundred and three years old. Studying each one, he let out a frustrated sigh.

"I thought there was only going to be one of you." Pointing to Otava he shook his head. "I'm sorry, the queen will not allow your type to enter in. No beasts or soldiers are allowed, and you appear to be both. You may wait in the courtyard though."

"I can wait with him," Merope offered, feeling out of place and uninvited.

"No. The queen would not forgive me if I let *your* kind slip past her without a meeting. Both of you come with me." The butler motioned for them to follow him.

Instead of leading them into the castle, he removed his satin shoes, replacing them with a pair hiding behind a fern outside the door. He walked them past the courtyard to a wall filled with closed doors. He removed a key from his pocket and opened one.

"You are not yet fit to enter Her Majesty's halls. Boy, this is your room. Please scrub the dirt and the jungle smell from yourself, and put on the clothes set out for you." He opened another door. "I'm sorry, my lady, this will have to do for you as we were not prepared for another. I will send a maid presently with hot water and a change of clothes."

After a thorough cleaning and a change of clothing, the Old Miser instructed them on all the proper behaviors in the queen's presence. When he felt they were informed and prepared, Jackson and Merope were escorted back to the front door. They were both wearing dull gray clothing of the same satin material and coloring as the butler's. Jackson wore pants and a tunic that displayed a crown created with jewel-sized mirrors; Merope stood draped in a plain gray dress with a mirrored sash around the middle. At the front door, the butler handed them both satin slippers to put on their feet.

The inside of the castle displayed a complete contrast to the bright colors, encompassing greens, and lively disorder of the jungle outside. The world became a mirror: floor tiles, walls hangings, and chandeliers; nearly every part of the inner palace reflected back on itself. It didn't take much light from the outside to fill the entire empty hall, for one ray of sunshine endlessly bounced off each mirror filling the room with light. It might be an amazing sight if there were more colors bouncing around than the orange, yellow, or red of each sun, but there were no other decorations and everyone dressed dully. Every maid and manservant they passed wore the same gloomy gray, though it was evident that Jackson's and Merope's guest clothing was set apart with unique designs and embellishments.

"Wait here." The butler walked in and announced them. "My most beautiful Queen Cassiopeia, who displays splendor beyond all others"—he bowed—"Jackson, a Son of Earth, and Merope of the Ilmatar sisters have traveled quite far, requesting the most honored privilege of looking upon your countenance."

"Interesting guests, indeed, Shedir. No doubt they are eager to delight their eyes with the glory of my presence." She gave a dramatic pause. "I will be gracious to grant their request. Allow them to enter," declared the smooth regal voice.

Walking in the throne room, the grays reflecting through every other passage were suddenly replaced by sparkling colors everywhere. Sitting atop a diamond-crested glass throne, the queen's colorful adornments radiated through the mirrors, filling every inch of the room with her visage. Though a bit intimidated by the formalities, Jackson and Merope did well following Shedir's odd advice. Unlike most royalty where the servants and guests must look at the ground to show their submissiveness, this queen would be highly offended if they did not look directly at her face the entire time in her presence. In a room full of mirrors, however, it was difficult to determine which of her images to focus on.

Queen Cassiopeia's rainbow-colored hair was intricately woven around the diamond crown, not a strand out of place. Her dress flowed to her feet, puffing out with visible ruffles of purples, blues, and pinks. Clusters of tiny, shiny ornaments sparkled off her bare arms and the sides of her eyes like stars. If you surveyed the entire room, the queen consumed all the walls, the floors, and the ceiling minus the little specks of gray people echoing vaguely amongst her grandeur.

The castle and everyone in it existed for one purpose: to provide contrast to and reflection of the colorfully decorated beauty of the queen. Unnaturally thin at the waist and voluptuously accented in the bust and hips, it was also apparent that she was accustomed to the pain of a quality corset.

"My daughter, Princess Andromeda, explained to me that the Ilmatar has entered our realm because she lost her sisters to Gurges Ater. What a happy fortune for you that these circumstances have led you to seek the face of the royal flower of the Eridanus." The Queen, referring to herself as the royal flower, continued talking, but instead of looking at Merope or Jackson, she moved her eyes from reflection to reflection recognizing how sharply she glimmered in the room in comparison to everyone else.

Jackson could no longer hear a word. His eyes were

glued to the figure next to the Queen. In an elegant but simple periwinkle gown, wearing a tiara on her head, sat the purple-eyed, amber-haired jungle girl. She had transformed into a princess with wavy hair lying down past her shoulders, her dress in pristine condition, and her face stoically solemn, lacking the vivaciousness the forest brought out of her. Andi caught his confounded gaze, enjoyed his surprise with a slight smile, but then quickly reminded him with a flick of her eyes that he must return his focus to the queen.

"I am surprised though, Merope, that your hair is so dark. I've heard so much babbling through the years about the Ilmatar and their silver hair, purple hair, blue hair, but I can hardly see the purple in your hair at all. Poor thing, you can out sing the birds but their heads are still adorned more radiantly," the queen continued as if she were giving the gift of knowledge and wisdom and the secrets of the world to all who had the privilege to listen to her brilliant proclamations.

"And Jackson, Son of Earth, how common you look for one from another world. What a pity that you must return there soon, for you will surely live a life with no mate, waiting endlessly for a woman of beauty to enter your life again. Then, you will plead and beg with Cygnus to fly you with his colorless wings back to our world, so that you may sit at my feet and serve me the remainder of your days." Cassiopeia paused, looking at Jackson with a hint of sincere compassion.

"Coming from a world of darkness like you have, it is a

haunting and consuming thing to look upon the flower of the Eridanus. Alas, most leave my presence only to live a thousand lives consumed with their own inadequacies. My beauty is a large enough burden for my kingdom. I cannot feed and clothe every mouth drawn to my splendor and desiring to gape at my glory every day." Putting her hand on her daughter's shoulder, she barely stopped for breath.

"My Andromeda knows a little of this burden. She has my noble blood within her, so she far exceeds the common creatures, but the half of her that is her father's leaves her plain and rough-looking. You must understand I tried to get an heir worthy of me. I brought every magician and sorcerer from the edges of Arcas, and none of them could create a child of my likeness out of a single strand of my precious hair. So, I finally agreed with my relentless husband, King Alderamin, that I would allow this temple of worship the torture and disfiguration of bearing one child, and one child only, so that *someone* on Arcas could share at least half of my unparalleled beauty and unequalled burden. Pity she looks so much like her father."

Cassiopeia stroked Andromeda's hair gently while Jackson and Merope were astounded to silence. Shedir, being seasoned in his interactions with the queen, knew just how to respond.

"My Queen, our guests are delighted by your exquisite words and your magnanimous ways. The fair Cassiopeia already knows that Lord Cygnus has asked us if the fair royal flower who rules graciously over the Altair Kingdom would allow the Son of Earth to visit the old pillar. I dare say they are eager to hear your response to their request, though it will pain them greatly to leave your beauty and grandeur for the dullness of an ancient ruins."

"You speak truth, Shedir. Undoubtedly, you have learned much from the unmerited advantage of being in my presence more than most unfortunates. Here is my ring. Do tell the pillar guards that I am sorry I did not grace their eyes in person, but my burden is heavy enough without being exposed to the burning of the suns above, the wretched dirt below, and the gloomy old ruins of a past misfortunate age before the royal flower bloomed to her reigning glory. Good-bye, Lady Ilmatar and Son of Earth. I feel great sorrow for you as you part. But I implore you as you go, do not pluck your eyes out for their lack of observing my beauty in the flesh. There may be another day when good fortune brings you back over the Eridanus River to gaze upon Queen Cassiopeia of the mighty Altair Kingdom, and on that day, when you are blessed to enter my courts again, I would hate for you to mourn at your loss of sight."

Swiftly and awkwardly, Merope and Jackson gave a short "thank you" and multiple bows as they exited with Shedir, never turning their back to or their eyes from the queen. Returning to the entrance of the castle, Shedir attempted to justify the oddities of the queen.

"You must pardon Her Majesty. She inherited the kingdom at a young age. It's a complex duty to carry such power and responsibility for thousands of years. We who choose to serve her have a fairly good life here. Queen Cassiopeia never leaves the castle and seldom receives visitors anymore, which proves advantageous for many of us in the Eridanus who desire to be left alone and have no desire to resurrect the politics of the past."

Opening the great castle doors, they met quite the commotion outside. More servants and palace guards had gathered near the fire in the courtyard. Laughter and drinks flowed freely for all, while the crowd's attention fixed on a gruffly voice instructing them behind a column of rising smoke.

"Now, if you want the meat to hold its juicy flavor on the inside while getting a crispy, smoked flavor on the outside, you must be long-suffering. No cooking over a petite fairy fire, and no hastening the moment. So, while the pan heats up to a sturdy sizzle, I say grab a friend and grab a goblet!" recommended the large, furry brown chef.

"Heed, heed!" the entertained audience cried out in agreement, raising their cups and their faces.

"Heed, heed, indeed!" Otava emptied his drink with one swig. "Ahh, I see we have more friends gathering to enjoy these moments of culinary excellence! Noble caretakers and guards of the lush Altair kingdom, I present to you Jackson, a sensitive-stomached Son of Earth and

Merope, a refined Ilmatar beauty from my very own Starling Forest." Otava invited them to the party as people made room for the two to sit. A burly guard next to Jackson thumped his hand upon the boy's shoulder.

"Fret not, Son of Earth, if you can't handle the brawny ways of a charred pisces, I'm sure we can bed some delicate turkey on bread just for your fragile viscera!" he joked heartily followed by roaring laughter from the crowd around.

"True, true. White Wings feeds him like a boy of Earth, but I saw him face the mighty Eltanin like a man of Arcas," Otava complimented him and the crowd echoed back.

"Heed, heed!"

Being far from home, it felt comforting for Jackson to be around friends, to hear good-natured jokes and feel fortified safety all around. It was a nice change from constantly feeling chased since he arrived in Arcas. He enjoyed the quiet kingdom with relaxed guards who couldn't remember the last time they worried about threats and wars and palace upkeep.

Otava, Merope, and Jackson took their time eating, amusing, and enjoying the good company. Underneath the smiles, however, darkness wove around their hearts like string circling a finger, slowly swelling it to tenderness while choking out its life and color. One companion was still missing. Every once in a while, Jackson would glance at the open entry past the courtyard, hoping to see The Hunter stride through. Merope would listen for the howling songs of Procyon and Sirius darting through the jungle, and Otava would laugh extra loud anticipating that his sounds of merriment would guide their friend safely back to them.

CHAPTER 15

THE PILLAR OF ALTAIR

Moss covered the rock path leaving a thick carpet of green to hike upon. The various stone trails branching from the castle were the only areas of the dense jungle without trees, bushes, flowers, and ferns bursting out of them. The levels of overgrowth and moss made it apparent which paths were regularly used. The trail to the Pillar of Altair seemed to be the most idle, the most abandoned.

Shedir walked carefully, leading the group with a stick in each hand to support his withered body. Jackson couldn't help but notice the difference between the butler and everyone else he'd met so far on Arcas. The others looked strong and healthy, like their bodies froze in age and growth by their late twenties. He couldn't contain his curiosity any longer while walking alongside the aged man.

"Shedir, can I ask you a question?"

"Ask me anything you'd like."

"You're from here, right?"

"Yes, I was born and raised in Arcas."

"Then why do you look so much older than everyone else?"

"Because, my boy, I spent the best years of my life on Earth." Shedir paused for a moment, his eyes already telling a story of both joy and pain. "I dealt in trade between the worlds at this very pillar. But I fell in love with a Daughter of Earth. Her name was KoChav. I left Arcas and vowed my life to her. My eyes were neither dim nor fearful in the black of Earth's night for she always glimmered with bright radiance. We enjoyed many days and many nights together, and we grew old and frail like all who dwell in your world. But the shadow of sickness overtook her suddenly, and she died before I could bring her back to Arcas for healing. When I buried her, the nights turned only to blackness. Neither the stars nor the moon could illuminate my heart again, so I returned to Arcas to resume my position serving King Algieba."

Small monkey heads bounced overhead from tree to tree as if they were excited fans following their favorite traveling band. Their smooth faces displayed a soft blue while their furry cheeks and heads blazed orange like the coral sun.

"Take this, Jackson!" Otava whispered handing him a dagger. "Merope! Protect yourself with this." He handed her a spear. "I've heard these jungle monkeys will jump right on someone's head and rip their ears off or worse, their nose! I can't live without my nose. It would destroy my keen sense of taste." Otava nervously tottered along pointing his crossbow at the trees.

"Aw, Otava, they look sweet. I think they want to be friends with us," Merope assured, trying to hand him back the spear.

"No, Merope." Otava refused to accept the weapon back. "That's what they want you to think. Underneath that colorful, furry camouflage are dagger nails and bladed teeth."

"I do believe, Mr. Ursa, that those sharp teeth and nails are for biting into the thick skins of fruit. In all my years, I've never seen them bite into a man… But… we do have one fur-covered fruit. The monkeys tear all the fur and skin off to reveal a sweet soft fruit that hides inside. As long as none of us are covered in fur like that, we should be fine," Shedir teased.

Otava did not quite get the joke though and pointed his crossbow all the more intently.

"Those long-tailed, flying rodents so much as touch my fur and I'll show them I have claws and teeth of my own!" He growled. Everyone else held their chuckles beneath clenched lips and amused looks.

"Ah, there it is, my friends, the ancient dwelling of the Pillar of Altair." Shedir pointed to a tan stucco building barely noticeable given that it was draped with vines and tree branches all around. Hanging from two trees on each side of the entrance were vine-woven hammocks. On the left side, one guard was carving a fish out of wood while the other gently snored as he swayed from side to side with the breeze.

"Ahem." Shedir cleared his throat, alerting the guards of their presence. The left guard jumped out of the hammock and threw the fish inside of it, leaving it swiftly swinging with a fin hanging down out of a hole between the weaves. He awkwardly ran over to his friend, shaking the hammock to wake him.

"Ruchbah! Ruchbah! We have visitors." It took a few minutes for Ruchbah to shake off his sleep and sit up. He grabbed his belt and sword, which were lying against the tree by the entrance of the pillar, and straightened his garments.

"Ah, Shedir. How can we serve the most lovely queen on this fine day when the crimson sun looks down on us from on high?" Ruchbah inquired.

"We have come with Queen Cassiopeia's ring and her blessing to enter the pillar."

"The most beautiful and knowledgeable queen must remember that there are no more gems in Altair. She had King Alderamin remove them years ago to add to her personal collection. There is nothing left here." Ruchbah wanted to make sure that he would not be held responsible for valuables that no longer ornamented the walls of the pillar room.

"The queen does not request any items from the pillar.

She has simply granted us permission to inspect it. She does send her regrets to you both that she could not personally grace your presence."

"Then tell the queen we covet her thoughts toward us and her regret." Though Ruchbah responded with the proper reply, his voice rattled off the phrase with a rote lackluster disinterest. "Give me the ring."

Ruchbah took the ring and pushed it into a precisely shaped hole next to the door. With a quick turn of the ring, a loud click vibrated the walls and then the door leisurely rolled, opening the entrance. Jackson and Shedir walked inside the dark room. Unlike Vega, where air swept through the pillar room keeping it dry, the Pillar of Altair smelled damp and musty from the tropical humidity.

Shedir pulled on a rope just inside the door, and several tiny windows flung open, throwing light to the path and a shallow burst of fresh air. They followed the waves of light to the right past a wall, which blocked the view from the outside doorway. Instead of a room covered in jewels like Vega, Jackson beheld a room decorated with empty holes. Just like the servants and the guards dressed in dreary colors to contrast the glamorous queen, all the gems sparkling with glory and beauty in the ancient pillar now adorned the queen instead, leaving the room empty, dull, and lifeless.

"Ah, I see you recognize the pillar." Shedir moved next to Jackson who was touching the top of the thin sheet of rock as if to bring back memories.

140

The last time Jackson's eyes met the three rock columns rising from the ground, he was short of breath, wet, and filled with a wildly beating heart. A dragon and a friend warred outside the grand grotto at Vega. This pillar, though desolate and ripped of its visual glory, remained quiet and at peace.

Three circles were etched into the rock with one empty hole sitting below the suns for the gem of Arcas, and again some foreign language was engraved into the wall across from the pillar.

"I saw this same writing at Vega. Do you know what it means?"

"Ah, yes, it is a poem, actually written from an ancient language of Earth. In the modern tongue, it would read:

Two worlds joined by gems so rare
Three suns shine on Arcas fair
One sun, one moon Earth's delight
Friendship and trade we unite."

"Huh. That's kinda catchy. Well I guess I'd better head over to Earth now."

Jackson grabbed the gem from his pocket, clamped a finger down on each point, breathed deeply, and drew a door. The gray walls in front of him collapsed underneath the blue and orange electricity pulsating in the air. Jackson carefully walked through, praying for safety on the other end of the portal.

As he entered his home planet, a loud noise throbbed

around him. It was the sound of a thunderous radio signal filled only with static. Jackson stood still, allowing his senses to adjust. The room felt humid and damp like the pillar he just walked out of, but tiny droplets of water seemed to be misting upon him. The shimmering lights from the portal verified that solid rock lie in front of his feet, so he stepped forward a few paces and then turned toward the sound. Thick streams of water rushed down beside him.

"Isn't it beautiful?" a voice whispered. Jackson startled a bit but then recognized the voice.

"Yes, Shedir. The waterfall is amazing."

"No, Son of Earth. The stars. They are as radiant as KoChav was."

Shedir took a few steps forward but slipped on the damp, algae-laden rocks. Jackson released the gem into his pocket and carefully ran to help the old man up. But instead of standing up again, Shedir simply used Jackson's hand to move to a sitting position and stared past the water at the dark sparkling sky. Tears streamed down the old man's face.

"Are you okay?" Jackson hoped he didn't sustain an injury falling on the hard rock.

"It is not my back that is broken but my heart," Shedir answered.

Jackson felt sorry for him, but he also felt an overwhelming confused curiosity about the old man's loss. After a moment of silence, he had to ask.

"I don't get it, Shedir. Why did you choose to live on

142

Earth? If you both could live forever, why did you risk getting old? Why did you risk death?" Jackson thought that if he loved someone as much as this old man did, he would run away with her and transport to Arcas in a heartbeat. Live forever with a worry-free youth and an everlasting love.

"Because when people do not fear death, they do not feel the immediate need to love. I don't mean the type of love that merely seeks pleasure. I'm talking about the type of love that sacrifices, pushes to be a better person, and quickly seeks to reconcile when hurt. The people groups in Arcas neither sacrifice much, nor work much, nor love much because time dwindles by in seemingly endless days. Each sun morphs into the next with little change in season and little change in people." He spoke with the raspy depth and bottomless wisdom of a sage. "Listen to truth, Jackson. I have lived a thousand lifetimes on Arcas and none of them compare with the one lifetime I lived on Earth. Love is truest and deepest when it feels both the pain and the pleasure of each fleeting moment leading you onward to death."

They both fell silent, watching the stars skip around on the gushing water. One bright yellow flame dazzled through the falls as it shot down across the sky. The warm mist bubbled tiny droplets upon their face and hands. Jackson tried to grasp the wisdom of Shedir's words, but he still disagreed. If he ever fell in love, if he found a girl worth spending every day with, why not go to a world where you could live forever? Surely, if he were consumed with love, the real kind, the fire wouldn't dwindle and the love wouldn't grow cold even if he were given an eternity of days to live it out.

Jackson noticed movement in the darkness contrasting against the still rock. A spot of moonlight shone off the gem, creating yellow sparkles on the wall.

"I need to get the gem, Shedir." Jackson slowly steadied himself, reaching the drier rocks near the wall. If nothing else on this journey made sense, at least the pillars all worked the same. A slab of thin rock was embedded into the sheltered wall behind the waterfall. The Earth symbols displayed in the same formation as he witnessed before: sun on top, crescent moon on the left, and a cluster of stars on the right. The yellow gem leisurely turned below within its slot. Jackson curved his fingers around it, pulled it out, and secured it in his pocket. He then grabbed the transport gem from his other pocket and drew another door.

"There used to be a path out of here, but it seems that part of this mountain collapsed. I stepped through that portal not planning on returning."

"Come on, Shedir. If you don't guide us back, Otava will start a jungle war with the monkeys." Jackson beckoned him, holding out his hand to help the wearied man back through the portal.

"It was good to see the stars one last time," Shedir noted on their way out.

As they walked back through the pillar room of Altair, weeping filled the air. Jackson ran ahead to find out what the distress was about. Otava hunched over, slumped against a tree with thick paws covering his face as low roars of sorrow exited his mouth. Merope sat curled in ball with her head buried in her lap, sobbing.

"What happened?" Jackson cried. Neither of his friends looked up. Ruchbah put his hand on Jackson's shoulder, but turned his eyes to the ground as he explained.

"One of our men just came across a secret burial. An unmarked foreign army just next to the river had dug a large hole. He saw them throw two bloodied dogs into it. He did not see the body, but they spoke of The Hunter's death as well. The guard immediately returned because Andi, I mean Princess Andromeda, asked us all to look out for your friend, The Hunter, traveling with two dogs. I am sorry that we must bring you this solemn news."

Jackson felt as if his heart had been shoved into his stomach and then ripped from his body. People were supposed to live forever on Arcas. The Hunter was supposed to live forever. They should have gone looking for him. They should have stayed awake in pairs. Despair, sorrow, pain, and revenge cringed at every muscle in his body. What sicko would kill the dogs, the very dogs that saved Jackson's life?

He'd escaped the threat of death several times, but this

was the first time Jackson really felt the presence of evil on Arcas. It was the first time he felt both righteous anger and fervent passion well up within him. He would get the last gem away from Gurges Ater even if he had to fight the entire army by himself with Otava's little dagger.

But now was not the time to fight, and they didn't have time to mourn. The unmarked army was now approaching the Altair pier bridging over the Eridanus River and would soon be upon them. Breathing deeply, Jackson pulled up his two sorrow-filled friends, giving them each an arm to grasp as they left the pillar. A few kingdom guards would take them to a natural bridge—concealed by the jungle—over the water a little farther south, but they must flee before the army reached the castle. The only way to honor The Hunter right now was to beat these villains to the Pillar of Deneb and finally beat the evil schemes and brutal tactics of Gurges Ater.

CHAPTER 16

THE CHARIOT AND THE RIDERS

Three bodies walked along in heavy despair. Though three suns overflowed light in every crevice of the flat grasslands, darkness laid hold of their souls. Each moved and breathed, but their vitality was gone. Jackson, Otava, and Merope shuffled silently together yet each tread alone in their thoughts. Neither words, nor looks, nor touch were safe interactions, for connecting openly to the sorrow of another soul would only awaken the silence back into tears. And no vigor remained for more tears. All of their slight enduring energy must focus on the next stride, one foot in front of the other. Each step confirmed a bit of progress though the destination seemed unreachable.

Jackson thought of how he would have loved to have

147

The Hunter as a father. He longed for an adventurous outdoorsman to walk side by side with him, teaching him to survive off the land. He had a good dad. He just didn't feel a deep connection with his dad's way of life. Jackson tried to relate a few times with his father's work, following him in the body shop, listening to motors, changing oil, and replacing spark plugs and belts. He wanted to spend that time with his dad. He wanted to enjoy the work his dad did, but there was no passion there.

In Jackson's mind, why be walled inside a moving iron horse when he could run with the breeze rushing at his face on a warm-blooded, breathing horse? Sure, when he saved up enough money, he would buy a car, and he was excited about driving to school, but he didn't want to wake up every day and spend it with a rumbling machine. He wanted to spend every day in a world that smelled and breathed and felt of life. The world The Hunter had lived in.

He wasn't chained to schedules or customers or backordered spare parts. The Hunter lived surrounded by life and air and trees and freedom. Jackson wished he had just one more day with him, one more day to learn how to fish with a hand-made pole, how to pick a good dog, how to know what wild plants to eat, and how to get a woman as amazing as Merope to love him to the point where it's obvious to everyone else even when she can't admit it to herself.

The dark-haired Ilmatar had only one mission left that

kept her from collapsing and neglecting her bodily needs until death welcomed her from the throbbing pain. There remained one flicker of hope that her sisters were still alive, awaiting rescue or awaiting reunion. Merope's life, which had always been so sheltered, so secure, so surrounded by love, now faced the threat of utter loneliness.

She walked along in the solo of her mind, longing for the harmony of her sisters. Their combined song livened the forest and brought healing to those in need. Their home—known in Arcas for safety, beauty, and healing—lie in rubble. The song had left the forest, and Merope felt the song drifting from her soul, floating above her out of grasp. The very life that she clung to, the noble purpose that separated her from the one man she ever loved, no longer existed. Everything of meaning vanished with her sisters, with her home, with her Rigel.

Merope had only one hope now. She must somehow get to White Wings and find her sisters no matter the cost. The lady of peace would wage a war to the world's end to retrieve just a piece of the love she once dwelt with. Just a sliver of a beating heart could warm her from the stiff concrete ready to crack within her chest. Just a strum of notes could remind her of the songs of life and the songs of joy that still must be heard to bring healing in the bleak world around.

Otava turned his grief into schemes. He grumbled within about the woes of getting close to others, the woes of getting involved in the affairs of men. Visions of his vanished people flooded over him. The Ursas had relied on men in ages past, and the Ursas were no more. They trusted their strong, furry existence to the fickle frailty of men. His people blindly believed others and forgot their own mortality. Otava, on the other hand, survived alone and would survive this new age of war as well.

Otava was always prepared, but there was more work to be done. He needed to update his cave decoy by the river, make it look a little homier inside so it really appeared as if someone lived there. He then would move the rope switch for the trap portcullis door to work from farther away. Otava's underground escape tunnel from his cabin would also need to be lengthened. He plotted adding more dead-end paths. And the new genius idea, two more houses built next to his cabin! Underground, he would make a cozy fourth living space behind a fake wall from one of the paths. His stockpile of food and weapons would rest here, awaiting battle or holding out under siege from above ground.

In order to cook while remaining hidden in his secretive underground location, Otava would create a piping system zigzagging up and eventually exiting out one of the decoy home's fireplace. But he still needed one more escape exit from the bunker in case Gurges Ater followed him through the underground world. That's it! He would create a pulley system to collapse the path once he escaped with his weapons and his favorite cooking utensils.

Ursa Major! Otava thought as he remembered his favorite ladle still lay in the thick of the pot sitting over the fire at Cassiopeia's courtyard. News of The Hunter's death disrupted his usual diligence for grabbing his tools. At least he remembered all his weapons. *Why didn't The Hunter remember them?* If his weapons took down a dragon, they could have taken out any threat facing The Hunter. *If people would just listen to me, if they would just prepare for the dangers*, Otava thought.

He wouldn't be caught unguarded. Once Jackson grabbed the last gem, Otava would return home and finish his bunker. He'd preserve himself underground until the wrath of Gurges Ater and the looming wars in Arcas ended.

A deep rumbling began echoing through the fields as the ground and grass throbbed with growing vibrations under their feet. The travelers awakened from of their inner world of grief for a moment, sensing the changing presence.

"What is that?" Jackson asked the other two. Merope placed one ear to the ground and listened.

"Horses. Either a small, wild stampede is galloping through the plains or we are being hunted," she replied as their heart rates increased.

"We can't outrun horses! Is there anywhere we can hide?" Jackson panicked. They were so close to finishing the mission, only one more pillar till the breathtaking nightmare ended for Arcas and for him. His eyes raced around the plains looking for some escape.

"Speak for yourself, Son of Earth. I can hold my own against racing a horse," Otava piped in.

"I'm sorry to tell you, Jackson, but you're the slow one here. I can run like a gazelle when it counts," Merope added.

"So, one of you take the gem." Jackson offered it to them. "We'll split up, and when they catch me, it will buy you some time to reach Deneb."

"I'm not touching that gem! Only the hands of an Earthian can survive it," Otava proclaimed.

"Otava's right. You must keep the gem, and you must make it to Deneb. The army isn't looking for Otava, and if they catch me, I'll gladly suffer in chains if it reunites me with my sisters. Hurry! Lie flat in the tall patch of grass over there," Merope pointed. "Otava and I will run the opposite direction to lead the horses away from you."

Once Jackson fell flat on the ground, concealed by the lofty greens speckled with white and purple flowers, the horses came in sight. It looked to be a team of about five horses running toward them with a chariot tethered behind.

Immediately, Otava and Merope took off running from Jackson's hiding spot. The charioteer steered the horses to follow the two. Jackson couldn't see anything, and didn't want to risk popping his head above the grass, so he put his ear against the ground as Merope had and listened for clues.

Once Otava and Merope ran to a safe distance, the friends turned, grabbed weapons and stood their ground to meet the pursuers. Jackson remained frozen, waiting for the horses to gallop away with or without prisoners. He could hear a faint mumbling of voices across the plains, but could not gather what they were saying. Then, cantering hooves were moving again. Plastered to the ground, Jackson could tell that a smaller group of horses separated from the others who still must be near Merope and Otava. They were moving back toward him!

Jackson never heard any warnings from his friends nor did he hear cries of pain or death, but he couldn't risk being caught with the gem. He quickly began digging a hole to hide it, and then threw bits of grass on top. If caught, he would tell them that the eagle already took the gem back to White Wings. If they were going to capture or kill him, he would grab the transport gem from his pocket, run as fast as he could, and then risk transporting in hopes he would land somewhere safer on Earth than he was right now. Two horses stopped about twenty feet away from him. There was no way he was still hidden from sight, especially with the enemy so close and on horseback, but he dared not move or look up just in case.

"You know, for declaring to your friends that I'm just a harmless girl, you sure do act like I'm dangerous," teased a familiar feminine voice. Jackson poked his head out of the grass.

"Princess Andromeda?" He was beyond perplexed.

"I believe I commanded you, lowly Son of Earth, to call me Andi." She smiled after using her most authoritative but ridiculously royal voice. "So, what is your conclusion, little Earthling? Is the Princess of the Eridanus dangerous or not?"

Jackson managed to unearth the buried gem from Altair and stick it back in his pocket before standing up, hoping she didn't see as it might lead to further teasing.

"I don't know if you are particularly dangerous, *Andi,* but I sure don't feel safe around you either."

"Good. Do you know how to ride?" She motioned to the horse that tagged along beside the one she rode. Andi's horse resembled a white Arabian but sparkled with blue as if hazel glitter were melted into its smooth, shiny coat. The unoccupied horse next to her, meant for Jackson, sparkled pink.

"Yes, I know how to ride. But of all the horses in Arcas, do I really have to ride the glittery pink one?"

"Well, you're not riding *my* horse. And you've met my mother, did you really expect anything less flamboyant to come from her stables?"

Jackson grabbed the sparkly royal saddle snuggly resting on top of the sparkly pink horse and swung his leg around. Finally! A task in Arcas he felt skilled at. Despite the horse's delicate, feminine color, he could feel the strength and power underneath him. The two began trotting over to join the others who had already created a small campsite for resting the horses and themselves. Merope and Otava waved at Jackson when they saw that he was coming to join them.

154

"How did you get your mom to let you leave? Don't you have to sneak out of the castle just to play in your backyard?" Jackson wondered why she followed them and whether the queen even knew Andi had left.

"My mother may be bound to the security of the castle"—her purple eyes looked directly into his—"but I am no chained lady."

She loosened the reins, gave a few quick nudges to the horse's sides and took off ahead of him, her amber hair twirling in the wind behind her and a competitive smile illuminating her face. Jackson accepted the challenge and rode beside her as the two galloped across the pasture.

When the horses were unsaddled and grazing, Jackson and Andi sat with the others for some food and rest. The man driving the horses and chariot was Auriga. He was a large man with fiery red hair, which appeared to fly off his scalp like wild flames, and a red beard. As he bit into his sandwich full of meat and jungle vegetation, a little gray goat lay at his feet, chewing on his pant leg. It was his pet, Capella, who was said to be as smart and loyal as a dog though he still nibbled on everything like a goat.

Auriga often journeyed between Altair and Deneb because Queen Cassiopeia sent fruit and other delicacies from the Eridanus to the Cephid people, and they returned payment with sparkly treasures from their mined caves. King Alderamin grew up in the Deneb Kingdom and returned there when he grew tired of hassling to find new ways to please his wife's beauty obsessions. Cassiopeia remained relatively content with him as long as he continued to send her gifts from the Cephid Caves.

The princess would often accompany Auriga on his trading route in order to spend time with each parent. When she spotted the unmarked army nearing the Altair Kingdom, Andromeda convinced her mother that it was time for her to visit father again. She promised to handpick many beautiful jewels to adorn the lovely queen upon her return. Though she would not admit it openly, Andi was concerned about Jackson and his friends traveling on foot. She knew she could bring extra horses along to help her new friends reach Deneb quicker.

"Wait till you meet the Cephids! They are an amazing people. Their skin is dark and shiny—it somehow absorbs the light of the three suns. When they enter the dim caves, their golden eyes glow, creating their own personal torches to illuminate the mines," she explained excitedly. It was apparent to all that Andi loved to visit her father and the Cephid people. As their conversations continued, she slowly turned into a softer, more joyful version of herself, a happy combination of the untamed jungle girl and the proper pristine princess.

"Look to the sky, friends. There is a large bird hovering toward us from the south." Auriga pointed out the creature with a suspicious voice and a head nod to the sky. Fearing the worst, Otava, Merope, and Jackson immediately thought it was another black corvus from the southern ruins of Trifid. Everyone stopped eating and conversing to watch. Though slightly shadowed under the suns, it was not a dark raven. Brown, white, and golden feathers silhouetted against the blue sky, which coordinated nicely with the sharp blue specks on the bird's feet.

"Blue talons! Jackson, haven't we seen that bird before?" Otava questioned.

"Aquila! It's Cygnus's eagle!" Jackson replied just as the bird circled around him and released a small bag landing right into his lap. He pulled a note out of it and read it aloud:

Jackson,

You are close to locking all the pillars from Gurges Ater and saving both of our worlds! Thank you for your faithful service.

I'm not sure if you have heard of The Hunter's demise into the hands of Gurges Ater. I am sincerely sorry because we all have lost a friend. It is clear that no one is safe from the capture or the control of our powerful enemy.

I will return to you shortly, and together we will rid our worlds of the gems and of Gurges Ater's grab for power.

If the fair Merope still travels with you, tell her that her sisters are rescued and safe within my care. Please send the gem from Altair with Aquila for safekeeping.

—Cygnus

"Thank the Creator of the three suns that my sisters are rescued! Cygnus is a true and kind heart." Merope spoke with joy, knowing she would reunite with her sisters soon, yet also with renewed sorrow from being reminded of Rigel's passing.

Jackson placed the gem of Altair in the bag and held it up as Aquila once again swooped his claws around it and flew off. He felt relieved to once again be free of carrying the hunted gems.

Once rested and filled with the non-turkey-meat sandwiches that Shedir sent along from the castle, they all mounted their rides. Otava rightly refused to ride horseback, so he stood in the chariot next to Auriga and Capella the goat. Andi would continue to ride her blue-glittered horse while Jackson managed to obtain some compassion from Merope, who switched him the pink glittery horse for the yellow glittery one.

They all thanked Andi and Auriga for allowing them to ride along and for the fresh meal. For the first time, they felt ahead of Gurges Ater and his trailing army. On the swift, gliding trod of the horses' hooves and with some good news from Cygnus about the sisters, they felt they were gaining a little favor and luck in the midst of their horrible loss. A speck of life returned to their trampled souls, and a little hope that the end of a long journey was nearing. Soon, Andi would be with her father, the gems would be with Cygnus, Merope would be with her sisters, Otava would be in his cozy cottage, and Jackson would be home again. Safe. Predictable. Home.

The rolling rock caves reached their arms both above and below the ground. Hills and bumps covered the landscape, a city of curved rock homes. The band of travelers had smiles on their faces and a skip in their hearts as they rode through the gates of the Deneb Kingdom that fenced in the cave lands. But the smiles quickly vanished into concern and panic.

A war zone with refugees was spread out on the outskirts of the caves. A fresh tent was raised and filled with the wounded and wailing. The Cephids not only worked in the caves; the caves were also their homes. *BOOM! BOOM! BOOM!* Little Cephid men ran from the noise, the danger, and the flying particles. Women and children huddled and cried underneath a few small trees, struggling to keep root in the shallow layer of soil above the rocky land. As they neared, a crowd of short people parted and a tall, light-brown man walked through, carrying a little Cephid man in tattered clothes with several bloody, oozing pierces on his limp body.

"Father!" Andi yelled, jumping off her horse and running to meet the man. "What's going on?"

"Andi?" He set the injured man down on a table near the hospital tent and gave her a long, tight hug. King Alderamin's hands and face were darkly streaked from dirt, soot, sweat, and blood. He didn't wear the clothes of a king, nor did he act as one who demanded worship and

159

adoration. But he did carry the concerns of a king, a king who loved and cared and led those around him with dignity and respect. He was a king who did not sit in the castle and watch his people die, but a king who joined his people side-by-side in a fight no matter the cost. King Alderamin pulled his daughter away from his chest and looked despondently into her eyes.

"You shouldn't have come, my dear. We're under attack."

CHAPTER 17

GUESTS OF THE WHITE PALACE

The smells of dampness, musk, mold, and human stench filled the air. The ground felt cold and hard, and the back of his head was pounding. He slowly reached around to feel the tender, throbbing, inflamed knot protruding from his skull but hidden underneath a thick mixture of dried blood and hair. Remembering some sort of attack, his eyes sprung open in shock. The damp darkness was almost blinding for a man used to the light of many suns and the freshness of the wooded lands. Sitting up, he squinted and blinked, surveying the prison around him that slowly moved into focus.

"Welcome to the luxurious palace. Quite a view from here, isn't it?" The voice was raspy but pure and kind. The Hunter peered through the steel bars, struggling to concentrate on a white-haired man sitting on a pile of straw a few cells down. "Don't worry. Your eyes will adjust to the darkness." The old man smiled then heaved out three dry coughs. "Just don't let your heart adjust to it."

The Hunter was about to ask him where they were when a door opened from the top of the stairs, sending light flooding through the dungeon in its rectangular shape. Heavy boots clanked down the concrete stairs toward his cell. One man in knightly robes and four soldiers stood before his personal prison door.

What now? The Hunter thought. *Questioning? Torture? Death?* He could care less about those. What he did care about was the fate of his beloved friends who apparently were not sharing the same dungeon as he. When the cell door was unlocked and opened, he braced himself to be surrounded or bound or at least forcibly grabbed by the soldiers. Instead, the cohorts remained outside. The leader who bore a fresh welt across his face and a bandage on his arm talked first through gritted teeth.

"A thousand apologies for your treatment, sir. My name is Sulafat, and His Lordship has instructed me to bring you to your proper room."

With a cold, emotionless countenance, The Hunter studied the men and did not move.

"Where am I?"

"You are at the most glorious palace of Lord Cygnus the White Winged."

"Where are my companions? Where are my dogs?"

162

The soldiers uneasily shuffled their feet slightly and threw their eyes to various points around the room, fleeing The Hunter's gaze. Sulafat remained unmoved by the question. He looked directly in The Hunter's eyes to give his reply.

"Your dogs stayed back in the Eridanus Jungle. The woman, the boy, and the beast also remain there untouched and unharmed. Again, I apologize for my lapse of judgment. Lord Cygnus meant for you to enter the castle as an honored guest, not a prisoner. He will meet with you soon to explain."

Slightly appeased with Sulafat's answers but refusing to let go of the fact he was forcibly abducted and thrown into a dungeon, The Hunter stood.

"Well, then I look forward to hearing a full explanation from Cygnus." He moved to edge of the cell mere inches from Sulafat's face and glared in his eyes. "As for you petty thieves, I'd rather stomach this dungeon than the stench of your presence. But I suppose I can't receive the pleasure of your departure until you've finished your *proper* task of escorting me to a *proper* room. So lead on, bandits, lead on."

The Hunter hoped his captors would feel the sting in his voice and the lack of trust in his words. He wasn't the type to trifle with others, and he didn't forget quickly when others toyed with him. As he walked past the barred gate of his cell, the raspy voice called out.

"Friend!" The Hunter turned back toward the old man.

"Remember, if you give your eyes time to adjust to the darkness around you, your vision will become clear again."

"Thank you, kind sir. I hope you enjoy your stay at the *luxurious palace.*"

The old man chuckled as Sulafat and his soldiers escorted The Hunter away. While walking in between them, he noticed one of the soldiers had a lump and small split on his head that was dried with blood. A head wound for a head wound and a welt across Sulafat's face, it appeared that Cygnus had divvied up a bit of justice already for the soldier's maltreatment of The Hunter.

Though the dungeon's darkness shocked The Hunter's eyes, leaving it for the blazing beams of the three suns was equally shocking. Light overwhelmed the castle. Large windows filled the hallways allowing radiance to stream in at every hour of the day. Each opening appeared to be placed strategically to harvest the warmth and illumination needed during the different positions of the suns.

The palace's visual essence indeed revealed its master. Like Cygnus, the walls were clean, chiseled, and decorated to elaborate perfection. Large, smooth white stones covered both the interior and exterior. Etched designs and emerald jewels ornamented each section of flat wall divided by pillars and windows.

"Your proper room, sir." Sulafat once again clenched his teeth to control his wounded pride. He loved giving the orders and maintaining control over others. He did not like the feeling of being humbled by Cygnus and challenged by The Hunter who he was now forced to treat amicably.

Once The Hunter entered his room, the soldiers left and immediately shut the door behind him. Waiting a moment or two, The Hunter reopened the door to verify whether he was being guarded or not. The white halls remained empty and silent, so he shut the door again and studied the room.

Red, round beams ascending on the horizon glowed through the windows which were accented with brown mesh drapes hung back to reveal the scene outside. The Ligeian Sea crashed upon a jagged white rock cliff extending vertically to the flat ground above. The Hunter's room was not decorated in typical Cygnusian fashion. Bronze hunting dogs accented the sides of the fireplace, and protruding from the walls were various mounted animal heads native to different lands all over Arcas.

The bed rose up with smooth but rugged wood beams, which must have cost quite a price and taken some time to import. Steam rose from a stone bathtub and fresh towels and clothing were placed nearby. Upon one wall hung a small armory. The Hunter's sword, freshly cleaned and polished, rested upon wooden knobs next to the others: his bow, a new spear, and a new shield. The Hunter examined the emblem on the shield. He'd never seen it before: large white wings with a golden sun centered over the relaxed "V" shape at the top of the wings while two suns, one coral and one crimson, were positioned underneath each curved bow of the wings on the opposite side, creating a triangle of sorts with the suns revolving around the wings.

The Hunter shook his head. He'd worked so hard to stay out of the kingdoms, out of the politics and laws and formalities and titles. But with all his efforts to remain elusive, not only was The Hunter an expected guest at the White Palace, it seemed as if the very room was created and prepared just for him. He bathed and reluctantly changed his clothes. Surely, Cygnus's servants could wash his own soon enough, so he could be rid of the formal crested cloak before he left.

Knock. Knock. Knock. The soft but direct connection of knuckles to thick wood traveled through the room. The Hunter tightened his belt and opened the door.

"Rigel! It really *is* you!" exclaimed a woman, throwing her arms around his neck and crying tears of joy and anguish. "I've knocked on nearly every door in this place trying to find you!"

"Alcyone? How are you here? I thought you all were taken captive."

"We were, Rigel. It was horrible. Out of nowhere, we were attacked and bound, and these awful black birds carried us away. But by the light of the three suns, White Wings, I mean Cygnus, found us and rescued us. He's been so kind, letting us stay at the palace." Her face journeyed with her story from fear and distress to relief and joy but then grew somber again, and her eyes teared up. "But I must tell you, Rigel, Merope isn't here. We don't know what happened to her. She escaped and was supposed to find…"

"Alcyone," he compassionately interrupted while motioning gently with his hand for her to stop talking. "Merope is fine. I was just with her."

"She's here? She finally made it to the palace?" she asked, excited and relieved.

"No. I'm sorry. She's not here. She found me while looking for Cygnus. During the last golden sunrise, I was with her in the Eridanus. She is safe with good companions, and Procyon and Sirius are looking after her as well."

"Well, she's not as close as I would hope, but that's wonderful news."

The Hunter looked out the window and turned the conversation away from Merope as it only upset him that she was just within his reach such a short time ago.

"How are the others?" he asked.

"They're okay. Maia's been spending a lot of time following around Cygnus, but always sounds very official about it. Either she's falling in love or she's about to *croon* his army to victory against Gurges Ater." Alcyone giggled. "Celaeno and Electra have been fairly preoccupied with entertaining the soldiers in the barracks and the interesting array of palace guests. You know Asterope and I aren't too interested in castle business, so we've been taking a lot of walks around the gardens. And Taygeta, poor Taygeta, the whole abduction was very traumatizing for her. She mostly sits in the corner of our room, rocking back and forth, singing some horrid tune about darkness."

"That's odd."

"You don't know the half of it! Her terrible little song has scared away every rodent and scampering creature within a thousand walks. She won't talk to anyone, and she won't come out of her room, but I dare say, the castle maids are so pleased, they might just pay her for her varmint-ridding services!" They both laughed with the craziness of it all but also with a hint of sadness for the poor girl's trauma.

"Well, I will rid the palace of one less varmint soon enough… though Taygeta is not the Ilmatar whose songs will drive me away."

Alcyone put her hand out to squeeze The Hunter's.

"Then, I shall pray my Merope arrives quickly, so you have good reason to stay."

"You're very kind, Alcyone, but I'm not sure we can sing that song together again."

"Sometimes, you must suffer through the verses of the past to reach the chorus of the future."

Knock! Knock! Knock!

"Lord Cygnus requests that The Noble Hunter join him presently to dinner," announced a deep official voice from the hall.

"Very good. I will join you presently," The Hunter answered back with a loud voice through the thick door.

Turning to Alcyone, he added quietly, "It was a true pleasure to see you again. Forgive my untimely leave, my lady. I must go listen now to the less lyrical squawks of Lord Fluffy Feathers." After a wink, a chuckle, and a hug, they parted ways.

CHAPTER 18

AN UNSAVORY DINNER

A colorful array of rich and delicate food spread out on the long, white stone table before them, every morsel untouched as Cygnus sat waiting for The Hunter to join him. But The Hunter walked in the room and stood firmly several feet away from the table.

"Old friend, you must be famished. Please sit and eat."

"Forgive me, *friend,* but since when does The Hunter of Arcas become the hunted? If you needed to speak with me, you should've come to me yourself or at the very least dropped a note. I will not eat from the bounty of your table until I am satisfied with the bounty of your answers." The Hunter replied with face as unmovable as the stone surrounding him. His eyes locked coldly to Cygnus's, challenging him.

"In days past, I had the luxury to travel and personally give appeals," Cygnus began with a calm sincere tone, which rose gradually in intensity. "Now, I have to protect my shore and the rest of Arcas from Gurges Ater while also trying to protect and conceal the Son of Earth. Forgive me, but I do not sit stagnant, soaking up my wealth and slumber like the useless remaining royal kingdoms of Arcas. Unlike them, I have always worked to protect Arcas. Unlike them, I care about protecting Earth as well."

"Oh, I'm sure you are pleased with the present circumstances. A politician always grows more popular when there is a crisis to avert, a world or two to save." The Hunter was not yet convinced.

"I understand the complexities and pains and mishandlings of our past policies with Earth. But what do you recommend now? Do we sit back and allow Gurges Ater to conquer the pillars and have sole access to Earth? Should we freely release the fate of both worlds into his hands? Should we allow the seven Ilmatar to be snatched away as their home crashes down around them?" Cygnus challenged back, knowing that he struck a crucial nerve by mentioning the sisters. "You know the answer to these questions. It is no longer my duty to deal with mere policies and treaties and communications throughout the kingdom realms. It is my duty to lead."

The Hunter's face turned from deep irritation to deep thought as he relaxed his guard slightly and joined Cygnus at the white table. The seven sisters of peace, beauty, solitude, and song had no business being thrown into a struggle over worlds and power. The Hunter wished he were there to protect them, to protect their home when it mattered most. He usually visited the Ilmatar sisters while traveling through the Starling Forest to share stories and a few meals, though mostly he came just to see Merope's face. Another day, and he would have been dining with the ladies in their beautiful treetop home.

In the quiet of the Starling Forest, the sisters were unprepared, unprotected, and easy targets for outside threats. But for what purpose? The Hunter found his anger toward Cygnus subsiding as it grew against Gurges Ater. Witnessing The Hunter's deep silent thoughts, Cygnus took the opportunity to continue his appeal.

"I am thankful we were fortunate enough to find and free the Ilmatar before they entered whatever bondage or service he premeditated for them. Justice was also brought upon those who carried them off… but I do hope that Merope is safe."

"Oh? Didn't the ignoble Sulafat tell you? She was under *my* protection when last the golden sun rose over the horizon."

"I'm sorry for that. Please accept my apologies for the manner and swiftness with which you were brought here. May you also have the wisdom to forgive Sulafat for the wrongs he unwisely committed against you."

"I have the wisdom to forgive you both, but likewise the wisdom to not forget."

"Then also do not forget the wrongs already committed by Gurges Ater. Coming here was the only way for you to really protect Merope. It is one thing to face a dragon alone, but it is entirely different to face an army alone."

"What are you proposing?" The Hunter was done with talk and ready to hear an actual plan.

"If you want to protect Merope, if you want to protect the boy and the Ursa as well, lead one of my armies out. Find the ones hunting the Son of Earth, the ones who abducted the Ilmatar and destroyed their home. Hunt them down. Help us take out the enemy now before they destroy further. If you succeed, Jackson will have the time and safety needed to retrieve the gem from Altair and to reach Deneb. After that, Merope will be reunited with her sisters with you to thank for it. No more hiding or running or ignoring Gurges Ater. Let's take the fight to him, and show him that there are still men of strength and valor willing to die for the good of Arcas."

Cygnus held out his hand, offering The Hunter to meet him as a partner in trust, understanding, and ultimately, war. The Hunter could care less about dying for Arcas, but he was honored to fight and even die for the sake of Merope, Jackson, and Otava. His hand met Cygnus's with a clasp while his eyes met with a nod of agreement.

When the meal ended, Cygnus escorted The Hunter to

the barracks to meet the army and devise plans for the departure and attack. Recalling Merope's descriptions, the militia in the woods was mainly on foot. Some higher ranks rode horses but none wore uniforms. The enemy's greatest strength was its stealth.

Cygnus insisted Sulafat needed to aid in the offensive attack, though The Hunter remained uneasy and irritated by the proposition. His lyre's magic could not carry off the entire enemy army, but it could help find their location, which was essential for the success of their mission. The army was already not far behind his friends somewhere in the jungle of the Eridanus.

The Hunter neither liked nor trusted Sulafat, yet there was no time to argue for a different second in command. A swift departure was essential to protect his friends who hopefully had reached Cassiopeia's by now. The Hunter vowed that he would not remove Sulafat from the edge of his eye, and he would not forget the edge of his sword. A short rest followed by a short meal was all that was left before they would head off with Lord White Wing's one hundred horsemen and several thousand foot soldiers.

Alcyone, Asterope, and Taygeta were a welcome sight for The Hunter's eyes as he excused himself from the ranks to meet with them in the palace gardens. Taygeta grasped her sisters' arms with white knuckles, walking stiffly with wild eyes as if she sensed an unforeseen assault.

"Taygeta, it's great to see you walking about the

gardens. They are manicured to perfection, are they not?" The Hunter looked directly at her, but her eyes would not focus on him. She nervously continued shivering and darted her eyes about, quietly singing her song:

Darkness takes, Darkness lies
Darkness kills, Darkness flies

"She calmed down for a while and was only humming," Asterope explained. "We finally convinced her to get up and go for a walk, but the minute we left our bedroom, the song resumed."

"Taygeta, it's Rigel." He reached out and touched her arm. "You're safe. I'm going to find the men who did this. Justice will come to them for their crimes. Don't worry, you are protected here. No one can hurt you."

"Rigel?" The weak voice's owner lifted her eyes to his. "Did the dark ravens take Merope?"

"No, Taygeta, Merope is safe. Cygnus killed the black ravens. They can't hurt anyone anymore. They are gone."

"But no one is safe from the blue claws," she whispered. "The blue claws reach out from the darkness. The blue claws fly with the darkness. The blue claws are one with the darkness." Her eyes grew increasingly wild again as she shook more violently and resumed her song loudly.

Darkness takes, Darkness lies
Darkness kills, Darkness flies

A loud "caw, caw" echoed through the gardens as Aquila left the castle and flew off on another mission from Cygnus. Taygeta screamed, fell to the ground, and curled in a ball. She was now weeping hysterically and her broken song only echoed the last line:

Darkness flies. Darkness flies. Darkness flies. Darkness flies.

Taygeta lost consciousness, sagging against her companions. The Hunter picked up her wilted, slumped body and carried her back to her room in the castle. Sitting next to her and stroking her forehead, Alcyone hummed over her sister's slumbering body. Though Taygeta finally lay silent and still, one could feel the battle raging within her mind. Asterope followed The Hunter into the hallway.

"There's something off about all this."

"I know. It's heartbreaking to see a girl who was rescued from evil continue to act as if she's still captured." The Hunter felt true compassion for Taygeta and her sisters who were fervently struggling to repair her.

"That's just it. I'm not convinced we were really rescued. We were told the ravens were killed, but when we landed, I was able to see through a small hole in the sack that carried me. The ravens flew away unharmed and unstressed. Why would they lie to us about that?"

"I don't know. Maybe they found and killed the ravens

later, maybe they didn't want you to be afraid of the birds coming back, or maybe they just wanted you to feel safe," The Hunter reasoned.

"Maybe. But there's something murky floating in the air. I'm not going to breathe easy until I figure out what it is."

"I will keep my eyes open, Asterope. I promise. If you find anything else amiss, let me know. We forest people must watch out for each other in these strange lands." The Hunter gave a reassuring smile and left to return to his chamber.

The Hunter did all he could to rest before the looming battle, but his mind was abuzz. He replayed every conversation, every sight since he reached the castle. Something did feel amiss. Asterope was not one to create conspiracies or jump to false conclusions. What if there were traitors in White Wings' castle right now? What if someone was obeying different orders or had a different agenda?

Sulafat! It could be Sulafat. He could have captured the girls, and then made himself out to be a hero to gain Cygnus's trust. *What if he's working for Gurges Ater to find out more about the gems or to thwart the coming battle? But is there any real proof?* The Hunter searched his thoughts for answers.

It was no secret The Hunter didn't like Sulafat, but calling him a traitor was a heavy allegation. The only one outwardly proclaiming something foul was Taygeta, who was obviously fighting madness. Taygeta's eerie song echoed through his mind. *Darkness. Darkness.* There was somewhere else he heard the accusation of darkness since he entered the palace...

The dungeon! Just before The Hunter left with Sulafat and his soldiers, the old man said something about adjusting his eyes to the darkness in order to see clearly. It seemed superficial enough at the time, but now it felt as if the messenger told a deeper tale, perhaps a cryptic tale of warning.

The Hunter suddenly felt a strong urge to get back to the prison. A locked-up criminal had little to lose by simply talking him. If his information was good enough, perhaps it could earn the prisoner some leniency from Cygnus for his past crimes. If they could get evidence to prove that Sulafat is an emissary from Gurges Ater, then The Hunter would vouch for the prisoner to receive pardon.

The Hunter quietly and quickly wound through the halls and stairs of the White Palace. Whenever he met guards and servants in his path, he reminded himself that he was not in the woods hunting for prey. No, he was the commander of an army now, merely going about official business. He looked every passerby in the eye and gave a stern nod of acknowledgement. As The Hunter reached the dungeon door, he was surprised to find it unlocked and unguarded. The smell of mildew and dust flooded over him. Leaving the door open a crack so he could see the path without lighting a torch, he made his way down the stone stairs toward the lone prisoner of the White Palace, which didn't look so white down there.

Noticing the ranked clothing that The Hunter was wearing, sporting the emblem with white wings surrounded by the three suns, the prisoner called out to him.

"What is someone of your high stature searching for in the pit of the palace?"

The Hunter crouched down next to the cell, so he was eye to eye with the sitting old man.

"What did you mean when you told me to adjust to the darkness around me to see clearly?"

"I don't think you will believe any answers coming from an aged prisoner."

"On the contrary, your age tells me that your information may be quite valuable. Your gray hair proves that you have spent time on Earth. And being the only prisoner in White Wings' castle, I assume that you have worked with Gurges Ater. I need to know who else is working for him."

"You're right that I have spent many days on Earth, but I do not know Gurges Ater," the man straightly answered.

"Look, if you help me, I will talk to White Wings to lessen whatever sentence you've been given. I give my oath to you that I will help you and not bring more punishment upon you." The Hunter tried to lift any fears of retribution a prisoner may feel under such questioning.

"It's a nice offer, but I'm telling the truth. I've never heard that name before." Not thrilled with the man's answer, The Hunter took a deep breath and probed further.

"Gurges Ater is our enemy, the creature living in darkness and spreading it throughout the land. If you do not know him... do you know Sulafat? The man who brought me here and then escorted me out."

"The twisted fellow who carries around a musical turtle shell?"

"Yes. Is he a traitor to White Wings? Did you hear him say anything of an unsavory nature when he brought me here."

"Every word he speaks sounds unsavory to me, but I don't think he is the darkness you are looking for."

"Then who? Who is working against White Wings? Who is orchestrating calamities against innocent people and feeding information to the enemy?" The Hunter was growing increasingly frustrated and impatient. The old, dirtied man kept silent in earnest thought. After a few minutes, he responded.

"I can see you are man who seeks truth. So, let me tell you a little history from Earth. You already know that Earth dwells in a double nature each day: light and dark. Now, the greatest man born to our planet was called 'the light of the world.' But he did not bring light to the visible darkness of night. He did not change the double nature of the Earth. Instead, he brought light to the darkness within us and changed the double nature of people's hearts." The man became increasingly animated and earnest through his story and ended by lightly pounding his hand on his chest.

"I have seen many things on Arcas by the light of the three suns, but I have never had the gift to see in someone's heart, though it would have served me well many times." The Hunter's mind flashed back to visions of Merope. "I cannot even conquer this darkness in my own heart, let alone another person's."

"You cannot see a person's heart, but you can test it."

"But if you are right, and Sulafat is not treacherous to White Wings, then whose heart am I testing?"

"Your enemy's. This Gurges Ater."

"What?" the Hunter growled lowly. "My mind has not been aged by Earth as yours has. What type of trap are you trying to lead me into?"

"No trap. You just seem to already know who your friends are. Cygnus you believe to be good while Gurges Ater you believe to be evil." He spoke not as an outsider or servant who typically used the name White Wings, but as someone who knew him more personally and called him by name. "Tell me, have you ever seen Gurges Ater?"

"No."

"Then shine light upon the darkness of your ignorance. If you do not know the strategy of your enemy, you cannot fight him. If you do not know the identity of your enemy, then how do you know he is not riding out to battle next to you?"

The Hunter didn't have time to respond further to the old man's advice. The dungeon door came flying open.

"If you preferred the prison cell to your room, you should have requested it from White Wings himself. Or do you delight in the counsel of criminals?" Sulafat and his men slithered quickly down the stairs, surrounding The Hunter.

"Maybe I just prefer to speak to criminals who are caged rather than criminals who roam free." The Hunter stared them down, then brushed past them up the stairs, unmoved by their threatening tones and larger numbers. Turning back one last time, he asked the prisoner, "Old friend, for what crimes are you in this dungeon?"

"Petty theft," he replied with a smirk.

CHAPTER 19

THE VENOM OF SHAULA

"Cygnus told me the Son of Earth would be coming here, but that was many suns before this wretched beast dug her way into our caves. I'm afraid the way to the Pillar of Deneb is going to be difficult to reach. The cave entrance is sealed at this moment for everyone's protection," King Alderamin explained.

"Dad, they don't have much time. An army from Gurges Ater is close behind us," Andi pleaded.

"We can help get rid of the beast! Otava is very skilled with traps and weapons, and Merope has a powerful song that even put Eltanin the great dragon to sleep! We can help you, King Alderamin." Jackson promised with great enthusiasm and courage, trying to impress Andromeda while also attempting to reach the gem before the pursuing army could arrive at their heels. Merope and Otava nodded in agreement.

"After all these years of sending gifts to please my pretentious wife, perhaps she has finally sent me a worthy offering. We will accept your service, Son of Earth. If you and your friends defeated the mighty Eltanin and his flaming breath, then perhaps you also have a chance to triumph over Shaula and her poisonous venom. If you succeed, then Errai—the chamberlain of Deneb—will guide you to the pillar hidden within our caves. If you will kindly excuse me, I must go rest now. When I return, I hope to give you the thanks and praise worthy of a king for your service to our kingdom."

King Alderamin retired from the dining room of his castle, followed by Andromeda, who appeared weary from visiting the wounded and suffering lying in the makeshift hospital outside of the Cephid Caves. She longed to return to her bedroom for rest. Her father made sure her room was always stocked with clothing and gifts for her visits, though everyone knew she cared little for such things. At this moment, she desired only solace and comfort to recover from the intense heart-wrenching activities since her arrival.

Jackson, Merope, and Otava remained with Errai. Immediately after their arrival, the three were taken to the castle and given time to rest and clean up before meeting the king and Andi in the grand dining room to discuss their business.

"Come." Errai motioned. "I'll show you Shaula, and my people will help you in any way that we can. She is a wicked and vile creature who has robbed us of our homes and our safety. Perhaps the suns have shined mercifully upon us by sending you here."

Otava grew a little nervous about confronting this unidentified cavern beast.

"What type of creature is Shaula?" Otava probed.

"A horrible monster we have never seen in these parts before. She has a pale white, slippery body with red eyes and a red heart. If Shaula cannot grab you with her giant clamping hands, she attacks with a raised dagger-like tail full of poison."

"Scorpius!" Merope uttered with a look of deep concern across her face.

"A scorpion? But scorpions are the size of a large spider or, at most, a rat... How could one scorpion do that much damage?" Jackson asked.

"Shaula is taller than a centaur," Errai answered.

"What?" the guests gasped as terror filled their minds and eyes.

They left the castle and continued along the trail leading them back to the main cave entrance, which now rested with boards nailed over top of it. Merope grabbed Jackson and Otava, pulling them to walk close to her. Errai continued ahead, not noticing their changed pace.

"We have a problem," Merope whispered. "No songs of mine will work on this creature. I may be able to lead him toward us but only in attack. I cannot alter his behaviors or put him to sleep. I have no sway over a creature that has no ears to hear."

Jackson's brilliant offer of chivalry did not look so wise now. Their stomachs only tightened as they walked past the trembling locals, quivering in fear that the scorpion would dig its way out of the caves to attack. Other Cephids lay crying over the dead and wounded. The main weapon of defense so far had been a form of dynamite, which was growing short in supply.

The cave passages were many, connecting and intertwining between homes and mining spaces. Every time they thought they outsmarted the beast and threw a stick of flaming explosives through the boarded up entrances, the creature would feel the vibrations and escape before the explosion, or clamp down on the wick, cutting the flame from the dynamite.

Several days prior, the Cephids were digging and picking away at a section of rock inlayed with precious metals. The glowing eyes of one man saw something shiny and red around the corner of rock. When he walked over to examine the interesting chunk of minerals, he came face-to-face with not a red ruby, but a red, beating heart. Shaula greeted him with a claw around his stomach and a sting to his chest. The Cephid stayed conscious, moaning until the claw released him, and the venom charged from his heart through his body, instantly paralyzing him.

Others were injured with broken limbs and venom-oozing wounds as they attacked back with rocks and axes. Shaula would not give up her motionless meal easily, however, and fought back, standing over her prey. The men eventually had no choice but to drag their own wounded bodies out and leave their lifeless friend behind. Since then, no Cephid has felt safe entering the caves or their homes, for Shaula waits silently in the darkness, eager for her next victim.

"This entrance was our last sighting of Shaula." Errai pointed to the black hole still simmering with soft dynamite smoke through the slits between the log barriers. "I will go gather what bodies and tools we have to assist you." Though an entire civilization encompassed the fields surrounding the caves, once again, Jackson, Merope, and Otava were alone.

"I'm sorry. I shouldn't have volunteered us. I didn't even know what we were fighting," Jackson apologized.

"It's okay. There really is no other way. If we wait for White Wings to arrive, it may be too late. If we fail to reach the pillar, I'm sure the army behind will not fail to reach us. We must at least try or Gurges Ater will walk right in and take over the Deneb Kingdom whose people are already weak from fear and suffering," Merope reasoned.

"Look at me!" Otava jumped into the conversation with a bit of zeal. "Do I look like a beast?" No one knew how to respond to his question correctly. "I *am* a beast, and I know how to fight a beast. We can't throw a stick of explosives at it, and we can't fight it claw to claw." Otava proudly displayed his own dull but powerful, dark brown daggers.

"So, what do we do?" Jackson asked just the question Otava was striving to hear.

"We fight with better weapons, better traps, and better smarts."

"What do you suggest?" Merope asked.

"Well, here's what we do. They still have enough explosives to throw a stick in all the openings except for one. Once each stick has exploded and each passage is clear of the scorpion, we'll send some of the Cephids through with wooden shields the same size as the tunnels, top to bottom, side to side. The shields will close off those passages from the beast. In the one remaining entrance, Merope can sing a deep tune, so the creature will feel the vibrations through the rocks. Shaula will then follow the vibrations, thinking it's a snack. When she enters the last passage, my net will be waiting overhead to drop on her. Before she can claw her way out, I will send an arrow from my crossbow right through her bloody heart!" Otava was quite proud and satisfied with his plan.

"There's only one problem with that plan, Otava." Merope felt bad crushing his dream, but she must.

"What?"

"Your net remains at the lair of a certain dragon. We can't list it among our assets."

"Oh, right."

"Can we build a cage outside the entrance to trap it, instead? I've witnessed first-hand that Otava makes a great falling door to cage dangerous beasts," Jackson added eagerly.

"It is unlikely the scorpius will come out into the sunlight," Merope informed. "If given the choice, it will stay in the darkness."

"Then, my fair lady, we don't give it any other choice but to come face us in the light!" Otava confidently announced.

Errai arrived with a hundred Cephid men armed and willing to help take out Shaula. Using a stick on the grey dirt outside, Otava asked Errai to map out the cave areas where the scorpion had direct access. When the sketches were complete, Otava began adding to the drawings with arrows, structures, and a battle plan.

By the time Princess Andromeda and King Alderamin arrived, everyone was bustling around, cutting and nailing wooden structures together. A smaller side entrance was just wide and big enough for the creature to pass through. On this opening, they built a wooden cage all around the outside of it. A thin gap between the cave and the cage afforded enough room for a door to crash down the moment the beast entered the container.

While Cephids built the various battle structures,

Otava oversaw and ordered out instructions. Merope went with Andi to visit the sick, hoping she could give them a few songs to fight the venom and quicken the healing process. Her warm hum hovered on the wind, encompassing the exterior campsite as it joined in the beat of the pounding hammers and the driving handsaws.

Jackson assisted a group of Cephids who were adding spear holes and handles to the large wooden shields. It took four of them to hold up each shield and an additional Cephid in the center would jab and angle the spear as needed to keep the scorpion at a decent distance. The shields were small enough to freely travel through the passageways, but large enough the pinchers and stinger should not be able to maneuver around them to attack.

Many of the Cephid homes were separated by rock from the larger mining passages, but they were still too scared to occupy their homes in fear that Shaula would scratch or dig her way in to find food. Days ago, they did manage to find and collapse the original entry hole into a pile of thick rubble. Around the front of the city, there were five arched caves openings, which all eventually led to the larger mining room, the same room where Shaula was first discovered.

When construction was complete, weapons had been sharpened, and prayers lifted, the large boards were pried off each entrance simultaneously. The bravest Cephids held the shields, stood in their appointed places, and waited for the first command.

"Ready, men?" Otava made eye contact with each of the five groups to verify.

"Kindle stick one… and throw!" *BOOM!*

"Push forward with the shield!"

Four little men lifted the heavy shield and shuffled forward through the passageway while the fifth man held a spear through its middle in defense.

"Kindle blast two… and throw!" *BOOM!*

"Good! Go forward, men!"

Otava called the shots, looking nearly as focused, obsessed, and excited as he did while cooking a rare specialty for a crowd. It was all science. Just as each ingredient and spice had its place, time, and temperature for entering the main dish, each trap, person, and weapon was precisely mixed to form a satisfying and successful attack.

Two more blasts. Two more advances.

The Cephid men pushed forward to the end of the tunnels and waited and waited. Nothing happened, and the scorpion was yet to be seen.

"Merope, see if you can bring the beast out," Otava asked.

"I'll try."

Merope pressed her hand against the outer stone wall near the caged opening. She then sent a hummed melody through the air, through her body, and through the thick walls of rock. The sound echoed around and around, bouncing through and upon each cavern wall. Mere minutes passed, but it felt like hours for all those holding their ground behind the large shields and those waiting at the cage to catch a glimpse of the beast. Slowly and stealthfully, a pair of red eyes emerged from the end of the long, empty tunnel, following the trail of Merope's vibrations.

"Keep singing, Merope!" Otava yelled.

The cherry eyes crept closer and closer. When Shaula appeared to be well within the last tunnel and out of the main cavern, Otava yelled to Errai who struck the dinner gong. The shields moved forward in the caves, joining together in the large cavern as they marched as one to block Shaula from retreating.

At first the scorpion froze, not knowing which vibrations to follow: Merope's steady melodic sensations toward the remaining entrance, the gong near the largest mouth, or the firm but light treading of twenty feet closing in on her. As the four shields marched side-by-side, the giant whipped around to face them, thrashing its claws out. Shaula's pale, translucent white pinchers lunged at them and grabbed two spears, splitting them in half. Her stinger flew between the cracks of two shields meeting together and pierced a glowing-eyed Cephid in the shoulder. He screamed, grabbed his arm oozing with blood and thick, yellow venom out of a deep hole, and then fell to the ground, convulsing.

"Get a healer!" one man yelled as the shields continued to push forward.

They needed to get the scorpion to back up farther so

they could get just one shield lodged snuggly in the last tunnel. One Cephid threw his severed spear end at the creature, getting it to scurry slightly backward. Outside the cave, many could see little parts of the struggle. Occasionally, the glowing yellow eyes of the little miners shone through the small peepholes in the shields, but mostly the waiting crowd could see the blazing, red, beating heart of the giant villain pumping more rapidly each moment as it felt more threatened. Jackson, who stood on top of the cage awaiting the signal to cut down the door, had a good view. He watched clearly as the severed spear ricocheted against the side of the beast and tumbled to the ground below. Then, he had an idea.

"Aim for his eyes! Send the spears toward his eyes!" Jackson shouted, peering through the wooden slates of the cage underneath him.

The men inside got the message, and one spear shot through the hole in its shield, grazing Shaula's scalp. The Cephid, looking through to see if his shot made it, jumped back as the moist stinger flew into the open hole inches from his head. Only one spear remained, and the shield holes were only big enough to allow new spears to be inserted from the front side. Each weapon was placed in backward so that the tip of the spear stayed intact on the outside, facing the threat.

"Hurry! Men on the edges, turn sideways!" one man ordered.

"Are you crazy, Alfirk? Shaula will grab the shields right from us!" another responded.

"That's what I'm hoping for! Then her hands will be full long enough for me to aim," Alfirk replied.

"Let's do it!" yelled another. "She's almost right where we need her!"

"One, two, three!" Alfirk shouted.

The two shields on the ends opened up sideways. *Snap! Snap!* Shaula grabbed the wood and swung her claws inward. Flying in the air from the lifted shields, two Cephids jumped off and rolled away while the other six hung on, their feet dangling above the ground. But in grasping the shields, the rest of Shaula's body stood still momentarily and Alfirk's spear flew directly into one eye. Reflexively, she dropped the shields, leaving the one on the right with the men on top of it exposed to attack and the men on the left buried beneath theirs.

Running backward, she flailed her arms, pinching and grabbing at the spear lodged in the red eyeball and discharging red fluid. Shaula could not release the spear from her eye, but tugged at it so fiercely the eye came out, still stuck to the spear with white nerves and muscles hanging off it. While she struggled to see and move and protect her maimed body, Alfirk's group led the charge. They closed off the final tunnel and slowly moved forward, pushing her back toward the sunlit cage.

The four remaining Cephids, holding to a now-unneeded shield, dropped it and ran to help steady the moving shield against the wildly enraged creature. The others picked themselves up and worked together to unpin those trapped underneath the large, wooden structure. The healthy assisted a few healers in carrying out the one paralyzed by a shoulder sting and another with a crushed leg from the force of the heavy shield falling upon him.

Outside, everyone waited with weapons ready and adrenaline pumping as Shaula writhed and snapped and pierced violently all around. The wooden cage rattled as she entered it, twisting, and the Cephids jumped back as her pinchers and stinger flew through every crevice.

"Jackson, cut the rope!" Otava commanded. Jackson raised the sword and started sawing away at the rope, but out of her good eye, Shaula spotted him. Rising up on her lower legs, she threw her dagger tail out toward him.

"Jackson!" Merope screamed.

He jumped just in time as the stinger, dripping with venom, pushed vainly into the rock next to him. As he leapt to escape, one of Jackson's legs fell between the cage and the cave. Otava shot arrow after arrow into the beast, enraging it to snap and pierce ferociously, but its red eye remained fixed on Jackson.

Jackson pushed up with his arms, but his leg would not budge. The Cephids' swords were too short to reach the scorpion, and the jabs from spears and arrows didn't seem to break her vigor. Jackson reached out for the sword lying on top of the cave, and Shaula reached back for her final strike. Just as her tail passed through the cage to sting his dangling leg, he struck the rope overhead, sending the gate flying down on top of her tail, pinning it flat to the ground.

The Cephids jumped out from behind their shield, climbing on top of the gate to ensure her poisonous tail was rendered immobile and useless. An array of weapons flew in at the beast, piercing and stabbing from every angle. The cage shook as she attacked the bars and snapped the air so ferociously her body flipped upside down with her tail still caught under the gate and her beating red heart exposed on top.

"Otava! Otava! Otava!" The crowd shouted for him to deal the deadly blow. Otava grabbed a spear, dipped the end in tar, and set it ablaze. Instead of throwing it, Otava walked over to the king and handed him the flaming spear.

"King Alderamin, you should finish this battle. Shaula stole her way into your kingdom as a thief and a murderer, but you have opened your doors to us as friends. Please, take the triumph for your people." Though proud of his accomplishment and ultimate victory, Otava's nobility and humility radiated out of him.

"My friends and my companions, today the Deneb Kingdom has victory over Shaula, and we will now sting her back with everlasting death for her crimes of terror and murder!" The king shouted triumphantly and threw the fiery spear directly into the large, contracting, throbbing heart. The crowd cheered as the sharp fire seared into the scorpion, and she burst into flames.

"And now, my friends, go back to your homes and bring out your songs, your bread, and your wine! Today, we will honor our dead and our wounded and our brave men. Today, we will celebrate victory together!" And such commands as this coming from a king are always obeyed with swiftness and gladness.

It seemed as if this little city had prepared for such a feast months ago. In what felt like mere moments, music strummed, clanked, beat, and piped. A fire blazed high in an outdoor pit and people grabbed hands and danced. Otava laughed and reveled with the cooks, comparing strategies and smelling each unique seasoning from the cave lands. Merope strummed a stringed instrument created with wood and pegged with jewels. She smiled and laughed, enjoying the unbridled joy of a people freed from bondage and fear, a people whose lives were restored to them. Jackson sat and watched all the little men, little women, and even littler children bound around through their meadow of dance. From the top of the caves, a smooth cool voice starting singing.

> *I asked my pa,*
> *"Where should I take a gal to ask her to be mine?*
> *Should I row her on the lake?*
> *Should I stroll her through the forest?*
> *Should I sit her on the meadow green?"*

The rest of the crowd joined in on the song, raising their cups and their voices enthusiastically:

No, no! Don't take her to the lake!
No, no! Don't take her to the forest!
No, no! Not the meadow green!
Hold to your axe and hold to your lass,
Walk her through the caves that are cool and clean.

A group of Cephid men brought out their large picks, performing a synchronized dance. Experts with their tool, they flung the heavy dangerous picks up in circles, catching them effortlessly, then pounded them on the ground, and twirled them upon the flattened axe heads. But someone did not belong in the group and stood out vibrantly. Andi grabbed a pick and joined in the dance as if she was born for it. Though a powerful and dangerous tool, she twirled it around with grace and beauty. Her wavy, amber hair bounced around, dancing with her purple dress. She carried such a unique combination of wild beauty and dangerous innocence.

Yep, she's definitely not safe, Jackson thought, smiling.

A second verse rang out from another Cephid singing,

I asked my ma,
"Where should I take a gal to give the perfect token?"

Errai noticed Jackson's eyes were fixed upon Andi and

whispered something to the king standing next to him. Alderamin nodded with a straight face, whispering something back to Errai. Maneuvering effortlessly through the crowd, Errai approached Jackson and sat next to him.

"You really should go out there and dance too. This party is because of you and your friends. Enjoy it. Join in." Errai nudged.

"Thank you, but I'm afraid I would look a little tall dancing out there, and not quite as graceful," Jackson answered, lightly joking.

"I believe I see one other out there who would match your height well enough." Errai smiled and pointed to Andromeda.

"I think she's a bit out of my league. Anyways, don't kings chop off the arms of boys like me for dancing with their royal daughters?"

"Not tonight he won't. Tonight, you are a hero. You have earned a dance with the princess. Come, come! Are Sons of Earth brave enough to fight with a venom-tailed monster but not brave enough to dance with a girl?" Errai wasn't going to let up on him as the crowd roared out the chorus one last time.

No, no! Don't take her to the lake!
No, no! Don't take her to the forest!
No, no! Not the meadow green!
Hold to your axe and hold to your lass
Walk her through the caves that are cool and clean!

"Not a girl wielding a pick axe like it's a baton," Jackson replied with a smile, but just then the dance ended and the picks were placed on the side in a pile.

"Well, now you have no excuse."

True, Jackson had just faced a venomed, giant scorpion beast. How hard could it be to ask a girl to dance? He tried to keep the butterflies from bursting out of his gut as he steadied his feet and walked over to the tree-climbing, axe-wielding princess, the girl who grew up sleeping in castles but also dwelling in cool, mazed caverns and hot, unkempt jungles. Perhaps Midwestern girls were just as dangerous, just as scary for Jackson to approach, but at the moment, the most lovely and frightening female in the universe stood on the sidelines, clapping and swaying and smiling, just waiting to shoot him down and grind his heart underneath her feet as he lay it out before her.

"Hi, Andi," Jackson started.

"Hi, Jackson." Andi smiled at him, then continued watching the dance.

"Hey, I was wondering if you could teach me this dance. Our dances are a little different on Earth." It seemed like an eternity before Andi turned to him and responded.

"I don't typically dance with just any boy who shows up from another world." Andi allowed a dramatic pause as Jackson was thinking about how to bow out of his embarrassing invitation mutually. "*But*, considering I don't see any *boys* here, I'd gladly dance with the man who brought the scorpius to the ground."

When Jackson finally snapped out of his assumed rejection and swallowed her words with accuracy, he smiled, puffed up his shoulders slightly, and held out his hand to her.

"Well, then, show me how this dance floor works, princess."

CHAPTER 20

THE FACE OF GURGES ATER

The Hunter did not return to his room alone. Asterope caught The Hunter's eye and he delivered an unspoken warning as she passed him and the stalking soldiers in the hall. Sulafat and his men followed The Hunter all the way to his room and kept guard at the door. He sent two of his men to find White Wings and describe the precarious nature of The Hunter's prison visit. Sulafat himself and two of his soldiers stood watching the closed door and would follow him until they received orders from White Wings himself.

Typically, one higher in command would not perform the menial tasks of a guard dog, but Sulafat wanted to be the first one to see The Hunter's face, the first one to look in his eyes, punch him in the gut, and throw him back in a cell where he belonged. He was not about to follow the orders of some freelance, traveling woodsman. Sulafat was determined to lead Cygnus's army out to meet the resistance, and The Hunter would not share in his glory.

Heeding The Hunter's warning, Asterope immediately gathered Celaeno, Electra, and Alcyone to help her. Even Sulafat could not say no to a few innocent little songbirds. Three sisters swayed up the stairs near The Hunter's chamber singing a soothing soft trio:

> *My heart flew out the window, the window, the window;*
> *My heart flew out the window in search of my love.*
> *A voice floats in the window, the window, the window;*
> *A voice floats in the window; its sound is my love.*

Upon reaching the hallway and seeing Sulafat with his two men, they blushed and giggled as if they didn't know anyone would be listening.

"That was beautiful, ladies. It is nice that others in the great White Palace carry a love and a talent for music." Sulafat spread the flattery thickly like someone who desires repayment for complimentary words.

"We have also heard of your musical fame. Why don't you join us? We would be honored to finish our song with your skillful accompaniment. There are only two verses left." Asterope spun her offer with ease and grace, masterfully containing her inner disgust. Though Electra and Celaeno had enjoyed entertaining and chatting with many leaders in the kingdom, they too were neither fond of Sulafat's treatment of The Hunter nor his demeanor, which would cause most women's skin to crawl.

"Yes, please do!" echoed Electra and Celaeno. The three ladies each sat down in front of the three men.

They complimented the beauty and rarity of Sulafat's white turtle shell lyre that displayed large, black spots, mirrored on both sides of the spine. Two black, wooden columns curved slightly out, then slightly inward from both sides of the shell. A black neck rested across the top set in a groove on both columns, and the strings ran tightly from pegs on the neck down the middle of the shell and over the yellowish-white turtle skin stretched over the hollow body.

"I desire nothing more than to play a delicate tune with you ladies, but I cannot play my own lyre in the castle. The music is a bit too powerful for indoors," Sulafat responded with obvious pride about his magical instrument.

"No worries, you can play ours." Asterope took a small wooden lyre from Celaeno and gave it to Sulafat. They were prepared.

The Hunter listened to the conversation through the door. It wasn't typical for the sisters to seek out attention or purposely flirt with any man, let alone one like Sulafat. His mind raced to figure out their schemes as the song continued, accompanied now by the rhythmical plucks of a lyre.

My eyes fall down the window, the window, the window;
My eyes fall down the window to gaze at my love.
His lips fawn at the window, the window, the window;
His lips fawn at the window to bind with my love.

"The window, the window!" The Hunter whispered when he got the message and ran to look out. Beneath him, Alcyone peered out from a window directly below and waved at him. He could never jump as far as the ground, but he could make it to the room beneath him if he could find something to hold on to. On the wall hung a large fishing net whose current purpose was simply to add to the rustic décor in the room.

The Hunter tangled his sword along with the bow and arrows within the net, and then lowered them down to Alcyone. When he pulled the empty netting back up, he hooked it to one of the bronze dogs bolted into the fireplace bricks. He meticulously climbed down the netting, using only the strength and grasp of his arms. The Hunter knew not to risk getting his feet tangled within the mess of interweaving cords. Once his waist reached the top of the window beneath, he swung his legs inside.

"Rigel, what is going on?" she asked, concerned.

"I don't know, Alcyone, but I'm going to find out. Thank Asterope for recognizing a problem and bringing help, and thank Celaeno and Electra for helping distract the guards. You need to get back to your room quickly, so they don't interrogate you about my escape. I'll come back for you all when I have some answers." He grabbed at the door handle.

"Don't go through the door! We found a better way." She pulled back a rug, which revealed a hidden, hinged door underneath. "The acoustics always bounced a little differently in this room. It goes down quite far and exits by the beach, but thanks to Taygeta, you don't have to worry about any rats down there."

"Perfect. Thank you again."

"When you come back, Rigel, I'll expect you to bring a dark-haired songbird with you." Alcyone eyes were earnest and slightly watered. Her face was always an open book of her emotions. That is why she was chosen to hide out in Celaeno and Electra's room to meet Rigel. She never could have played out the deception of Sulafat with a straight face.

"I'll do my best. I promise, I'll do my best." Rigel replied with a firm hug. He walked down the steep stairs, feeling the walls for balance and direction. All light disappeared when the door overhead shut.

The Hunter's mind felt as awkward as his body, feeling around, grasping for answers, looking for truth, and hoping for light to shine on the many lingering questions. He felt certain that Sulafat must be a traitor, but there was only one way to find the truth. The Hunter would walk up to the ancient ruins of Trifid where The Bridge of old lay in a pile of rubble and where Gurges Ater made his shadowy home.

It was time for the cat and mouse games to end with the enemy. It was time for the uncertainties to end.

The Hunter journeyed alone now just as he had for several thousand years. Even if the truth cost him his life, he would have more than he did now. Ripped from the only friends he had, parted from his trusted canine companions, and holding on to a thread of hope from love lost long ago. If he could just decipher the truth, if he could just know who the real enemy was, maybe the truth would set him free from the confusion. Maybe he could live another thousand years with more vibrancy and purpose than ever before, knowing he was fighting for something good, for something true.

Light peered through an opening at the end of the tunnel. The Hunter was no longer treading down stairs but walking straight. When he reached the end, he had to duck low to exit the small entrance, which from afar appeared to be just another deep groove in the jagged rock wall surrounding the narrow white-sand beach.

A dense fog hued with reds and purples settled on top of the water. Between the fog and the rippling tides, his footprints and shadowy silhouette were covered well from sight. Of all the places that Sulafat may try to search for him, the shoreline headed straight toward Gurges Ater would be the last place.

Suddenly, a dark head emerged from the thick fog. Black like onyx, his mane surged in the wind as if it were ablaze. It was Alnitak, the famed black stallion who galloped without a herd and only appeared when it was time to choose a rider, when it was time to ride to war. The Hunter walked up to the mighty beast as its nostrils flared, and his front feet thundered to the ground from their reared position. His eyes looked into The Hunter's with a challenge as he pawed the sandy ground just inside the concealment of the shallow waters. The Hunter extended his hand for the wild beast to smell.

"My name is Rigel." The grandeur and power of this horse demanded a proper and honest introduction. "Good to meet you, Alnitak. I've heard many legends about you. Let's say we ride to the dark fortress together and look the devil in the eyes."

Alnitak nickered, moving his head to the side and pushing Rigel's hand up toward his mane. He grabbed at the top of the thick cords of black and swung his leg over. The time of the lone horse was over; the time of the lone hunter was over. It was time for Rigel to ride to battle, prepared to fight the fires of the famed enemy with the blazing fires of the famed warhorse. As they rode southeast across the shoreline, blue flames flared up with the dust beneath their feet.

The ocean breeze tasted surprisingly fresh for carrying the weighty flavors of salt and fish upon it. A journey of several hours felt like mere minutes riding upon the gallop of Alnitak. The fog gradually lifted revealing a well-constructed fortress in front of where the ancient ruins of Trifid and The Bridge once dwelt.

The enormous Trifid Fortress towered high above on a plain of rock next to sand and eventual grass, but the backside rested directly against the Ligeian waters. Rigel was taken aback to find the fortress freshly dressed in white bricks where it was rumored to be as dark as the nights of Earth. The large black ravens, the same ravens that carried off the Ilmatar sisters and chased Jackson, perched upon the white walls, sending their *Caw! Caw!* throughout the fortress alerting them of his arrival.

As he rode up to the gates, he expected shouts or arrows pointing down at him, questioning his arrival. Instead, the iron portcullis was raised and the huge steel and wood doors opened inward to grant him entrance. Rigel would not turn back now. Alnitak softened to a canter through the corridor surrounded in stone and underneath a second raised portcullis protecting the main courtyard. Rigel dismounted just as a lieutenant with a few soldiers approached him.

"My name is Albireo. Why has Lord White Wings sent you? Tell me, what does he demand of us?"

How do they know I came from White Wings? Rigel thought. He fought the inner panic remembering he still bore the cloak sealed with Cygnus's emblem from the White Palace. Rigel breathed deeply.

"I am here to seek an audience with Gurges Ater."

"Who?" Albireo seemed to scan his thoughts attempting to find a face to match the name.

"Gurges Ater. Is he not your leader?"

"No. There must be some mistake. I am in charge here, underneath His Lordship of course." Albireo examined Rigel becoming skeptical as to his purpose.

"Forgive me. The long ride has made my head dizzy and my mouth parched. Please tell me the name of your lordship again." Rigel teetered on his legs, holding his head and playing a victim of the road to seem innocent while attempting to peer into the illusive face of the enemy.

"Get him some water and food, boys! Come and sit for a minute." Albireo led him to a table and chair in the courtyard of the fortress. "You'll remember everything in moment, I'm sure. We serve Lord Cygnus. The powerful and wise White Wings who is soon to rule over all of Arcas."

Now, Rigel really did feel dizzy but not from the long travel. He drank the water and ate the food provided to him, nodding his head in agreement as if he understood. While pretending to recover, he examined the surroundings. Familiar white bricks constructed each wall, but he now noticed the banners and flags decorating much of the interior: three suns surrounding white wings in the center.

The face of Gurges Ater was an empty hole of nothingness, sucking the life out of Arcas. Cygnus uprooted all of his friends from their homes and swirled them into a journey of dangerous nothingness. They were running from an enemy who didn't exist. Fighting for a fabricated cause. *But for what purpose?* Rigel searched.

"Ah, yes, thank you. My thoughts are returning to me, Albireo. Lord Cygnus sent me here to bring back news of progress and your status before he sends an army out to destroy the resistance."

"Please inform him that four compounds are finished with more to come as needed. Each building sleeps a hundred and twenty servants, and we lie in wait for White Wings' command. Would you like to have a tour while you are here? The Bridge to Earth has been completely restored." Albireo seemed quite proud of the facilities, but Rigel knew better than to stick around for long.

"I would very much like to, but I have strict orders to return without delay. Your progress will be well received by His Lordship." Rigel gave the official soldier salute of his fist against his chest, which Albireo repeated.

Grabbing hold of Alnitak, he mounted the horse in one motion and flew past the entrance as if he was fleeing the very gates of hell. Rigel first headed west back toward the White Palace, but once at a safe distance, he bore hard northeast.

His mind raged with fury. Taygeta was right. The darkness wasn't sitting around some distant place; it was flying around, over, and through every detail regarding the gems. Cygnus had deceived and endangered everyone Rigel

211

cared about. The Ilmatar sisters were the first to tell Rigel of the strange events surrounding the name Gurges Ater. A few years prior, Cygnus visited the sisters and informed them of this dark creature making his home in the old ruins of The Bridge. At the time, the information seemed not only eerie and bizarre but also trivial and inconsequential.

Always the politician, White Wings cared neither for Arcas nor for Earth. He was after nothing more than his own fame, glory, and power. He rebuilt The Bridge hidden behind a web of lies while effortlessly deceiving everyone into helping him attain the power to use it.

Rigel needed to find Arcturus and the resistance. It was time to know the full truth. If his ally turned out to be his enemy, perhaps his enemy would turn out to be his friend. In their present ignorance, Jackson, Otava, and Merope should be safe from the wrath of Cygnus, but Cygnus was no longer safe from the wrath of Rigel. Alnitak ran hard with fire beneath him while Rigel rode hard with fire inside him. It was time for the flying angel to fall before he took down all of Arcas with him.

CHAPTER 21

THE ENEMY OF ARCTURUS

"Queen Cassiopeia, I have come to ask that you help us find the Son of Earth. Is he here or has he already been to the Pillar of Altair?" Arcturus spoke with command and authority while remaining respectful to the ruler of a realm belonging to another. He even took off his sword and garments to wear the proper castle attire of gray though he loathed the idea of having to follow the absurd rules of the dying, yet everlasting, breed of royals on Arcas.

"Oh, yes, the Son of Earth! How enraptured those creatures became when they entered my presence. Do you know it is the vivid memory of my beauty that has sustained life on their dark, aging planet so long? Have you ever seen a Son of Earth? Some of them look so pale as if their skin never saw the light of day, yet for never seeing the sun, their skin wrinkles up to something awful. It's only natural for the poor creatures to paw and scratch their ways through the ancient portal of Altair just to glance upon my splendor." The queen paused for a moment of silent compassion for the misfortunate Earthians.

"Fair Queen, I implore you, the safety of your kingdom, of all of Arcas is at risk here. Everyone has heard that Gurges Ater means to control the pillars, but we have good reason to believe that White Wings is also working with him." Before he could say more, the queen piped in.

"Oh, I know White Wings very well, such a fascinating man-bird he is! If only he wasn't so colorless. I'm sure in his pale, overwhelming whites, he wishes he bore the vibrant colors of the flower of the Eridanus. I've tried to advise him on it. I even gave him some small jewels to adorn his wings with. Of course, no number of adornments would make him my equal, but it would vastly improve his ashen appearance. I would look marvelous with wings. But I dare say wings would burden me with more beauty than anyone could handle. My burden is great enough as it is, sitting here every day while every knight, statesmen, and Earthian comes to gape at me and learn from my tireless wisdom."

"The Son of Earth, Queen Cassiopeia, where is he now?" Arcturus increased his urgency, frustrated that time was moving ever onward, but he had learned nothing yet from the queen about the gem-stealing travelers.

"Isn't it obvious where he is? He is sitting alone, staring

214

at the flowers and the birds and the plants around my marvelous river and wondering why they pale in comparison to my beauty. He's dressed in dullness and dreaming visions of grandeur that he can never attain just as you shall be when you leave my presence."

But Arcturus was not dreaming visions of grandeur. He was imagining busting every piece of glass and yelling with all his might until he could snap the queen out of her self-absorption into a world where she could give at least one speck of valuable information.

"Queen Cassiopeia! I beg of you, did you grant the Son of Earth access to the Pillar of Altair?" His voice was tense and slightly raised though he grasped to maintain self-control with all his might.

"Shedir! This man and his questions have wearied me. Sir, I understand your distress with meeting a beauty you so obviously have never encountered before. I know you are one who dwells in the nether regions of Arcas away from the manners of the court. But treating me in such a vile manner will not win you more audiences to glance upon my splendor. So, please, go now and be miserable knowing your time to revel in my glorious, glimmering presence was cut short. If you ever wish to return to my courts, I suggest you bring gifts worthy of my beauty, and instead of bringing me questions as dull as your countenance, bring me the praise I most certainly deserve."

Queen Cassiopeia nearly shook with frustration, fanning herself in attempt to hinder the waters welling in her eyes. Arcturus turned abruptly and stomped out as Shedir faced the queen giving her adulations of praise and comfort as he exited behind.

Shedir hobbled as fast as his old feet could afford him to catch up with Arcturus.

"The queen was very gracious to let you enter her presence. You can't be angry she doesn't hold the answers you are looking for," Shedir explained as Arcturus continued out of the castle into the courtyard. Ripping off the gray shirt and throwing the slippers given to him for castle entrance, he grabbed his sword and clothes from his son, Nekkar.

"And if not your queen, then who *does* hold those answers, old man? My questions were simple enough, but you all are living in your sparkly fantasy world while your kingdom and the rest of Arcas slowly crumbles around you."

"Not so. We are a people of peace. We stick to the Eridanus and do not barge into the sovereignty of other kingdoms or try to steal the ancient gems and force our way into power." Shedir held his ground firmly and politely but with an accusatory edge.

"Forced power? No, we have not forced ourselves upon anyone nor do we wish to rule over anyone. The problem is you subservient dogs who lick at the feet of royal ruins. You who have lived under the rule of a ridiculous monarchy, obeying her whims and lust for beauty, yet you cannot see when the very devil has entered your realm and defiled your precious queen for his own pleasures."

Cassiopeia's men had heard enough of Arcturus's accusations. Enraged, they pulled out their swords, surrounding Arcturus and his few knights who were allowed to cross the river and enter the kingdom. Though smaller in number, the foreigners also pulled out their swords, standing their ground.

"So, aged counselor of the queen, was this the plan you agreed upon with Gurges Ater? Have you joined ranks with the Earthian and White Wings and the serpent lord to destroy us now? Perhaps your decorated queen will earn a few extra adornments for her service as she joins the rest of you subservient dogs before your new ruler."

At his insults, the castle guards lost their cool. Clanging, slashing, and swiping, everywhere their metals edges flew together. But Arcturus and his men were stronger from their long travels and rigorous training. The soldiers of Altair were weak and fattened from years of inactivity. In moments, the kingdom soldiers all lie at the edge of a sword while Arcturus's men awaited his command to usher them into a never-anticipated death. Just then, a shout echoed and a flame blazed through the courtyard.

"STOP!" When all eyes moved to the man sitting upon

the black horse, they saw an arrow aimed directly at Arcturus.

"We thought The Hunter was dead. Have you also joined ranks with the monarchies and tyrants?" Arcturus asked, keeping his sword at the throat of the soldier in front of him.

"The Hunter *is* dead. I am Rigel, and I have joined ranks with no one. Tell me, what are men of the Free Realms doing fighting with the ancient kingdoms and hunting down a mere boy?"

"We care not for kings or castles," Arcturus declared. "We are here to keep Arcas free and unblemished by Earth's darkness. We know White Wings secretly holds the three gems of Arcas. We also believe that he is working with Gurges Ater and…"

"There is no Gurges Ater," Rigel broke in, his words echoing through the courtyard with resolve and authority.

"What do you mean? Does he not dwell in the forsaken Trifid ruins at The Bridge? Surely you have heard he seeks to control the pillars once again and access Earth. He desires to gain unnatural powers and wealth from that dark, water-destroyed land."

Rigel lowered his aimed arrow while Arcturus and his men gradually relaxed their swords from their captives' necks, but did not yet sheath them.

"I just rode here from Trifid. A freshly built fortress rises around the ruins. No part of Trifid bore a face or a symbol of Gurges Ater. The fortress bore White Wings, the symbol of Cygnus."

"Then where is this Gurges Ater whom the whole of Arcas trembles about?" Arcturus probed, still skeptical.

"He was nothing more than a great lie, a decoy. Gurges Ater was the enemy everyone was fighting with, whom everyone was looking for. You were right. It is White Wings who carries the gems of Arcas. But it is also White Wings who brought the Son of Earth to our world and fooled him to retrieve the gems from Earth. He's fooled us all to chase around a phantom enemy while he rebuilt The Bridge in secret."

"Why rebuild The Bridge to Earth? Isn't it easier to just open the pillars again?"

"That was also part of the lie. The pillars are too spread out, too small of entries, and too remote in both our worlds. They enter Earth in isolated places without easy access, places of no use to Cygnus. The Bridge gives him full control over the portal, allows him to alter its destination, and makes the passageway large enough to bring in armies, weapons, and wealth all under his solitary control. He means to bring Earthians to Arcas as his servants. He already has compounds built for them to dwell in."

"But if he hasn't opened the pillars yet, how did he get the boy here?"

"I know how." Shedir had been listening and trying to piece all the stories together. Now he spoke up. He had a new look on his face, one of solemn anger. "He must have captured my friend Charles and stole a most unique gem from him, which carries both the red of Arcas and the yellow of Earth's gems. I saw the boy use it at Altair. It creates a small portal anywhere on either planet. My friend, an aged Son of Earth, found it in his world and came here many years ago. Cygnus told me he found the gem in Charles's cabin after Gurges Ater captured the Earthian. I fear now that Cygnus took both my friend and this powerful gem to use for his own purposes." Shedir looked to the ground. "I, too, have been fooled. The boy already has Earth's gem from Altair. They left when last the crimson sun flew high. I'm sorry. We thought you were an army sent by Gurges Ater, coming here to overthrow the pillar and capture the Earthian."

"He speaks the truth," Rigel affirmed. "I met this Son of Earth inside of Cygnus's dungeon. He is the one who implored me to meet my enemy face-to-face. Your friend has been trapped in that dark prison, knowing who the real enemy was, while the rest of us wandered in the shadows of our own ignorance." Rigel dismounted Alnitak, who pawed at the ground, waiting for action. He put his fist to his chest as a sign of friendship and a unified cause. "Arcturus, let's quit fighting each other and together figure out how to confront this feathered deceiver."

They sat at the same pot and fire that Otava entertained with in the courtyard, his ladle still stuck out of the large pot though it rested in a new recipe. Arcturus introduced two of his sons, Nekkar and Muphrid, who accompanied him to the castle along with several knights of high rank. His other two sons, Seginus and Asellus, remained back across the Eridanus with the rest of the army.

Arcturus and his sons commanded an army of volunteer soldiers under the highest leadership of Regulus, who currently waited in the Starling Forest with another legion of warriors. They dedicated their lives to the autonomy and liberty of the Free Realms. They usually stayed within their own lands, abhorring the waste, politics, and archaic systems of the regal kingdoms. As long as the kingdoms kept to themselves, everyone could continue with their own systems and beliefs, but the threat of one power possessing all the gems and gaining access to Earth brought them together to stop the threat of a unified empire under one sole ruler.

The Free Realms were created after the great, ancient battle that left The Bridge in ruins. They wanted nothing more to do with kings and powers and all their corrupt rules. They simply wanted to be left alone to live honestly and raise their families as they saw fit. They became profitable, large, and strong, but unlike the lax kingdoms, they continued to train hard and would fight to protect their autonomy in Arcas. They feared the people of Earth were a cursed and diseased people who would threaten their lands and their way of life. Just like long ago, they believed the Sons of Earth would always grow greedy for the health and beauty of Arcas and would want to take it for themselves.

Rigel and Arcturus began forming a plan. His army would never reach Jackson, Otava, and Merope in time, especially since Shedir informed them the trio had received horses to hasten them through the prairie lands. Arcturus and his army would head straight for the Trifid Fortress, and if they met the legion displaying the emblem of White Wings on the way, they would be ready for them.

Rigel would ride upon the swift flames of Alnitak to reach his friends, hopefully before the last gem left Deneb in the grip of Aquila or Cygnus. Arcturus hastily sent a messenger to inform Regulus of the new developments.

"Rigel, if we do indeed battle with White Wings' army, do you want us to capture or kill the man who attacked you?" Arcturus asked.

"Sulafat? Why would you capture him?" Rigel wouldn't care if he never had to see that turtle-strumming, slimy magician again.

"Because I thought you might want to kill him yourself after what he did to you."

"My head is healed from the blunt of his sword. He is no threat to me now."

"What about your noble dogs? You care not to repay him for taking their lives?" Arcturus wanted to make sure that Rigel received proper justice for both his abduction and the murder of his faithful hunting partners.

"What have you heard about my dogs? I was told they still traveled with my friends. Shedir, my dogs were with them, right?"

"No. We looked for them as your friends requested, but only found them bloodied and lifeless at their burial."

"AHHHHH!" Rigel yelled and threw a spear sitting next to him, which stuck in the stones of the castle wall.

"I'm sorry we must bring you this news. We found your dogs speared and stabbed through the chest across the river. We assumed you were dead too. We gave them a proper burial." Arcturus sympathized with Rigel's heavy loss. After a few moments of silence, Rigel responded with a deep rumble through his gritted teeth.

"I will not ask you to hold the serpent in your hands till I return. But if your sword does not pierce through Sulafat's heart, mine surely will. Either way, make sure he knows his body will lie wasting in the blazing suns without burial just as he intended for Procyon and Sirius."

CHAPTER 22

THE PILLAR OF DENEB

The caves felt dry and cool. Jackson lifted his torch next to the walls to see the dull, faded drawings decorating the long narrow paths.

"What are these pictures of?"

"They tell the history of our people. This is how we record the major events in our kingdom. As we carve out new precious stones and new paths, we add to our story along the walls. Look over here, this wall shows the building of the pillars." Errai proceeded to explain the story behind each picture as he pointed them out.

"This drawing was remade from the actual pillar walls so our people would not forget the past, though we no longer enter that area of the caves. It shows the very first days of our worlds when two large gems created The Bridge, a giant, open pathway for trade and travel between Earth and Arcas. Over time, however, the darkness of Earth began to overshadow the light of Arcas, making people grow pale, weak, and old. One powerful king of Earth became greedy to conquer the light and life of Arcas for himself. But here, the three kings of Arcas and three kings of Earth defeated him together. They then cut the two gems, one belonging to Earth and one to Arcas, each into three pieces and created treaties to maintain open but more secretive trade between the worlds. Over here shows how each kingdom built a pillar to hold the gems and to provide safe, guarded locations of transport."

"That's so cool. The history of Arcas makes a lot more sense now. I'd definitely remember my own history much better if it was etched in the walls around me."

"Next, our artists will add the death of Shaula, then *your* face will be forever etched into our history."

"Really? No way! Maybe I can convince Cygnus to bring me back when all of this is over, so I can see it completed. I'll never make it into our history, but I'd love to bring a camera back to have a record of my little moment in Arcas history!"

"Jackson, you will always be a welcomed guest in the castle and amongst the Cephid people." Errai remembered the other in their company and added, "And Otava, one of the great Ursas, your magnificent face will grace our walls as well. Our caves are always open to your kind."

"Thank you. You know I am also a great lover of caves. There is much potential here for hideouts and trap doors. You could fight off an army quite well." To Otava, these caves were of greater value than any castle or fortress above ground. He did not believe that safety rested in walls or numbers, but in solitude and bunkers.

"If we ever have the need to fight off an army, we would gladly take some secrets from a fellow cave dweller." Errai stopped walking. "Well, what do we have here?"

"Is that the way to the pillar?" Jackson pointed at the pile of rocks, which appeared in front of them as soon as they rounded a new arm of the underground world.

"I'm afraid it is. It must have collapsed, perhaps as we were hurling explosives at that beast. Hold your torch higher. Do you see that opening at the top?" Errai asked.

"Yes. I think I can fit through. But is it safe to climb?" Jackson examined the pile in front of him. It looked sturdy enough with large boulders intermingled with medium rocks and smaller stones, but he wasn't sure how stable the crumbly roof was above it.

"I cannot say, but I will go with you if you want to try."

"It's definitely not safe for my robust body!" Otava patted his belly. "I won't even attempt to fit through that tiny space. I'll stay out here and wait. You'll need someone to run for help if you two get trapped."

"We're too close to give up now," Jackson declared,

226

putting his foot upon the first stone. The boulder was large, heavy, and solid. He climbed up near the wall, using its steadiness to grasp onto with one hand, while the other hand tested each rock before he grabbed hold.

The rocks felt cool and dusty. Some were slightly rounded, though most obtained a jagged rough exterior from breaking apart from the cave. The jaggedness increased the ease of clutching them and finding footholds, but the awkward shapes and sizes created varying degrees of stability. It didn't take long to reach the top, and feeling confident, Jackson forgot to check his next hold. His firm grasp loosened the rock, which tumbled down along with pebble-filled debris.

"Watch out!" Jackson yelled as Errai and Otava jumped out of the way.

Thump! Thump! Clunk! Clunk! Pound! Trickle. Trickle. Trickle. The substantial rock along with its puny pebble companions rested their echoing tumbles as the dust settled to the ground once again.

"Sorry!" Jackson apologized, wishing he had been more careful.

"I think I'm going to wait for you a little farther back…" Otava retreated from the pile.

"It's okay. Just grab the wall as you slowly slide your legs through the hole. Then, I'll pass you the torch," directed Errai.

Jackson held his fingers into grooves within the stable

wall, slowly edging to the top with his feet and knees. One knee slid over the top of the pile into the darkness. He tested different positions, verifying the stability underneath him. Solid. Cautiously, he curved his body and remaining leg up and over the pile.

"Okay, I'm good," Jackson announced as Errai effortlessly shimmied up the boulders and handed him the torch. Jackson guided himself down using the torch and an increased awareness to gravity and touch. Errai, used to this underground world, beat him to the solid rock floor. When they both were steady with two feet on firm ground, they yelled out to Otava, so he would know they made it.

"I'll be right here waiting," Otava yelled back.

Errai and Jackson walked along, turning corners and watching multiple scenes of the Cephid's history unfold before them. Jackson saw a royal wedding scene filled with flowers, Cephid people, and olive-toned, taller people. The bride with bright, amber-colored hair and the groom with darker skin and black hair had a familiarity about them.

"Whose wedding is this?" Jackson asked desiring to know why it felt familiar.

"Ah, yes, this was the wedding between King Alderamin and Queen Cassiopeia. They were very young, even younger than you, but they were noble and brave. Their families were all nearly extinguished in the Pillar Wars. Vega was decimated to a desert wasteland, and

228

Alderamin and Cassiopeia were left parentless to control the remaining two kingdoms. They married to unite the East and West and to bring peace out of the midst of war, a peace that has lasted us a long, long time. Their marriage helped heal us few who survived the bloodshed."

"Wow," seemed to be the only word Jackson could utter after such a tale, which brought out in him a new compassion for the obscure ways of the queen.

"Here we are." Errai motioned to a hole the size of a large doggy door near the ground with an unlocked metal gate attached to it. "Just follow the path as it curves. There is no other way out or in to the pillar room. I will not enter the Pillar of Deneb, for it is believed among my people to be either a sacred place or a cursed place, and I am not sufficient to enter either."

"I don't know if I can travel on my knees for long while carrying the torch. I might fry the hair off my head..."

"No, no. After you crawl through the doorway, the room opens up again. The small opening was just a way for the old king to control what entered and exited our world from Earth. Just crawl in, then I will hand you back the torch."

Jackson opened the creaky gate and crawled into the darkness. Just a few paces into the tunnel and he could feel the rock overhead disappear. He turned around and stuck his arm through the gate, taking the torch from Errai. He stood and held the torch high.

The light revealed murals of gold, silver, and copper.

There was The Bridge with riches and animals coming to and from it, extending over the top of a large ocean and then disappearing into the huge, colorful portal. In the next scene, an army came through The Bridge, but was soon surrounded by three armies in front and then three armies behind it. As he followed the path, six kings joined together, watching the two large gems being split apart. One gem traveled with a tall king and a short army with yellow eyes. The king led them to a now familiar place for Jackson: the caves of Deneb. Lost in a world of deep history and beautiful art, Jackson didn't notice a light shining past the last curve in the path.

"Jaaack-sooon. Jaaack-sooon," the voice called out in a sing-song whisper. "If you get here any slower, the rest of the cave is going to collapse on top of me while I wait!"

"Who's there!" Jackson yelled back, startled, realizing there should neither be a light nor a voice coming from the pillar room around the next corner.

"Keep your voice down!" she answered back in a whispered yell. "It's just me, Andi."

Jackson ran around the corner.

"Andi? What are you doing here?" Jackson was pleasantly surprised it wasn't some creepy cave creature waiting to devour him, or the face of Gurges Ater waiting to steal the last gem.

"This is the last chance I have to see Earth. There's no way I'm going to miss it!"

"You shouldn't have come here by yourself. You could've been trapped or killed coming over that rock pile alone." Jackson lightly scolded her, feeling a bit protective and worried.

"I know these caves like I know the Eridanus. You don't need to worry about me."

"Is your dad going to be mad that you're here with me? Does he know you're here?"

"My dad knows I can handle myself. And he knows I often come to the pillar to visit it." She paused for a moment. "Do you know what it's like to grow up with stories and history right at your fingertips, etched on the walls, but you never get to be a part of it? Whether you approve or not, I'm coming with you. And one day, I'll tell my children I saw Earth, that I walked through the portal the last time the Pillar of Deneb opened to the other world."

"Ok, you win. You can come with me, but you have to let me step in the portal first to make sure it's safe, and you have to come back out of the caves with me, not alone."

"Thanks, but I don't need an escort, and Errai won't be pleased if I return with you. It'll freak him out that I came ahead by myself and that I was here with an open portal."

"Believe me. I know you can handle yourself." Jackson chuckled. "But I'm not leaving you here to crawl over the fallen rock pile alone. I'll sit here and yell for Errai to bring us food if I have to until you agree to leave with me."

Andi thought for a moment, studying Jackson's face.

"Fine. We have a deal." She stood then led Jackson over to the pillar, explaining everything in the room with great passion and excitement.

"My grandfather King Denebola designed the pillar. Here are the three suns of Arcas and the empty hole where the gem of Arcas once spun as it aligned with the gem of Earth, creating a constant open door. Over there on the wall is the poem that each portal holds to remind us of the unity and treaties between Earth and Arcas. It's written in the language that all Earthians spoke at that time:

Two worlds joined by gems so rare
Three suns shine on Arcas fair
One sun, one moon Earth's delight
Friendship and trade we unite."

Of course, Jackson already had seen the other two pillars and the empty spots for the gems and Shedir even translated the poem, but he let her explain it all again anyway. She seemed to know so much and care very much about the history of Arcas and the pillars. Some girls wait in eager expectation to get a pony or a new dress or a castle... Andi already had all these things. What Princess Andromeda had waited in expectation for her whole youthful life was to become part the stories of old, to gain access to another world.

Andi had traipsed through jungles and caves, seeking out adventure, but at last, the ultimate adventure was right in front of her. Jackson smiled as he listened to her explain why the precious metals decorating the walls still remained in the Pillar of Deneb though they were stripped from Altair. Looking at this beautiful pixie with dirt on her skirt and her nose from crawling around fearlessly in caves, Jackson couldn't help but feel nervous and excited at the same time to be sharing this moment with her and her alone. She ended her monologue of history by pointing Jackson back to the pillar.

"So, Son of Earth, are you ready to place the gem of Deneb into the pillar for the last time?"

"I don't have the gem of Deneb. Remember, Gurges Ater has the all gems of Arcas. Cygnus gave me a different gem to transport to Earth." Jackson pulled out the red-and-yellow stone, pressed on the sides, and watched Andi's amazed face as the lightning-like beams shot from between his fingers.

"Remarkable!" Andi watched every detail intently as he drew the door into existence.

Jackson was glad to have someone else just as amazed by the portal as he was every time he used it. He was glad that he could bring this moment, this experience to Andi. For a girl bursting with spiciness and flavor, at least he would always be remembered for adding one little sprinkle of seasoning to her life. Now when he returned to Earth for good, she would not likely forget him.

"Incredible!" Andi added as she played with her fingers through the dazzling door, watching the lights swirl around them as they disappeared.

"I'll step through first, then send my hand out for you to grab if it's safe."

Andi watched him disappear, and moments later, a hand reached out through the celestial doorway. Remembering the gentle warmth and subtle strength of this foreign hand many hours ago as she taught him to dance with the Cephids, she reached toward it and clutched tight, walking into an unknown world.

Coming from the dark, stale air of the caves, Andromeda's senses were shocked by a swift breeze and bright yellow sun setting down the shoreline. They were in a deep groove on the side of a large ocean mountain looking out at the crashing sea below. There were stairs descending from one side, but they crumbled halfway down as if they dissolved into the sea.

"So, when this one sun passes the horizon, everything is dark?"

"Yep, it happens every day here. Hours of sunlight followed by hours of darkness. On a clear night you can see the moon and stars though. They're pretty cool."

"Is that a star?" Andi released her hand, which had still been holding onto Jackson's, and pointed at the grayish-blue ball in the sky.

"Oh, no, that's the moon. It's a full one tonight. We don't always see it this well before the sun goes down."

"It has a sad face."

"Yeah, we call that the 'man in the moon.' We sent a

rocket ship up there once, and it's just a bunch of gray dust and craters, but it looks like a face from here."

Andi stood near the edge and breathed in the salty ocean breezes.

"I'll have to get my father to take me to Cygnus's castle. I hear it rests on the face of the waters just like this. I've never seen the sea with my own eyes."

"My family doesn't travel much, either. I've been to a great lake that feels kinda like an ocean, but this is the first real ocean I've seen."

They sat soaking in the warm rays of sun glowing red over the rippling waters. If only they had hours to sit here in the peace and seclusion with the crashing sounds of waves and the salty breeze. It was a place so untamed, wild, and free that it demanded peaceful admiration into the wildest of hearts, even a cave-exploring, jungle princess. Jackson fought his conscience, which told him they needed to keep moving. He wanted to stay here with the girl, with the sunset, with no worlds to be saved or gems to be delivered. As usual, though, his conscience beat out his desires. He lightly touched her shoulder, not wanting to disturb her as she breathed in every detail of this new world.

"I'd better find the gem, Andi. Errai and Otava are waiting for me to come back." Noticing the yellow stone rotating on the wall, Jackson then thought of something that may interest her. "Hey, come look at the gem of Earth. In each of the kingdoms here, they were placed into walls, not placed on pillars like in Arcas. See how the design is different? There's the one sun, the one moon—it changes shape from the round one that we see in the sky tonight to that crescent shape often—and then there is a cluster of stars."

"And that is the gem of Earth." Andi moved toward the rotating yellow stone with outstretched arm.

"Don't touch it!" Jackson warned, afraid for her safety.

"I know, silly Earthling." She then turned her voice to a spooky tone, teasing him. "Imminent death awaits those Arcasians who wrongfully touch the gems of Earth." Andi returned to her normal voice and spunk. "I'll just watch you take it out to make sure you really are an Earthian and not a spy."

For the last time, Jackson reached in and released a gem of Earth. He held it up so Andi could see it, and then placed it safely in his pocket.

"Well, you did it, hero! You got the last gem of Earth." Andi congratulated with a soft punch to his arm.

"Hero" and "man who brought the scorpius to the ground"—those were titles he could get used to, especially coming from an alien princess. They sounded good; they felt good. But soon, it was all going to be over. Just a memory of another world, an amazing place he likely could never return to. Friends he could never replace.

Sure, Jackson realized an army could be arriving right now outside the caves for King Alderamin to distract or ward off or fight, but he still didn't want it to be over. He didn't want to hand Cygnus the last gem. He didn't want to forget his lost mentor—The Hunter—or Otava, or Merope, or Andi. Perhaps he could barter with Cygnus to let him come back every once in a while for a visit.

"Look, up there! Do you see that sparkling diamond in the sky?" he asked.

"Yes! Is that a star?"

"Yeah, in few hours this whole sky will be as dark as your caves, but will sparkle with thousands of these diamonds all over it." Jackson motioned through the expanse of the heavens.

"I wish we could stay and see it. It must look amazing."

I wish we could stay too, Jackson thought, though he replied reluctantly, "Yeah, but we'd better return before Otava brings all of the cave lands down looking for us."

He held out his hand to Andi. He knew it was a safe return. He knew he no longer needed to guide Andi through the portal, but it sure gave him a good excuse to clasp her hand once more as the waning sunset shimmered off the waters beyond them. Andi reached back and intertwined her fingers with his as he drew the portal once again. Just before he walked through the door, she squeezed his fingers.

"Jackson?"

"Yeah?" He turned his head and met her purple eyes, just a short arm's length away from his. During most of their former interactions, their eyes shot mere glances or challenges or jokes at each other. This time, their eyes looked deeply, into the other's soul.

"Thank you. Thank you for taking me on this little adventure." She smiled warmly.

"Yeah, sure, no problem," he replied as if her words and her smile didn't just send shivers throughout his body. He turned to lead her back through the door.

Now, as Jackson pondered this moment, he kicked himself for not looking into her rich, purple eyes and asking for some type of proper payment for the adventure, like just one kiss in the shoreline sunset from a beautiful, very-human, yet quite exotic alien princess. It would make a good story, a good memory to take back with him. But Jackson had enough problems asking for just one dance, and he was a gentleman. He didn't want to put that emotional pressure on himself or any girl when he would soon be gone, probably never to return. Plus, he wasn't quite sure yet if something like a kiss would cause him to be slapped or kicked or pushed off the cliff by this spitfire angel clasping his hand and returning to her world forever.

But something in the slowly appearing stars lined up for him that night because, unaware, he opened the portal in a slightly different spot than before and walked back to Arcas straight into a cold cave wall. Turning around abruptly to keep from bruising his nose, he was met with warm lips and a warm body pressing his back against the cold wall as she followed through the shimmering doorway. A thousand sensations traveled down their surprised bodies, but they stayed there, soaking in the warmth and the electricity until they realized what happened and opened their eyes in surprise.

"I'm so sorry! I didn't mean to run into you!" Andi breathed out inches from his face, and then let go of his hand.

"Don't be sorry. You can run into me anytime." Jackson smiled, releasing the gem and closing the portal behind her. Andi smiled, blushed, and turned her head toward the ground. The air beat thick around them with their thumping hearts, tingly lips, and moist hands as they grabbed their torches and walked back to Errai quietly. Andi crawled through the small door first.

"Errai, it's me, Andi," she shouted out. "Will you grab the torch?"

"Andi? What are you doing in there?"

"You know me, always exploring."

"But, Andi!" Errai protested.

"I know, I know, it wasn't safe. I'm sorry. I was just saying good-bye because I probably won't get to visit the pillar any more for the rest of my five thousand years on this planet."

Jackson followed as Errai grabbed his torch, and they made their way back to the barricade of rocks. This time, Errai went up first so he could carry Andi's torch to the other side of the pile and light the way for her. Jackson would follow to keep the path behind lit. Andi climbed skillfully, but as she threw her legs and fluffy, dirt-covered dress over the top of the pile, her skirt got stuck on a jagged piece of rock. She couldn't pry it loose, no matter how hard she tugged and pried.

"Wretched garments! One day, I'm going to make it suitable for a princess to wear more practical clothing!"

"Or maybe, there will be a day when a princess chooses more practical activities!" Errai laughed as he headed up the rocks to meet her.

"I've got it, Errai!" Jackson bounded up the back to meet her, then yanked up and around to release the princess. *Rip!* She was free, but her dress was now torn as well as dirtied.

"I'm sorry about your dress."

"That's okay. It was a wretchedly evil garment anyway!" Andi answered, finishing her turn through the opening near the roof and inching her way down rock by rock.

Jackson followed, sliding his legs over the top, careful not to catch on the same jagged rock, but instead, his legs landed on a loosened bolder. His body slipped down as he attempted to grab at rocks to stop the momentum of gravity. The jabs, pokes, and tumbling stones bruised and jolted and scraped his body. His bleeding fingers reached for one last rock, but as he grabbed it, this rock also came collapsing down. He jolted his head and upper body to the side and out of the way, but as he hit the ground, a huge bolder bounced and landed hard on top of his left leg.

"AHH!" Jackson yelled, grabbing at his pinned leg while more small stones and pebbles attacked the ground and his body.

Otava and Errai jumped to action while Andi talked to him to get his mind off the pressure and pain in his leg. They first tried to push the boulder off, but the more they pushed, the more the boulder dug into his leg, sending shocks of searing pain throughout his body. Otava opened his bag of weapons—he never left them behind. He pulled out a spear, and Errai pulled out his pickaxe from his belt.

Errai dug around and underneath Jackson's leg as Otava shoved the spear underneath the rock. When the bulk of the weight rested upon the spear rather than Jackson's agonizing leg, they shoved the curved edge of the pickaxe under as well and pushed the rock over. Jackson yelled in pain and relief as the boulder rolled over next to him.

"Can you move it?" Andi asked, still holding one of his hands for support and comfort. Jackson sat up and attempted to stand.

"No. I think it's broken," Jackson answered, gritting his teeth and going pale as Andi helped him roll up his pant leg to examine it. Splotches of reds, purples, and blacks immerged underneath his swollen skin.

"Do you have any rope, Otava?" Errai asked.

"Of course!" Otava plumaged through his things and pulled out a rope. Errai grabbed the spear and set it next to Jackson's leg. Then, he wound the rope around both the leg and the spear to stabilize the bones.

"You're going to make him walk?" Andi asked, feeling both protective and sorry for him.

"Are *you* going to carry him all the way out of the caves?" Errai responded, not seeing any other viable option.

"It's okay. I think I can make it." Jackson stood and tried to walk, but he ended up hopping to the wall, moaning with each impact to the ground, and propping himself against the cave for steadiness.

"He most definitely can't make it!" Andi protested. "Can't he ride on your back, Otava?"

"Like a child?" Errai asked. "I don't think Otava has the hips for it..."

"No, like riding a horse." Andi was dead serious, and Otava was dead quiet.

"No, no, I can do it." Jackson hopped ever so slowly forward, clenching his teeth to silence his body's defiance, though pain echoed through his face with each movement.

"Come on, Jackson, you can ride on my back, but don't go spreading this around your world. Next thing you know, the Bear-Eaters will put us in corrals and strap saddles to our backs!" Otava mumbled.

Errai and Andi helped Jackson onto Otava's back, and

they walked, twisting and turning through each dark, cool path branching out from the main tunnels. Jackson seemed to get weaker and weaker as he tried his best to sit up tall, alert, and strong, while not pulling on Otava's hair for steadiness. When they reached the light outside, a large commotion of chattering and animation buzzed around the Cephids and King Alderamin.

"There they are!"

"Look, they're back!" Several voices yelled and pointed excitedly.

"Otava! Jackson!" Merope waved and called out to them, but her expression changed rapidly as she saw Jackson's pale face hunched over and the spear sticking up from the splint wrapped tightly around him. She ran to meet them.

"Jackson? What happened?" Merope asked once she reached him, but instead of waiting for a response, she helped Errai and Andi catch his wavering body and lower him to the ground as he groaned and grabbed at his leg.

"Everyone get back!" Jackson heard a familiar voice come forward through the crowd. "I'm sorry. We've no time to mend him. The boy has to leave with me now."

CHAPTER 23

DARKNESS FLIES

"I don't know if Cygnus should be taking Jackson back to Earth in his condition. Who knows what kind of barbaric healing they practice there?" Andi worried.

"Cygnus claims they are quite advanced. Perhaps he'll be better taken care of in his own world," Merope reassured.

"I don't know. I still think he should return to Deneb for healing. At least here, the Cephids would make him a sturdy peg leg to walk on. I do hope they won't they leave him to hobble along on one limb forever."

Andi wasn't happy with Jackson leaving injured or leaving at all for that matter. She'd grown fond of talking with him, surprising him, teasing him. She couldn't decide yet whether she was fond of the unexpected kiss in the cave, but when she thought about it, her stomach knotted, burned, and fluttered all at the same time.

Why did he say, 'You can run into me anytime?' Andi wondered. *Does he like me? No, no, he was just being nice and joking around to distract from an awkward moment. But did he like the kiss? None of this matters! He doesn't belong here. He's returning to his home soon. I do hope they take care of his health though. My main concern is his health,* she convinced herself.

For a royal, relationships were for expanding the kingdom, combining the wealth, and keeping the peace. And until a need arose for such measures, Andi was more than happy to not think of relationships, awkward courting games, and legal contracts. But it was nice to have a friend. She would definitely miss teasing and pestering and making her funny Earthling feel slightly uncomfortable by her playful antics.

"Well, Princess, if he ever returns to Arcas, I'll make him the finest peg leg contraption you've ever seen!" Otava promised.

"He certainly deserves it," Merope added. "Earth must be a great world now if it makes selfless and brave souls like Jackson."

"I hope you both know you're welcome to stay here as long as you like. We should be quite safe here while waiting for Gurges Ater's threat of war to simmer away." Andi hoped to keep some of her new friends around a little longer.

"Thank you. We're so grateful for your help and

kindness. I cannot stay though. I must join my sisters. I know they are safe now at the White Palace, but I can't bear being apart from them any longer."

"And apparently, I can't bear being apart from *you* any longer;" a voice rose up behind her. Merope jumped up, holding the stick she'd been fiddling with in the dirt and pointed it at the intruder.

"If you need to give me a beating, perhaps we could go somewhere more private so you can spare my ego and spare the young lady's eyes from violence." Rigel smiled.

"Rigel!" Merope breathed out as she turned white, dropped the stick, and flung her arms around his neck. "You were dead! There was a grave! They told us you were dead!" she cried as tears flowed down her face.

"There was a grave, but it was not for me. I was merely captured, but Procyon and Sirius were killed trying to fight the demons off." He pulled Merope back from his chest. "I'll explain everything soon, but I need to find Jackson. Where is he?"

"He just left with Cygnus," Merope answered.

"No!" Rigel's face fell in disgust.

"He broke his leg in the caves after getting the gem. We didn't want him to go in his condition, but Cygnus insisted that Jackson was needed immediately to finish ridding Arcas of the gems. We stabilized his leg, gave him some sleeping herbs, and Cygnus flew off next to his eagle who carried Jackson in a large sack," Andi explained.

"I can't believe it." Rigel shook his head. "He's been one step ahead of us the whole time!"

"Yes, for a Son of Earth, Jackson has remarkable stamina," Otava agreed.

"No. Cygnus. He's played us all, and we fell for his lies as quickly as he spun them. Once The Bridge to Earth opens, there's no telling what he'll do with Jackson, especially now that he's injured."

"The Bridge at the ruins of Trifid?" He nodded to answer Merope's question. "What do mean?" She studied Rigel, searching for the truth. "Cygnus has never mentioned anything about The Bridge. He hasn't lied to us or hurt us. In fact, he saved my sisters, and they are safe at the White Palace. Are you sure you're okay? Something has changed you. You seem different."

"I am different. I assure you, I am also in my right mind, but I am not okay. Listen to me, Merope. Cygnus sent spies to capture me by the Eridanus. He had everything prepared for me at the White Palace when I arrived— clothes, food, a room, and a commanding position. He entreated me to lead his army against this Gurges Ater to protect all of you. But after talking to your sisters and to a prisoner there, I knew something was wrong. I went to the Trifid ruins of old on the Ligeian Sea to confront the enemy face-to-face. I found Trifid standing anew, fortified behind white fortress walls. The fortress neither bore the name nor the emblem of any Gurges Ater. White Wings adorned the tower flags surrounded by the suns of Arcas, and the soldiers claimed White Wings as their leader. Make no mistake, Cygnus now has Jackson, all six gems, and is about to activate a rebuilt Bridge. We were all lied to. He is taking over Arcas lie by lie, realm by realm and is going to use his sole access to Earth to help him do it."

"It can't be." Merope breathed out in disbelief. "What about the unmarked army chasing us from Gurges Ater? Rigel, I saw them with my own eyes. They were real. And what about my sisters, my home? Rigel, I witnessed all these things," she gently challenged.

"That army was from the Free Realms. They are the true resistance led by noble Arcturus and righteous Regulus. They are not here to fight us. Together, Arcturus and I unmasked the truth about Cygnus. The Free Realms are now fighting directly against him and his grasp for power. As for your sisters and your home, Merope, with my own eyes, I saw the black ravens. They are still alive, and they guard the fortress by the sea. They do not answer to the phantom enemy we've all believed to exist. They answer only to Cygnus and his bird companion, Aquila. Some of your sisters also know this to be true. Taygeta saw the blue talons of Aquila while they were being carried off. Cygnus stole away your sisters for his own purposes, the same as he stole me away from you and as he stole Jackson away from Earth."

"This is very grave news. We must tell my father immediately. I'm sure he can help," Andi offered.

248

"Thank you, Princess. An army from him would show a united and strong Arcas. Entreat him if you can, but please forgive me. I do not have the time to meet with King Alderamin. I must leave now to stop Cygnus and save Jackson."

"I'm coming with you!" Merope announced.

"Me too!" Otava grabbed his weaponry, ready to go.

"Otava, I would be honored for you to join me." Turning to Merope and grabbing her hands, he looked at her sincerely. "You know, Merope, I have always wanted you to be by my side, but today, I need you to stay and plead my case with the king. Please, follow me with an army surrounding you." Merope shook her hands out of his and turned away.

"No! Rigel, no! Tell me. How many times must I lose you? How many times must you vanish from my sight? How many times must I hear of your death but never get to hold your body one last time? You think you're protecting me, but every time, you rip my heart out and take it with you!" Merope protested with righteous anger but ended with tears. Rigel held her shoulders and turned her around to face him, though she looked to the ground. He grabbed her hand and pulled it to his chest though she remained distant.

"I never meant to steal your heart. Take it back, Merope. If it will bring you joy, then please, take it back and live life again as you did before I followed your song through the woods," Rigel spoke quietly and tenderly.

"I do not want it back. I just want to be within arms' reach of it. I want to be able to feel that it's still beating." She opened her hand against his chest.

"Your heart is strong and Otava is well-armed." Rigel moved her hand back to her own chest. "But I need you to bring an army with you to protect my heart, for it is headed to the very gates of death." He held her tightly as her tense body slowly melted. "Please, Merope."

"Fine. But this is the last time, Rigel. I won't be left behind for another hundred years waiting for your return." Rigel threw his leg over Alnitak and nodded at Otava.

"My lady, this is the last time I say good-bye. This is the last time I will leave your side. For the next hundred years, you will suffer continuously in my presence."

"I'm going to hold you to that promise!" Merope yelled after him with a slight playfulness surfacing from the vast waters of her doubt and fear. Wiping her eyes, she attempted to compose herself from the uncharacteristic display of emotion.

As Rigel and Otava hurried off, Andi and Merope hastened to King Alderamin and imparted all that Rigel told them about Cygnus, the gems, and The Bridge.

"But what proof does he have? Cygnus has always been a trusted friend to the kingdoms. I cannot believe it," the king responded.

"It is a shock to all of us, King Alderamin," Merope sympathized.

"Father, can we please send soldiers to help him? The truth, whatever it may be, will be apparent once our men reach Trifid and The Bridge," Andi reasoned.

"No, Andi. We will find no truth there. The only truth on the battlefield is bloodshed and horrors and death. Haven't our people witnessed enough of that lately with Shaula ravaging our caves? Even if Cygnus means to open The Bridge, I must believe that it is for the good of the kingdoms, for the good of Arcas."

"But the Son of Earth helped us kill Shaula. Do we not owe it to him to make sure he's safe?" Andi challenged.

"Andi, if he is not safe with Cygnus, with whom would he be safe? Cygnus promised we are all safe now. He is taking care of Gurges Ater or whatever you want to name the evil force coming against us. I'm sorry, Merope, but The Hunter has had allegiance to no one. Cygnus has been our close ally since the three great kings fell in battle."

"Then let me ride with Merope, so I can find the truth and report it back to you," Andi offered.

"No. I will not have you riding toward an unknown battle with an unknown enemy."

"I'm not afraid, Father. I'm not going there to fight. I can be an ambassador for our kingdoms."

"Andromeda! I will not repeat myself again. You are to stay here in this castle until we receive word that the gems are secured and the battles have ceased. There will be no visits to the caves, no traveling to the Eridanus, and no horse riding."

"But, Father!"

"Errai, please, escort the princess to her room until she is ready to come out as a respectful and obedient royal daughter."

Andi stormed out of the room followed by Errai.

"Merope, I'm sorry. I cannot ask my men to fight a battle when we don't really know who or what or why we are fighting. We still have many wounded to tend to. May the three suns shine upon your path and shine upon the truth."

"I understand. Thank you for your time and hospitality, King Alderamin."

Merope respectfully exited, but immediately gathered her things to the horse that was waiting outside for her and rode off. She would not ride to Trifid with an army or even the chorus of her sisters, but she rode with resolve and courage. If death would meet them today, then she would meet it at Rigel's side. If death would take them today, it would take them together, for she was done living apart from him.

CHAPTER 24

THE BATTLE OF FORNAX FOREST

The eighth note whistles of a black-capped chickadee resonated over and over again through the Fornax Forest. Only, the black-capped chickadees did not live in the Fornax Forest, they dwelt in the Northern Starling Forest and in the Free Realms. The harmless whistles were really the warning of war, alerting Arcturus and his men that White Wings' army was in sight.

"Not an arrow, not a movement until I give the word," Arcturus whispered the command, and it spread rapidly and silently to his four sons.

Seginus quietly climbed back to the top, joining the other archers spread out in the trees. Underneath the archers were the men on horseback led by Nekkar. From atop his own horse, Arcturus would lead the charge for Asellus and the foot soldiers who lay on the ground, invisible to the world beyond the forest. Just inside the edge of the Fornax Forest, Muphrid with his hundred elite fighters would initiate the ambush.

Like Arcturus, most of the men were farmers at heart, but they were also trained fighters. After the three great kings fell, many people left the kingdoms to join the Free Realms. To protect their liberty and prosperity, the tribes united under the wisdom and direction of Regulus. Each tribe vowed to train their sons in the skills necessary to defend their lands and ward off any foreign threat, whether it came from the kingdoms of Arcas or from the people of Earth. Though fit and trained, many had never seen, felt, or experienced the realities of war. They should have been fatigued from their long travels, but the nervous energy of looming bloodshed and possible death kept their muscles tense and their eyes wide open.

It usually wasn't their style to ambush an enemy. They preferred to deal with conflict face-to-face; however, some unexpected news reached them several hours before they entered the Fornax Forest. The untimely news altered their battle plans just a day's journey after leaving the Altair Kingdom.

"Sir, I have word from Regulus." A centaur messenger cantered into their camp near the Eridanus River, speaking directly to Arcturus.

"Good. How soon can he join us?"

"I regret to tell you that he cannot come. A legion from White Wings came up behind us just before we reached Eltanin's desert. We have been fighting in the hills for many days. The enemy and their black ravens are blocking us from heading south, along with the iced mountains blocking the east. Our men are fighting well, but we will not make it to you in time for battle."

"This is disappointing news."

"Yes, sir, we didn't expect an attack all the way in the north. They waited for us to set up camp in a valley to rest, and then they assailed us without warning. Thankfully, some people of the forest had been watching them for many days and were not happy with their dealings. They joined in the fight and helped us push them out of the camp long enough that we could move to higher ground."

The farm-raised soldiers silently listened to the centaur as fear, anger, and unbelief rose within them.

"Listen to me, men of the Free Realms!" Arcturus stood and raised his voice so the whole camp would hear. "Our forefathers destroyed The Bridge because it became a road of greed and corruption. Some among us remember that the kingdoms also became pillars of greed and corruption. Now, Cygnus means to reopen our unfettered ties to Earth, a relationship that ended in unspeakable bloodshed throughout the ages. Every day, we learn more of Cygnus's lies and treachery throughout all of Arcas. Make no mistake, he will continue to steal, kill, and destroy until everyone bows at his feet. But I say if White Wings opens The Bridge, then today, we close it! If White Wings ambushes Regulus and our fellow brothers, then today we ambush him! Soon, we will enter the Fornax Forest that borders Trifid. May the suns shine brightly upon all of us today as we fight for the Free Realms and we fight for a free Arcas!" The men roared in agreement, pumping their fists and weapons into the air.

Hours after this change in battle plans, each soldier held his hidden position and his breath while thousands of soldiers marched out of the Trifid Fortress to join the thousands coming from the White Palace. The Trifid Fortress soldiers who were rested moved to the front lines, leading legions of men toward Fornax and then on to the Eridanus where they were prepared to battle. Sulafat made sure to greet the other sergeant but then retreated to the back of the army while servants passed out food and drinks to his men to eat and replenish themselves as they sat leisurely in the sandy grass fields separating the ocean beaches and the forest.

As the frontlines of White Wings' army neared the Fornax Forest, anticipation grew in the young and the smell of blood wandered into the minds of the old.

Wait, commanded Arcturus with his hand held straight in the air, directing the archers to make a unified strike as the opposing army touched the edge of the woods. He flicked his fingers out, signaling to ignite the arrows' ends.

"NOW!" Arcturus screamed.

The first round of arrows and fire rained down on the enemy's army. Shouts and screeches rang out as the wounded fell and fire consumed their clothing and the dry grasses. Immediate pandemonium and shock took hold of White Wings' army. The fields behind them blazed with fiery death though the woods remained quiet except for the *Thoom, Thoom, Thoom, Thoom* of flaming arrows flying from the treetops.

"Forward, men!" commanded the enemy officer in front, signaling toward the forest.

Cygnus's army collected their fears, angled their shields over their heads, and marched steadily together into the woods. Everything was silent and calm under the shade of the trees. No longer fearful of raining arrows, the men lowered their shields.

"Attack!" Arcturus commanded.

Muphrid and the elite fighters leapt out of the trees with arms raised and daggers aimed. As the forest swarmed with more men, Asellus and the foot soldiers jumped up from the ground and joined the battle. Then, Nekkar and the horsemen galloped between the trees, chopping off limbs and slicing throats as they charged. Seginus and the archers shot one last round into the fields, then turned their attentions to targeting individuals in the growing fight under their feet.

Arcturus's mighty sword clashed and clanked expertly

along the edges of the enemy's armor, sawing both head from neck and limbs from body. Blood ran down the forest floor like a river flows down to meet the sea while the legions of Cygnus battled with the three thousand men of the Free Realms.

"Where is your cowardly, lying leader?" Arcturus yelled at a battered enemy solider.

"You're too late! May Lord White Wings rule over The Bridge forever!" As the soldier raised his sword, Arcturus sliced his throat. Blood gushed from the sides of the blade as he drew it back toward his side. Screams, groans, zings, and clanks filled the air from the Fornax Forest to the Ligeian Sea.

Rigel and Otava had been watching since the flaming arrows of the resistance pierced through the tree line headed straight into Cygnus's army marching toward Fornax from the sandy grasslands miles away from Trifid. It was clear that Cygnus's men knew they were marching to battle, though they did not know the element of surprise was against them.

"Are you sure this is going to work?" Otava asked skeptically as they hid against the outer wall of the fortress.

"I walked right in before. It's worth a try. Unless you want to swim in the ocean or scale a wall, this is our best bet," Rigel answered.

"Alright, but I won't be able to pull off this dumb bear thing for long."

Rigel buckled a horse girth around Otava's neck. The

bear walked on all fours next to Alnitak as Rigel rode up to the gate wearing the White-Winged coat of arms once again.

"Where is your post, soldier? Don't you know there's a battle going on in the plains?" a voice cried out from the ramparts above.

"I was on a special assignment from Lord White Wings and have returned with a gift for him," Rigel explained.

"This is not a good time. You should have taken the gift to the White Palace."

"I was ordered to meet White Wings here. I know the battle in the fields was supposed to be near the Eridanus instead. I know that it is a dangerous time to open the gates, but believe me when I say His Lordship will not deal kindly with you if this valuable beast is captured or killed right outside the safety of his own fortress. For your own good, I implore you to open the gate quickly."

"Open the gate!" the soldier reluctantly yelled. Crossbows pointed at and behind them as they entered the gates. They proceeded swiftly but cautiously, ready for an attack.

"I must speak with Albireo. I met with him here a few suns ago," Rigel commanded.

"He's not here. Lord White Wings sent him out to lead the army... Perhaps we should lock up that creature. It does not look safe."

"No, it is not safe, but it is safe with me. I have trained

it, and this beast will be a personal guard for His Lordship as the humans arrive. Please tell Lord White Wings that his trusted servant has brought him a valuable gift to commemorate his coming victory and reign over Arcas."

"He's not here. He flew in moments ago with Aquila carrying a boy, then they disappeared."

Otava began to roar impatiently. Growing more nervous about Otava's large and dangerous presence, the soldier added, "Why don't you wait down by the waters near The Bridge? Lord White Wings said he would be returning there shortly."

Rigel walked through the courtyard down to the back of the fortress, leading Alnitak the wild stallion on one side and Otava the wild Ursa on the other. A brick road extended straight out over the water on top of the natural peninsula, which broke off on all sides to steep cliffs meeting the Ligeian Sea below. On one side of the paved ground, surrounded by ocean, lay a large, thick burlap sack with blood stains inside of it.

"What should we do now?" Otava asked Rigel as they examined the surroundings.

"We find a safe place to wait, and pray the boy shows up alive."

CHAPTER 25

RUINS NO MORE

A dense, acidic smell climbed in through Jackson's airways and grabbed his mind saying, *Wake up! Wake up!* When his eyes opened, Cygnus removed the smelling salts from his nose.

"Glad you're awake, Jackson."

"Ugggh, my leg hurts." He groaned. "Where are we?"

Jackson wondered what planet he was on now. He'd recovered all the gems, so he should be home, but it didn't look like home. Brown and tan rock walls jolted up on both sides of the stone-paved peninsula he was lying on top of. The walls arched into the sky over his head. Centered behind the arch walls stood a stone pillar with a flat top. The land beneath their feet rose steeply out of an endless ocean protected by the jagged, natural cliff fortifications.

"This is where I need you to hide the gems. It is remote here and safe. When we finish, Gurges Ater will never find them, and he will never gain access to Earth."

"So, I'm done after this? I don't think I can make it to anymore kingdoms or pillars."

"Yes, Jackson. After this, you can go home to rest and heal. You have done well, Son of Earth. Let's finish this now, together."

Cygnus hoisted Jackson up on his good leg and stabilized him. The huge rock arch towered up from the ground and domed high over their heads. Cygnus pointed to a hole on the front of the rock wall as he helped Jackson hop toward it.

"Put the first gem here," he ordered.

Breathing heavy and wincing with pain, Jackson reached into the satchel Cygnus held in front of him. He grabbed a yellow stone and pushed it into the perfectly sized groove. The stone slowly began to turn in its place.

"I don't think I can make it much longer," Jackson pleaded, feeling nauseous. "How far do we need to go for the next one?"

"It's just on the other side of this rock formation. You can do it."

Jackson tried to conceal his anguish, but every hop on his healthy foot sent shocks through the broken leg. The walk to the other side of the peninsula felt like an eternity though the misty ocean air and the shade from the towering arch provided a little respite from the three suns' heat. Though paved by men, the ground underneath was jagged and uneven, marred with the evidence of being created in another age and eroded by the suns, the water, and the wind. Seeing an identical hole, Jackson grabbed the second gem and shoved it within the gap. The bright yellow stone methodically turned.

"I'm glad we don't have to travel far, but isn't it dangerous to place the gems so close together?" Jackson asked confused. "They aren't hidden very well, and if someone found one, they could find them all."

"No, they are safe here. Trifid is well fortified, so they are always guarded and protected. And this area is known as a remote wasteland. No one will find them here. Trust me." Cygnus gave a reassuring squeeze to Jackson's arm while looking him in the eyes as if to say *you have no reason to doubt me*. "Grab the last gem. I will have to fly you to the very top of the arch to place it."

Jackson grabbed the last yellow stone, holding it in one hand while gripping Cygnus's shoulder with the other. Cygnus's powerful wings moved back and forth, swirling dust and wind around them. His arm firmly grabbed Jackson around his rib cage as both bodies rose above the ground. Jackson felt the weight and pressure of gravity pulling at his broken bones, shifting them around. They soared higher and higher until the agony in his physical nerves equaled the height-induced fear in his mental nerves, throwing him into a panicked frenzy.

"I can't do this! My leg! My leg hurts too bad. Cygnus, I'm slipping! I'm gonna fall!"

"No. You can do it, Jackson. This is our last task. You can do it. The hole is right in front of you in the center of the arch." Cygnus urged onward, masking his growing anxiety and impatience with verbal sympathy and support. Nervous and nauseated, Jackson tamed his thoughts, reached out and shoved in the last gem.

Cygnus seemed to forget about Jackson's condition as he landed quickly and dropped Jackson once his own feet met the ground. Not able to stand well without support, Jackson fell, wailed, and grabbed at his leg. Oblivious, Cygnus stood back and watched the stone arch anxiously.

The ground began rumbling as shimmering beams of light shot between the open air inside of the arched gate and the stone pillar that rose from the ground behind it. Vision became blurry within the arch, replaced by shimmering and rippling blues and oranges. The rumbling in the air stopped, but a new rumbling could be heard crashing into the land below. The ocean's tide swiftly and dramatically increased, violently rolling waves against the cliffs halfway up the peninsula.

Cygnus—usually composed, calm, and stoic—was laughing happily, heartily, and triumphantly.

"What in the world is going on?" Jackson cried out.

"Isn't it marvelous? Come and see, Jackson! I did it!"

Cygnus grabbed Jackson and dragged him through the portal. As Cygnus dropped him again and surveyed the destination, Jackson's pain fueled into anger as he saw what appeared to be a desert canyon on Earth. Behind him, the dancing portal lights filled the inside of a huge orange-and-tan natural rock arch.

"Cygnus, what have you done? I thought we were supposed to stop the portals from opening! What's going on?"

"Don't you see it, Jackson? Unlimited possibilities. Two worlds connected once again but with a strong and wise ruler controlling the passage between them. Come and watch! When I alter the position of the red Arcas gems on the new pillar, we will be at a whole new location on Earth!"

Cygnus turned back through the portal as Jackson hopped after him, pressing against the rock arch to steady his injured side. Entering Arcas once more, the world felt darker. The Bridge was blocking much of the light from the golden sun and coral sun. Only the deep crimson sun glowed a warm red over the land, unobstructed by the new portal.

"But you told me Gurges Ater wanted this! Now you've given him an entrance to Earth. That's what your enemy wanted!"

"Oh, poor boy, how confused you must be." Cygnus looked at Jackson with a speck of compassion. "Gurges Ater was just a phantom, just a name, and a threatening story that made people afraid enough to act. You should know by now that the only real enemy of Arcas has been the last thousand years of worthless royals, unused power, and unkempt kingdoms. It is time for the splendor of Arcas to rise once again under a leader who knows how to bring worlds and peoples together!"

"You lied to me about everything?"

"I did what was necessary to bring progress to both our worlds."

"Real progress is not built on lies. You can't win or rule people with lies! The Hunter was killed because of your lies!" Jackson was becoming angry.

"You short-lived, ignorant boy! Your people are diseased and pitiful. They squalor in pain and anguish as you do now and deserve to be put out of their misery. I will offer them a different life, a different world." He studied Jackson's disapproval, distrust, and anger. "But I can see you don't share my vision, and my rising kingdom has no room for the crippled or weak, so thank you for your service, Jackson Son of Earth, but it's time for you to go home now."

Cygnus used the transport gem to open another portal right next to him. He peered through it, and then smiled with approval.

"You know how to swim, right?"

"I can't swim with my leg like this! You have to take me home!" Jackson pleaded.

"Earth *is* your home. How fitting for you to share in

the fate of your predecessors who were consumed by water long ago. But fear not, I will be merciful on one condition. If you can tell me where the Sun Map is, then I will take you safely back to your little home near the woods."

"I don't know what you're talking about. I've never heard anything about a Sun Map."

"Where is the golden map that revolves around the red gems of Arcas and reveals The Bridge locations on Earth?"

"I told you. I've never heard of it! Please, just take me home," Jackson begged.

"Very well, Jackson. Feel at peace knowing you helped establish my everlasting reign. Thank you for your service to the new king of Arcas."

Cygnus pulled Jackson off the ground. As he tossed the boy at the open portal, a baseball-size rock whizzed through the air, striking his hand. Upon impact, the transport gem flew out of Cygnus's hand and the portal snapped shut in front of Jackson's nose. Cygnus ran after the gem and caught it just before it tumbled over the peninsula into the raging water below. He turned back to identify the attackers. Rigel stood next to Otava, who held a freshly snapped slingshot.

"Ah, if it isn't The Hunter and the Ursa coming to defend the little cub. Rigel, I should have let you die with your dogs. I placed the world at your feet. You could have had power and authority under a real king. We would have made a better and stronger Arcas together."

"You knew I would never give allegiance to any kings of this world. They are all corrupt just as you have become."

"No. They are all weak while I have grown strong."

Cygnus stowed the transport gem in the satchel on his belt and rose into the air, flying away to summon his soldiers. Suddenly, a spear sliced straight through Cygnus's satchel, grazing his leg. Bright red slowly stained his white garments as he reached down to the small wound. A look of horror crossed his face as he watched the gem fly out of the torn satchel and bounce across the roughly paved peninsula again and again and again until it landed on the edge, teetering above the roaring waters near Jackson. Relieved by her timing but frustrated with her accuracy, Merope jumped down from the fortress wall. She fell rapidly until a musical hum radiated through her body, slowing her landing to a soft hover inches above the ground. Merope then ran swiftly to join her friends.

"I hear The Hunter gives allegiance to no one but dogs!" yelled a familiar voice slithering in from behind. The cowardly Sulafat had abandoned his men in the fields near the Fornax Forest and ran to the safety of Trifid. Though he would not face the army in the woods beyond, he would not miss the opportunity to prove his skill and power in front of the audience of his newly self-appointed king.

"I'd rather give my allegiance to dogs than a serpent," Rigel responded.

"It's too bad your faithful friends are not here to defend you today," he scoffed.

"I do not need them to defend me today. I wield the sword of justice as my defense!"

Sulafat met the challenge by drawing his sword and pointing it at Otava and Rigel, but then he motioned his four elite soldiers to run in front and fight first. They circled Otava and Rigel, sizing them up and preparing for the first strike. At the same time, Jackson crawled through his anguish to reach the transport gem teetering on the edge of the rocks as the waves crashed wildly against the cliffs below. As he curled his fingers around the polished stone swirling with reds and yellows, Cygnus flew upon him with sword drawn.

"Give me back the transport gem," Cygnus commanded with a tone of threat and authority as his blade glided against Jackson's neck.

Between the peninsula and the heart of the fortress, the fight raged into action. Otava rapidly threw plumbata darts at the men from his belt. He knocked one to the ground with a pierce to the forehead, and then bound on top of him, finishing the villain with his machete. Two small darts imbedded into each eye of the other soldier. Shocked and blinded, he ran off screaming until he fell off the edge of the cliffs into the ocean. He flailed up from the water, gasping for air with blood squirting out of his sockets. The taste of blood attracted predators of the deep that pulled him under until he disappeared, leaving only a trail of red.

With a forward swipe and a side jab, Rigel quickly killed the other two soldiers, leaving only him and Sulafat. Sulafat removed his cloak and threw it to the ground, angry he had to dirty his hands with actual fighting. To keep the unfair advantage of horseback, he remained mounted and charged at Rigel full force while creating a whirlwind cloud in front of him with his lyre. Watching from the side, Alnitak sprang into action. He raced in front of Rigel, rearing his front hooves high in the air right before Sulafat trampled and stabbed through the vision-altering cloud. Frightened and alarmed by the powerful stallion, the other horse squealed, reared in the air, and threw off the stunned Sulafat, flinging his lyre out of reach. Alnitak chased the other horse away as Sulafat brushed off his clothes and pulled out his sword.

Though a cowardly weasel, Sulafat still bore much skill with his weapon of last resort. Their swords expertly clashed with power and proficiency in each strike. They exchanged blows as their blades whirled through the air, crashing and zinging when steel met steel. Sulafat swiped at Rigel's chest. He jumped back, returning with a strong overhead blow coming down toward Sulafat's shoulder. The blades clashed together leaving the men pressing their swords and their strength against each other with clenched teeth and eyes locked.

But Rigel was bigger and stronger and had much more to fight for than vain pride and ambition. He released his left hand from the sword. With his right arm weighing his sword down over Sulafat's, he made a fist with the left hand, and plowed it into Sulafat's kidney. As he hunched over, grunting under the blow, Rigel's mighty blade plunged through Sulafat's arm, sending his sword flying with the hand still clenched around it. Blood surged out as Sulafat fell to his knees, yelling and plunging his stub into his shirt to slow the bleeding.

"Is The Hunter really going to kill a defenseless, injured man? I never harmed you. I may have killed your dogs, but you hunt and kill all the time," Sulafat pleaded for his life in his gory squalor.

"I kill animals the Creator provides me for food. You steal, kill, and destroy what does not belong to you."

"Don't be foolish! Cygnus is too powerful for you to stop. He has the boy under his sword this very moment. Give yourself up and join us. Don't let a few wenches and a prisoner spoil your proper allegiance. If you send me to the darkness now, you will join me shortly!" Sulafat yelled in warning.

"You already dwell in darkness!" Rigel lifted his sword. "Make no mistake, Sulafat, I take no pleasure in killing a rabid dog, but it must be done before you infect others with your poison. Out of pity, I will give you a moment to beg the Creator's forgiveness before you meet Him and He exposes your dark heart."

"Ha!" Sulafat spit on the ground, responding with contempt in his eyes. "What Creator? I've made myself.

Though driven to my knees, I kneel before no one! I am just as good as you are!"

Rigel shoved his sword through Sulafat's heart.

"No man is good," Rigel avowed, then pulled the sword out of his chest. Sulafat gasped, sputtered blood from his mouth, and crumpled to the ground.

Near The Bridge, Jackson sat on the edge of the cliffs, holding the gem tightly behind his back. Cygnus hovered over the cliff next to him with his wings slowly expanding and constricting to maintain flight. He sheathed his sword, trying one more time to get Jackson to comply.

"The gem for your life, Jackson. Hand it over and live."

"I can't. My life and my family will never be safe as long as you can walk your way into my backyard again! I can't give you back that kind of power." Jackson flung his arm sending the stone as far as he could into the ocean beyond.

Enraged, Cygnus picked Jackson up off the ground with both hands, gripping him around his throat. Jackson grabbed at Cygnus's hands, trying to free his breath, which was constricted inside of him, fighting for a way out. Otava threw the bow to Rigel from the ground where it rested during the sword fight. Catching the bow, Rigel stepped forward on a small boulder with his left leg slightly bent in front and his right leg straight in the back. The three silver pendants on his belt blazed with reflected sunlight while his sheathed sword pointed straight to the ground. In one fluid motion, Rigel pulled two arrows from the sheath on his back, connected them to the bow's string and released the weapons. The two flying arrows spun and circled each other until they tore through Cygnus's right wing, causing him to release Jackson and fall back off the peninsula into the water behind him.

Rigel, Merope, and Otava ran to Jackson, who managed to grab hold of the side of the cliff. Rigel and Otava pulled him up as he coughed and crawled closer to the center, away from the water crashing higher and more intensely against the rocks below. Wheezing, sweating, and slowly writhing in immense pain from all the physical and mental trauma, Jackson rested for a moment with his head against the stone-paved ground.

Rigel spotted the turtle shell lyre of Sulafat. He walked over to it and raised his foot to crush it and kill its powers.

"Stop!" Merope grabbed his arm as his foot hovered mere inches from the strings. "Let me have it. We may need it to get out of here." Rigel nodded in agreement and gave the lyre to Merope.

"Well, Jackson, since the transport gem is buried under water now, it looks like we'll have to carry you through The Bridge and face those Bear-Eaters together to get you back home," Otava half joked, knowing Jackson wasn't going to make it far in his condition.

"Did you recognize that area of Earth?" Rigel asked.

"No… I have no idea where this portal leads. It's in the middle of a desert canyon or something. But if you can get me back to the cabin near the Starling Forest where I first entered Arcas, there is a stone at the cabin's door identical to the pillar stones. If I stand there, I think I should be able get back home with this." Jackson used Otava's strong paw to help him stand. He reached into his back pocket and then opened his hand, revealing the transport gem within his palm. "I just threw a rock in the water. I had the gem the whole time." He smiled slightly in triumph through his exhaustion and pain.

Wounded in body but not resolve, a wet and torn creature spread out his wings over the surface of the water to ride a large wave in to the side of the peninsula. When he met the jagged rock wall, Cygnus grabbed hold, and slowly slithered up to dry land. His hands finally reached the flat top. He quickly pushed himself up and ran, grabbing Sulafat's sword from the ground. He raised the double-edged steel up with both hands over his head and ran straight toward Rigel's back.

"Rigel, watch out!" Merope screamed, catching the movement out of the corner of her eye.

Rigel turned around just in time to meet Cygnus sword to sword.

"You've fallen so far from the heavens, Cygnus. It appears somebody clipped your wings," Rigel taunted him. Cygnus's eyes were wild with rage. His white wings appeared gray and limp as water dripped from every inch of his body.

"Don't worry, Rigel, my hands are still strong enough

to break the boy's neck when I'm finished with you. Then, I will choke the voice out of your songbird as well," Cygnus threatened back at him.

As Rigel and Cygnus clashed and swiped and jabbed, Cygnus's back moved toward Jackson. Aquila flew in, swiftly lunging his claws and beak down to attack Otava and Merope. Grabbing the sling from his belt and loose stones underneath him, Otava flung stones up at the gigantic bird. Aquila dodged and spun and dove to miss the soaring rocks. Merope shielded herself and Jackson by waving Otava's machete over their heads. One swipe from the large avian's blue claws would tear through them like a thick, curved harvesting sickle. Otava grabbed one fist-sized stone in his paw and aimed it right at the wretched bird's head. The speed and accuracy of the rock crushed Aquila's skull, and the large bird nose-dived in the water, surfacing up only to float lifelessly upon the tossing waves.

With the last ounce of strength he possessed, Jackson pressed down on all points of the transport gem, feeling the vibrations flow through him. He drew a large door with the gem's beam a few feet behind Cygnus's back. Merope ran to grab her spear, which was stuck between pavers in the ground. The sharp end broke off as she pulled it out. Once Cygnus was backed up to the edge of the portal, Rigel stepped back from the swordplay.

"What's the matter? The Hunter can't take down a real predator?"

"Cygnus!" Jackson called from the side and slightly behind him. "You know how to swim, right?" Otava caught the broken spear end from Merope and swung it like a bat into Cygnus's gut, sending him flightless and falling into the portal. Jackson immediately released the transport gem, closing the door between the two worlds.

Before they could share a moment of grateful victory, horns blasted through the air, and shouts echoed around the outside of the fortress.

"Retreat! Retreat! Retreat to Trifid!" officers shouted.

"White Wing's army is returning to the fortress. We must go!" Merope warned.

"What about The Bridge?" Otava pointed to the towering arch at the end of the peninsula still shimmering with dancing lights and surging the tides below.

"The Bridge will have to stay open for now," Rigel replied.

"Can't we just remove the Arcas gems?" Merope asked.

"We don't have time to risk it. Cygnus is gone and most likely dead, so our priority now is Jackson. We need to get him home. Then we can join Arcturus to destroy The Bridge and rescue your sisters."

"What's going on out there anyway, Merope? Are they fleeing from King Alderamin's army?" Otava asked as they hastened away from The Bridge and toward the wall of the fortress.

"No, they didn't come, but Arcturus seemed to be

putting up a good fight when I arrived. I think I was enough of an army for you," Merope joked.

"Haha! How did you get in here anyway, songbird? Croon until a wall fell at your feet?" Rigel asked her, teasingly.

"Nope. I scaled the wall. See, there's my rope."

"We can't get Jackson over that. He's going to have to dive." Rigel quickly scanned the ground. "Merope, run and grab that girth."

While Merope retrieved the girth that Otava was wearing when they walked into the fortress, Rigel instructed Jackson. Gritting his teeth in pain and struggling to stay upright while holding to Otava, Jackson did his best to listen. The overwhelming throbbing sensation was too great for him to be afraid or beg his way out of the new danger. Rigel tightened the girth around Alnitak as the fiery horse pawed his hoof on the ground next to them. Carefully lifting him, Otava and Rigel mounted Jackson on top of the stallion.

"Keep your head tucked here, next to his neck. Before you hit the water, close your eyes and hold your breath. Whatever happens, Jackson, do not let go. Can you do that?"

"Yeah, I think so."

"Alright. Alnitak, go!" Rigel yelled.

As the dark horse galloped over the bricks, steam puffed from his nostrils and flames flared under his hooves. Jackson clenched his hands and his teeth while his head tucked snuggly next to the warmed, flexing neck. At the edge of the peninsula, Alnitak jumped. A trail of blue flames and smoke followed him as his head and front legs soared down through the air and his back legs pushed off ground propelling them forward.

Down.

Down.

Down.

Rigel, Merope, and Otava held their breath as they watched the two soar as one unit then collide into the waves below. The water sizzled, smoked, and covered them. When Alnitak's head burst through the waves followed by Jackson's, the other three left the cliff and ran for the wall. Using Merope's rope, one by one, they climbed up and over the fortress.

With all enemy eyes focused on the battle beyond and the retreat heading back into the front courtyard walls, their escape went unnoticed. The friends met Alnitak on the outer shoreline as he climbed out of the water onto the beach. Jackson had held on. His fingers were still curved underneath the leather girth—but his white knuckles were now relaxed and his body slumped over. Alnitak bent to his knees and Jackson rolled softly to the ground, motionless and unconscious. He burned with the heat of a strong fever.

"The army is getting closer to the fortress! They are going to find us here!" Otava held tightly to his weapons as if he were afraid they would escape his grasp and run away, abandoning him to death.

"Perhaps it's time for this lyre to play a song of peace, a song of the forest." Merope kneeled next to Jackson as Otava and Rigel stood near, guarding them. She positioned the turtle shell in her lap and gently plucked the strings while softly singing and shedding tears of compassion, sorrow, and hope for the boy's fading life.

Lie 'neath the forest green
Listen to songs unseen
Where monoceros roam
Starling, my peaceful home

As Merope gracefully moved her Ilmatar fingers across the lyre, her voice carried effortlessly with the wind, mixing with a colorful cloud that grew and swirled around them. The cloud became thick, lifting the four friends into the sky and floating them on the winds above toward the Starling Forest.

CHAPTER 26

LOST AND FOUND

Cold water surrounded Jackson. He swam up and forward and around, but all he could see was dark, deep blue. Something brushed past his leg, and he shivered, turning to see what it was. Ripples of water swirled near him and a faint light flowed through the deep. He swam and swam and stroked up and up, trying to reach the light. As he neared the surface, faces surrounded the shoreline beckoning him toward them.

Otava dipped up water with his large ladle, drank it heartily, and offered it out to Jackson. Merope, Rigel, and Andromeda all crouched down in the grass with their heads peering over the bank, urgently calling him, though their voices were muffled, their faces blurred by the thick, dark blue. The large, strong hand of Rigel reached down for

Jackson. Jackson pushed his body and his arms up through the water to meet his mentor.

Chomp! Strong, razor-sharp teeth sank into his leg as he yelled for help underwater, still reaching up toward the light, toward the shore. Jackson looked down and Eltanin's mouth was biting and gnawing at his leg. The dragon carried him down from the light. His friends kept calling him, urging him onward and reaching for him, but their faces grew darker and their voices faded to silence.

Eltanin pulled him out of the water into a cold, damp cave. Jackson could not move or fight back as the creature bit and grinded and chewed on Jackson's leg over and over again. Suddenly, Eltanin scurried out of the cave and dove back into the water. All was dark and silent. Someone walked into the darkness. The quiet voice said, "He's going to be fine." Blurry arms and bodies surrounded him, wrapping and dressing the wounds on his leg. They covered him with one warm blanket, then another, then another until the wet, cold chills left his body, replaced by heat as he fell asleep, thankful for a little comfort.

Now different voices beckoned him out of his sleep. They were quiet and somber but clear. The darkness vanished slowly into light, but it was no longer the quivering silhouette of sunshine piercing through water. The light now completely surrounded him.

Everything felt heavy: both legs—though one rested weightier than the other—his arms, his head, his eyelids.

Jackson tapped his fingers against a clean, soft cloth underneath him. He fought with his eyes, fluttering them open several times against the strong urge to let them rest until his will overpowered the weighty sleep, and he looked around.

"Tim! He's awake! Thank God, he's awake!" a familiar voice shouted as a face jolted in front of his, simultaneously grabbing one of his hands and cupping his cheek with her other hand.

"Mom? Where am I?" Jackson asked groggily, knowing very well that he was in a hospital but needing to ask anyway. He hoped to distinguish the difference between the dreams and reality, between Earth and the world where he just made a lifetime of memories.

"You're at the hospital. The doctor said your tibia had a comminuted fracture, and your fibula had a greenstick fracture. They had to put a few small pins in your leg, and you'll be in a cast for several months, but you should be fine. It was a closed fracture, so thankfully there was no infection." His mom, a night-shift ER nurse, always answered with correct medical terminology for any ailment.

"Matt, my man, would you mind translating?" Jackson asked, knowing his inquisitive little brother would have already searched each term out on his parents' phone while waiting around at the hospital.

"It means that your big bone broke into a few floating pieces around the major break, and your little bone was partly broken and bent, but did not break all the way through," he read from his notes on the phone. "They were worried at first that the blood on your leg might be from bone breaking through your skin, but it was just from cuts and scrapes."

"Thank you, Dr. Matthew." Jackson smiled and nodded with understanding.

"Jackson?" a little sweet girl voice crept to the side of his bed. "Can I climb up and give you a hug? Mom said I had to ask first."

"Sure, Maddie." Jackson raised his bed up to a sitting position, and his little sister jumped up next to him and squeezed him around the neck as tightly as she could. "You can't choke me though!" Jackson pretended to use a wheezy voice, teasing her, though he did feel a little tenderness in the neck area.

"I missed you! Why did you leave us, Jackson?" Maddie grabbed his face, speaking earnestly and then went back to hugging him again. "I don't want you to ever go away again!"

"I'm sorry, sis, I didn't mean to leave you. I think I just got lost." Jackson lightly patted the back of her little five-year-old head.

In the midst of this reunion, Jackson was trying to piece together what happened. He remembered every detail of Arcas so clearly. Every person, creature, and adventure was as real to him as his little sister's grip. But now that he was sitting here, recovering in a hospital, he wasn't sure how to reconcile his memories with the reality around him. And he definitely wasn't going to start talking about other planets and portals and unicorns and kingdoms. He preferred to play this out in a way that would not land him in a loony bin.

"How did you find me?" he safely probed the questions back to them.

"Some hippie couple found you in the woods and brought you to Farmer John's house. Do you remember any of that?" his dad answered.

"No," Jackson answered honestly. "Hippie couple?" he asked, smiling with a look of confused but humorous inquiry.

"Yeah, they were wearing some weird clothes, looked like they travel around, living in the woods or something. The woman had long, dark hair and seemed to float about humming all the time like she was high on something, and the man was dressed like Davey Crockett, only instead of carrying a muzzleloader, this piece of work had a bow and arrow over his shoulder and a sword hanging from his belt. I'm sure if you saw them, you'd remember them."

"Rescued by hippies, huh? That's funny, Dad." Jackson laughed and felt pleased thinking of his Arcasian friends visiting his backyard.

"Well, if it takes hippies to find an injured boy in the woods, then we need more hippies in our world! The police, the search parties, no one else had any luck finding you over the past few weeks. We were beginning to think that you were…" As she became visibly anxious and frustrated seeking answers, his mom hid her face to block the tears that freely flowed down her cheeks.

"Lori, we can talk about all of that later," his dad interrupted. He was hoping to stop her ranting before it became uncomfortable and embarrassing for them in a public place.

"Do you at least remember what happened to your leg?" she probed.

"I don't know, Mom… I think something fell on it."

"See, Tim, I told you it had to be that storm the night he disappeared. We had lots of trees down, everywhere. And to think that my little boy was out there, trapped and lost and alone, all that time…" His mom broke down again, this time into sobs while his dad rested his hand upon her shoulder, trying to calm the traumatized emotions down once again. Managing emotions had become his full-time job since Jackson's disappearance.

"Well, after what Jackson's been through, I don't think you can call him your little boy anymore. It takes a man to survive all that time out in the wild."

"I don't care what he survived, or how long he's gone from home! He'll always be my little boy!" she snapped back.

"Mom, it's okay. I'm home. Everything's okay." Jackson tried to ease the apparent tension that his parents had obviously been struggling with lately while his siblings remained quietly invisible, a skill they had become quite good at since his disappearance.

"Do you remember anything else, Jackson?" his father asked, trying to fill in the black holes of confusion and ignorance hovering around them.

Yes! I remember everything! A lying angel who threw me into a new world during a storm. Three gems that I journeyed and fought and bled to retrieve. A quirky bear who specializes in weapons and cooking. The Hunter who knows how to track, fight, or vanish when he wants to, who is in love with the Ilmatar whose powerful song and strong spirit can heal hearts and mend wounds. The spunky princess who swung into my life from the trees: the kiss, the dance, the amber hair, the purple eyes. The Bridge awakened between worlds, possibly still glowing with its active orange and blue hues.

Not wanting to lie but not able to voice the truth, Jackson did his best to answer the question.

"I'm still trying to figure it all out, Dad. I think I blacked out a lot. I'm sure I'll remember more as I get rested and healed."

"Alright, son." His dad accepted the vague answer. "We're just glad you're home."

"I'm glad to be home too," Jackson affirmed, only he wasn't sure which home he belonged to anymore.

EPILOGUE

Jackson breathed in the crisp winter air, returning it as a cloudy fog in front of him. Each footstep crunched through the thick coat of frozen February snow. It had been three months since Jackson awoke in a hospital bed. After a few therapy sessions, his parents were satisfied that Jackson did not have the symptoms of an abducted or abused child, so the counseling appointments ended. The doctor visits were becoming fewer and fewer, and he was finally walking without the inhibitions of crutches or a cast.

Jackson controlled himself expertly the whole winter, keeping indoors and focusing on resting, healing, and catching up on schoolwork. But the very day he was medically released from all restrictions, he found himself returning to the clearing in the woods. A time or two, he tried to start a fire, but the mixture of snow and wind wouldn't allow it.

Jackson would lie on the wooden bench, looking at the

stars, secretly hoping Rigel would show up and take him back for an adventure or even just a talk. Maybe one day, he would wander back to find Otava cooking over the fire, sniffing and tasting different herbs before scattering them into his pot.

But they never came. No shimmering lights. No mysterious portals. No otherworldly companions. The woods were deafeningly silent, though the stars radiated with loud beauty and vivid mystery resembling these friends he had grown to love.

Most of his peers at school were chasing girls, or at least finding a date for prom. But the high school world around him of video games, gossip, and movies felt shallow and insignificant. He played along and went through the everyday, meaningless motions of school and life, but inside, he felt like the world was whirling around him while he stood still. The only girl Jackson could think about was an alien princess, and not the computer-generated type. She was real and unique and full of vitality. Andi didn't care a lick about make-up or rumors or impressing others. She cared about joy and adventure and living life in the moment.

At night, Jackson often dreamed of Andi. She was always smiling and laughing as she danced in the green meadow speckled with white flowers and illuminated with a trinity of sunlight. During the day, he dreamed about touring the cool, dark cave lands with her. He wanted to hold her hand and taste her lips again, even if it could only happen by accident.

Jackson rummaged through his tattered hoodie over and over again, hoping to find the transport gem, hoping to hold a proof of Arcas and a power to return. Deep down, he knew he wouldn't find the gem. So, he washed the hoodie and rested it on his desk chair as a reminder. Besides his dreams and memories, it was the only item that survived the journey home, the only other thing in his life scarred and changed by Arcas. As he rested with his injured leg elevated day after day, week after week, Jackson started to wonder what really happened when he disappeared from the woods.

Did I really go to Arcas? Did I really travel to another world? Maybe it was all a hallucination. Was my leg actually injured by a fallen tree like everyone else believes? What if the couple in the woods who brought me back really were hippies? Did they kidnap and drug me?

Jackson wasn't always sure what happened anymore, and as time passed, he decided it was probably best to forget Arcas. It was best to forget about the journey, the friends, the adventure... everything. It was time for Arcas to return to a more probable reality, so he could return to life in the tangible reality around him. Arcas was an incredible dream, nothing more.

Still, he wished he could at least share these dreams with someone beside his little sister. She listened intently and questioned fervently, but as far as anyone was concerned, the stories he shared with her were fun big-brother fairytales. If there was one person who would listen to Jackson without judgment, it was his grandfather. Now he missed the nights of stargazing with Grandpa even more. Returning to the clearing in the woods was as much to feel close to his grandpa as it was to feel close to Arcas.

Buzz. Buzz. Buzz. Jackson's phone vibrated in his pocket. His numb fingers reached in and retrieved it.

"Mom wanted me to tell you to please come home now," his brother texted.

These messages happened often lately, especially when he left the house near dusk. Jackson typed back that he would be in soon. He rubbed his cold, bare hands together, glanced around once more for any new footprints in the snow and crunched his way back to the house. After waving to his mom to ease her nerves, he walked upstairs and opened the door leading to the attic.

His grandfather left him a box of books and stargazing tools in the attic. He knew there were some old constellation maps and books about deep space objects. When it warmed up in the spring, he would carry out the eight-inch Dobsonian telescope to hunt for nebulas, double stars, and marvel over Saturn's rings. Perhaps looking through the dusty box labeled "Jackson" of Grandpa's terrestrial treasures would cheer him up.

Jackson opened the box and rummaged through it. He pulled out book after book, some familiar and some he'd never seen his grandfather use. One object in particular caught his attention. It was a round, hand-drawn, bright-yellow map made of cardstock with a wheel that spun in the middle of it. Jackson began to carefully spin the paper wheel, examining its contents. One line in bold ink rolled around to the center top and read *Earth*. Jackson played with it as it spun through three changing windows revealing various names and locations around the world. As he laid it down to sift through the box again, he flipped the map over.

The backside was not blank as he assumed. It contained another chart of sorts. This side of the map revealed three grids that each formed three-by-three rows of holes. When he turned the wheel, three red circles filled the holes in each grid, but always in a different combination. He flipped the map back to the other side, but something was familiar about a word scribbled near the center window. He moved the wheel slightly, turning it until the sketched word was fully visible. His heart skipped a beat. *DENEB* it read above curved drawings appearing like caves. Jackson spun the wheel quickly and read the word *VEGA* written in his grandfather's handwriting. He quickly spun it one more time and saw the word *ALTAIR*.

Jackson couldn't believe it. Heart racing, he went back to the box. He rummaged quickly but carefully through each item for any other connections to Arcas. All he found was a large wedding ring box at the bottom. He pried open the hinged box, and tucked snugly into the ring hole rested a yellow-and-red gem.

I guess I'm not the only one with secrets in this family, Jackson thought, overwhelmed with surprise and amazement.

He gently pulled out the gem and examined its familiar size, shape, and color. Alone in the attic, Jackson pressed each corner until the pulsating beam blasted out through the polished stone. With leisurely delight, he drew a small portal door and stared into the dancing lights.

APPENDIX

STAR CHARTS

No matter the race, language, culture, or location of a people, the stars play witness to their triumphs, their failures, and their history. These millions of witnesses pierce through the black sky, bringing light when eyes see dimly, bringing hope and beauty when hours feel darkest. Some look to them for enjoyment, some look to them for heroes, and some look to them for revelation. However you look at them tonight, know that it was under the same sky, the same ancient lights, that Jackson found himself the night that his life and his destiny changed forever.

Contained in the next few pages are simplified star charts of the constellations that were a source of inspiration for this novel. There are 88 modern-day constellations, 25 of them were used in *The Hunter, the Bear, and the Seventh Sister*. Familiar star names from the story are also labeled for your enjoyment and exploration of Arcasian mythology. Just as the people and creatures in the World of Arcas have ancient ties to Earth, these familiar constellations also hold an ancient place in our hearts and history. On any clear, dark sky, one should be able to find some of these constellations blazing through the atmosphere and waiting to be discovered, pointed out, and dreamed about. So grab a pair of binoculars or a telescope and explore the evening sky with us.

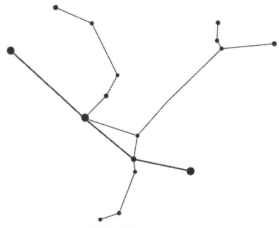

ANDROMEDA
an-DRAH-mih-duh
the Chained Maiden

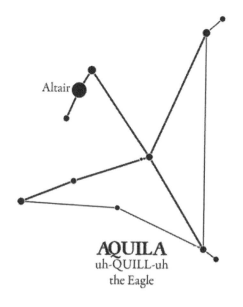

Altair

AQUILA
uh-QUILL-uh
the Eagle

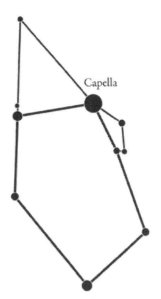

Capella

AURIGA
aw-RYE-guh
the Charioteer

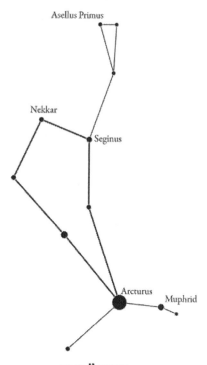

Asellus Primus

Nekkar

Seginus

Arcturus   Muphrid

BOÖTES
bo-OH-teez
the Herdsman

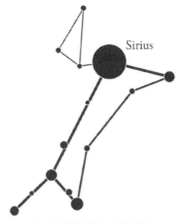

Sirius

CANIS MAJOR
CANE-iss MAY-jer
the Great Dog

Procyon

CANIS MINOR
CANE-iss MY-ner
the Lesser Dog

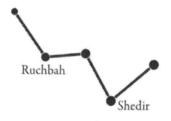

Ruchbah

Shedir

CASSIOPEIA
CASS-ee-uh-PEE-uh
the Seated Queen

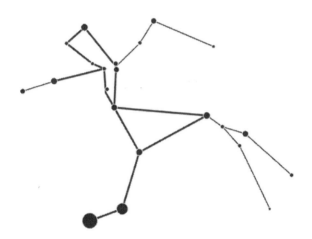

CENTAURUS
Sin-TOR-us
the Centaur

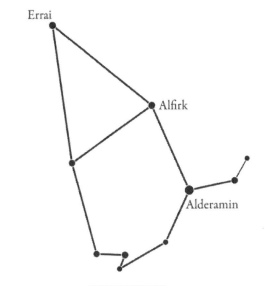

CEPHEUS
SEE-fee-us
the King

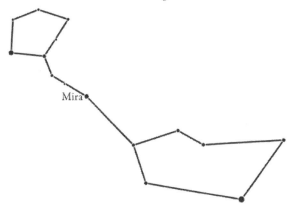

CETUS
SEE-tus
the Sea Monster

CORVUS
COR-vus
the Crow

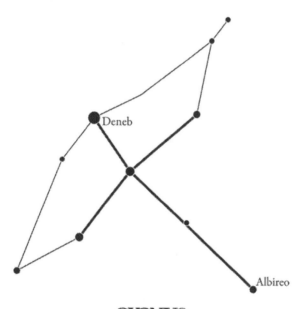

Deneb

Albireo

CYGNUS
SIG-nus
the Swan

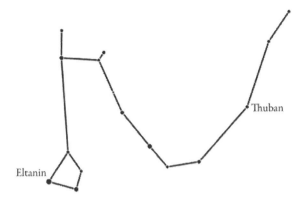

Eltanin

Thuban

DRACO
DRAY-co
the Dragon

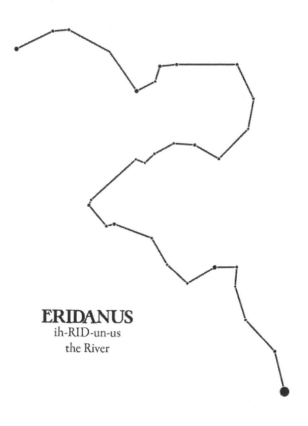

ERIDANUS
ih-RID-un-us
the River

FORNAX
FOR-naks
the Furnace

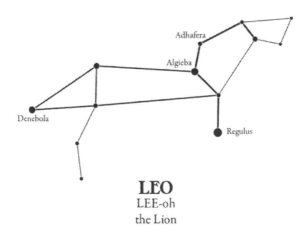

LEO
LEE-oh
the Lion

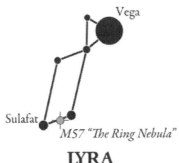

LYRA
LYE-ruh
the Lyre

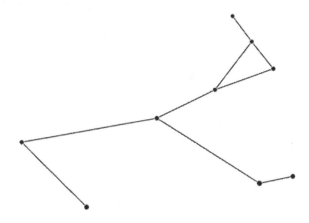

MONOCEROS
muh-NAH-ser-us
the Unicorn

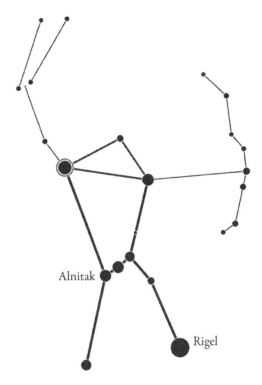

Alnitak

Rigel

ORION
oh-RYE-un
the Hunter

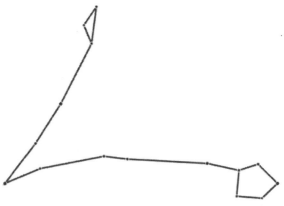

PISCES
PICE-eez
the Fishes

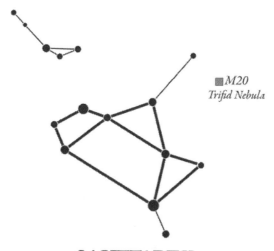

■*M20*
Trifid Nebula

SAGITTARIUS
SAJ-ih-TARE-ee-us
the Archer

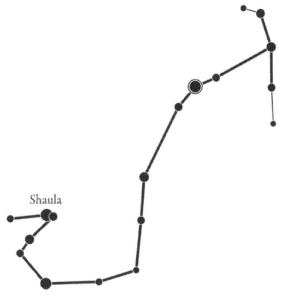

Shaula

SCORPIUS
SCOR-pee-us
the Scorpion

Asterope •

Taygeta

Maia

Celaeno

Alcyone

Electra

Merope

PLEIADES
plee-UH-deez
Seven Sisters

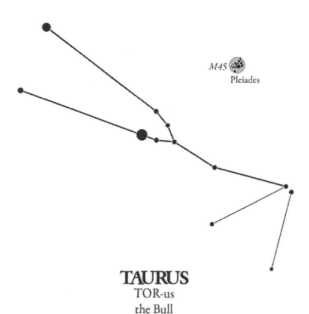

M45
Pleiades

TAURUS
TOR-us
the Bull

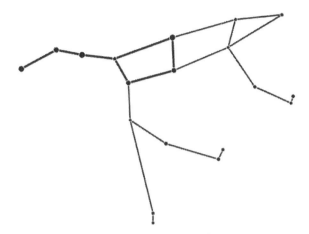

URSA MAJOR
ER-suh MAY-jur
the Great Bear

VOLANS
VOH-lanz
the Flying Fish

A SONNET OF
ACKNOWLEDGEMENTS

For God who created the stars above
That shineth in display of Thy glory
For friends who art true and showeth great love
To Ben and Barb'ra, honing our story
With Keith encouraging us in this prose
Leiters who conquered the tale with eyes clear
And Todd with Lauren for time that they chose
Regina and Amy, thy skills appear
For Langhofers, Woolets, and Riverside
We cherish and love our family tree
Advice and support thou surely provide
Through the shadows of life, our hearts you see
Thanks to all who believe in us and read
We hope to finish book two with swift speed!

B. I. Woolet is the author of *The Hunter, the Bear, and the Seventh Sister*. They enjoy creating lyrical and literary arts, playing music together, and exploring nature. They are happily married and live in Indiana with their children. This is the first book from the World of Arcas series.

Connect with the Authors

www.worldofarcas.com
www.facebook.com/WorldOfArcas
Twitter @worldofarcas

If you enjoyed this book, the best compliment you can give us is to tell others about it and give it to a friend. Thanks for your support!

Made in the USA
Charleston, SC
14 January 2014